Praise for

Welcome to your new favorite YA sci-fi series! *Landfall: The Ship Series Book One* hurls us into a frightening and fascinating future rich with action, mystery, and unforgettable characters. With elements of Orson Scott Card's Ender's Game and the best of Rick Riordan's Percy Jackson books, Landfall kept me burning through the pages. I hope Jerry Aubin is typing right now, because I can't wait to return to The Ship!

- Owen Egerton, author of *Hollow,* director of *Blood Fest*

RESURGENCE

THE SHIP SERIES // BOOK FIVE

JERRY AUBIN

For any information, please contact zax@theshipseries.com.

The main text of this book was set in Georgia.
The chapter title text was set in Avenir.

Lekanyane Publishing
Austin // Amsterdam // Cape Town // Sydney // Christchurch

ISBN 978-0-9970708-9-7 (pbk)
ISBN 978-0-9970708-8-0 (ebk)

For K, P, W, and Q.

THE STORY SO FAR…   IX

CHAPTER ONE
WHY THE HELL ARE THEY TORTURING US LIKE THIS?   1

CHAPTER TWO
THAT'S PRETTY CREEPY, BUT I UNDERSTAND WHY YOU DID IT.   9

CHAPTER THREE
I DON'T HAVE ANY PATIENCE FOR THAT NOISE RIGHT NOW.   15

CHAPTER FOUR
NOW!   21

CHAPTER FIVE
NUMBERS, DORAN.   27

CHAPTER SIX
CAG—DON'T LET HER GET AWAY!   35

CHAPTER SEVEN
I WON'T LET YOU DOWN.   43

CHAPTER EIGHT
ONE WAY OR ANOTHER.   49

CHAPTER NINE
I'M CONFIDENT I CAN GET THE BOSS TO DO AS I ADVISE.   55

CHAPTER TEN
I CAN'T WAIT TO HEAR WHAT THIS CRAZINESS IS ALL ABOUT.   61

CHAPTER ELEVEN
IT'S ALL TRUE.   69

CHAPTER TWELVE
I HAVE MORE EVIDENCE.   75

CHAPTER THIRTEEN
NOW WHAT?   83

CHAPTER FOURTEEN
YOU HAVE SIXTY SECONDS!   89

CHAPTER FIFTEEN
IF YOU WANT TO SURVIVE, PUT ON A HELMET.   97

CHAPTER SIXTEEN
THEY HAVE TO FIND OUT IF IT WORKED!   105

CHAPTER SEVENTEEN
ALL OF YOU WILL GET A TURN WITH IT.   115

CHAPTER EIGHTEEN
LET'S CRACK THIS THING OPEN.   123

CHAPTER NINETEEN
HOW MAY I REPAY YOU?   131

CHAPTER TWENTY
GET OFF MY BRIDGE.   141

CHAPTER TWENTY-ONE
THE ASTEROID HAS NOT DISAPPEARED.   147

CHAPTER TWENTY-TWO
MA'AM—THE ASTEROID JUST LAUNCHED A MISSILE!   153

CHAPTER TWENTY-THREE
THIS IS AN EXTREMELY BAD PLAN.   161

CHAPTER TWENTY-FOUR
THAT'S NOT GOING TO WORK THIS TIME.   169

CHAPTER TWENTY-FIVE
YOU FIRST, CAG.   175

CHAPTER TWENTY-SIX
YOU'LL BE CLIMBING THE WALLS BEFORE YOU KNOW IT.   183

CHAPTER TWENTY-SEVEN
SHE DID WHAT?   189

CHAPTER TWENTY-EIGHT
HOW DID THAT HAPPEN, ALPHA?   195

CHAPTER TWENTY-NINE
THIS ISN'T OVER UNTIL I SAY IT'S OVER!   205

CHAPTER THIRTY
HOW DO WE DO THAT?   211

CHAPTER THIRTY-ONE
I'M HAPPY TO STILL BE HERE.   219

CHAPTER THIRTY-TWO
WE HAVE A PLAN.   225

CHAPTER THIRTY-THREE
STAY FROSTY, EVERYONE.   233

CHAPTER THIRTY-FOUR
WE DID OUR JOB.   241

CHAPTER THIRTY-FIVE
A VIRUS.   249

CHAPTER THIRTY-SIX
IT'S GREAT TO FINALLY MEET YOU, ZAX.   257

CHAPTER THIRTY-SEVEN
THANK YOU.   267

CHAPTER THIRTY-EIGHT
HE DOESN'T CARE FOR US VERY MUCH.   275

CHAPTER THIRTY-NINE
ALL RISE FOR THE SUPREME TRIBUNAL.   281

CHAPTER FORTY
THE DEFENDANTS SHALL RISE.   287

CHAPTER FORTY-ONE
I WILL BEAR THE RESPONSIBILITY.   293

CHAPTER FORTY-TWO
HOW ARE YOU?   303

CHAPTER FORTY-THREE
I HAD ALREADY PLANNED ON IT.   311

CHAPTER FORTY-FOUR
CAG—WE NEED YOU ON THE DECK RIGHT NOW.   317

ACKNOWLEDGMENTS   322

THE STORY SO FAR...

LANDFALL introduces us to Zax and Kalare, two cadets approaching their sixteenth birthdays, as they work to establish their careers in the Ship's Crew. The two catch the eye of the Flight Boss, the second most powerful member of the Omegas running the Ship, and he offers to mentor the one who comes out on top after a series of training competitions. Mikedo, a Flight Lieutenant, leads their instruction and quickly forms deep bonds with the two cadets. The training culminates with a mission to explore a planet prior to colonization where Zax makes a startling discovery—what appears to be a spacecraft built by unknown humans. Mikedo convinces Zax that his discovery is a danger to the Ship's fragile society, and her fears gain credence when she dies under mysterious circumstances shortly thereafter. Zax identifies sufficient circumstantial evidence to suspect the Flight Boss of conspiring to kill Mikedo and hide the discovery of unknown humans, and he publicly confronts the man with it. The Boss laughs off the accusations and punishes Zax by banishing him to the bottom of the Ship's hierarchy.

REVOLUTION picks up one year later with Zax and Kalare moving in two different directions. She has thrived under the Boss's mentorship and loves the Pilot Academy, while he toils in the literal bowels of the Ship serving under the most clueless of its officers. The civilian uprising triggered by Zax's discovery of the human fighter boils over into full revolution. The two cadets, along with Zax's longtime nemesis Aleron, become enmeshed in a mission to help Sergeant Bailee, a fierce Marine, keep the Boss out of the civilians' hands in order to protect the Ship. Along the way, Zax runs afoul of Rege, a leader of the revolutionaries, and shockingly discovers their movement is led by no other than Imair—a civilian woman he had worked side-by-side with for a year. Zax accepts a mission to kill the Boss rather than allow the civilian revolution to succeed, but he fails when the man appears to betray the Crew in order to save himself and remain in power. The Boss rewards Zax and restores him to his position atop the Crew's hierarchy with an appointment to the Pilot Academy, but it is an uneasy truce as Zax continues to believe the man is a murderous traitor.

HOMEWARD opens with a trip back in time and introduces Adan—a brilliant innovator who designs a spacefaring ark to save humanity from Earth's environmental collapse. Along with his fearsome bodyguard and trusted lieutenant Markev, Adan travels to Earth's asteroid belt and returns with a massive space rock that becomes the foundation of the Ship. The Chancellor, the ruthless leader of the West, supports Adan in his efforts, but her cooperation comes at the steep price of Adan's independence. He regretfully compromises even further when he makes a deal with the General Secretary, a foe who has led the

East for decades in its battles against the West, to gain access to the East's consciousness transfer technology that Adan requires for the Ship's powerful fighter craft. Back in Zax's timeline, Imair leads the Ship along with her murderous lieutenant Rege as it starts a twelve-year journey back towards Earth in search of the mysterious humans. Zax's dream of piloting a fighter is finally within reach as he starts his training at the Pilot Academy and meets his new friend Mase—a precocious younger cadet who hacks into the Ship's Artificial Intelligence systems in his spare time. Zax thrives professionally and reaches the top of his Academy class, but his personal life gets thrown into upheaval when Kalare tires of his suspicions about her beloved mentor the Flight Boss and walks away from their friendship. Zax discovers his paranoia about the Boss is well-founded when he learns the officer has hit Zax with enough demerits to get him Culled, and Zax's timeline comes to a close as he descends into cryosleep.

RENDEZVOUS revisits Adan's timeline where the genius builder of the Ship is feigning cooperation with his adversaries in exchange for their consciousness Upload technology. The East's General Secretary recognizes something is amiss and dispatches a special agent to identify how Adan is preparing to betray them. Rilee discovers secret cryostorage facilities on the asteroid along with an illegal stockpile of nuclear missiles, but she is nearly killed by Adan's lieutenant Markev before she can report back and warn the General Secretary. When she awakens from a year-long coma, Rilee's worst fears prove true when Adan nukes Earth before launching the asteroid's journey. The Ship's creator initially convinces those around him that wiping out all life on their homeworld is necessary, but when Markev eventually pushes back Adan murders him along with the rest of his first Crew as part of a descent into evil that culminates with the abandonment of his humanity. Adan Uploads his consciousness into the Ship's AI system and transforms into Alpha, where he proceeds to secretly manipulate the Crew into doing his bidding across the thousands of years that lead up to the Ship's current timeline and Zax's awakening from cryostorage. It's been twelve years since he was Culled, and even though Zax remains a young cadet, Kalare has aged into a senior leadership role and is preparing for a final showdown with the other humans the Ship has battled during their voyage to Earth. His friend Mase discovers secret log files that reveal Adan's actions and Alpha's true identity, but Zax pushes the knowledge aside rather than risk running afoul of the Boss yet again. The Ship arrives at a restored Earth that appears devoid of human life, and Zax accompanies Kalare into a final battle against the other humans. Unfortunately for them and the rest of the Crew, they are quickly vanquished when their fighters are neutralized and the Ship's engine disabled.

RESURGENCE returns to the Ship as the Crew deals with the aftermath of their stunning defeat...

CHAPTER ONE

Why the hell are they torturing us like this?

Reveille sounded and Zax swore under his breath. He had no interest in waking up. It wasn't that he was exhausted, even though he was. The bigger issue was the toxic stew of boredom and foreboding affecting everyone on board for the past two months. He closed his eyes and dozed for a few additional mins until he was startled fully awake by a shout.

"The damned RTF has done it again! No showering until further notice. Why the hell are they torturing us like this?"

It was the female pilot who bunked next to Zax. She had become more and more agitated over recent weeks, and the stridency in her voice suggested she might have reached a breaking point. Zax had avoided discussions with her, but the same could not be said of the man from Engineering who bunked across the aisle. He enjoyed amplifying whatever upset the woman expressed even further and took advantage of the opportunity yet again.

"It's not torture, it's rationing. It's right there in their name—the Rationing Task Force." The engineer turned away from the woman and addressed Zax. "Are all pilots as stupid as she is? Maybe that's why the lot of you failed to do your jobs, and we're all stuck in this mess."

The pilot dropped her gear to the deck and charged across the aisle. The pitch of her voice rose and spittle flew from her mouth.

"We didn't do our jobs? You idiots in Engineering had one simple task—make sure the Ship could escape if necessary. How did you let the FTL engine fail when it was needed most?"

Zax didn't want anything to do with the drama unfolding yet again before him, so he hopped out of his bunk. It was time to get ready for work and, even though he wasn't enjoying his new job, it offered something to occupy his mind beyond observing the ever-increasing stress levels of all those around him. When he reached the showers, Zax discovered the sign which had triggered his bunkmate's ire.

By order of the Rationing Task Force, there shall be no showering effective immediately.

First introduced via morning newsvid ten days after the Ship's capture, the Rationing Task Force was charged with stretching the Ship's supplies as long as possible. The shower system recycled the vast majority of bathing water, so the supply situation must be dire if the RTF was forcing everyone to fester in their own filth. Zax activated a sink and was pleasantly surprised when water flowed out. Bathing was off limits, but at least he could scrub the sleep out of his eyes and brush his teeth.

Once he was done getting ready, Zax made his way to the prearranged location to meet his new trainee. The man was there waiting and extended a hand in greeting. He was a head taller than Zax and wore a red Engineering uniform.

"Hello. My name is Haydon. Thanks for escorting me to the hangar. I haven't been there for many years, and I remember it can be confusing to find your way around."

"I'm Zax." He paused for a moment to stare at the man's face. "You look familiar. Have we met?"

The man smiled awkwardly. "You were an instructor when I was in Gamma Cadre. I was hoping you wouldn't recognize me since I was a jerk to you back then."

The memories flooded back. Haydon was the boy who was so disrespectful the day of the Revolution, only to turn around and suck up to him a few days later once Zax's role in saving the Boss was made public. Like everyone else he had known from that time, the boy had passed by him in age during the years Zax was in cryostorage.

"Now I remember. You were a complete oxygen thief back then."

Haydon looked down at the deck. "Fair enough. I suppose I have that coming. We should get moving."

They had only gone a few paces when Haydon spoke again.

"I heard you flew with the CAG when we fought the Others. I wanted to be a pilot, but my scores were never good enough. What was the battle like?"

Zax grinned. He was well aware that Haydon wasn't cut out to be a pilot having delivered plenty of demerits to him during their time together. His smile evaporated immediately, though, once his mind flashed back to the last battle and its immediate aftermath. He responded with a tone intended to shut the conversation down.

"We lost. What more is there to say?"

The man was silent for a moment, but then he stopped walking and grabbed Zax's arm and forced him to halt. "Come on, Zax. They haven't told us any of the truth about that day. I gave you plenty of reasons to hate me back when I was a stupid kid, but I'm dying to know how we lost."

"Fine. You want to know how we lost? They rendered us useless with golden missiles that somehow neutralized our fighters. I was in the same fighter as the CAG and couldn't even speak with her. I sat there all by myself terrified about what might happen next. Then I get back to the Ship and have to stand there while some spacecraft I've never seen lands in *our* hangar and drops off warrior ants. We were so prepared to win, and then they not only beat us but they made it appear easy. There isn't anything else to say."

Haydon spoke quietly. "Yeah—I was in Engineering that day. Everyone geared up to fight as the ants approached on the security feed, but then the order came down to just let them in. They carried a bunch of crates and marched straight into the FTL compartment like they had a map of where they were going. They evicted the civilians and all of their explosives, so now the damned bugs control the engine and have us stranded. What do they even want?"

"If there hasn't been a single communication from the Others in two months, I have no idea what might happen to change that. Maybe they're just waiting for us to run out of food. Or to start killing each other so they don't have to do it themselves." Zax checked the time via his Plug. "Come on, we need to get going or we'll be late."

They started to walk and Zax enjoyed the silence until Haydon reached into his pocket and pulled out a nutripellet. Once the man had his pellet opened, he tossed the wrapper on the deck as had become customary for everyone in the month since the RTF mandated them for breakfast. The maintenance staff had kept pace with the new source of litter for the first few weeks, but Zax had noticed ever increasing trash piles forming in the higher traffic passageways. None of the empty wrappers belonged to him, though. Zax had once subsisted on the vile pellets for so long that just the sound of one being unwrapped threatened to trigger his gag reflex.

They entered the hangar just as the force field that covered its exterior entrance slowly flashed green. Zax pointed it out to Haydon.

"That means an ant shuttle is arriving. We need to double-time it."

They reached their workstations as the shuttle settled on the deck. A group of Marines lined up on either side of its exit ramp, and Haydon turned to Zax with his eyes wide.

"Those are the largest and most fearsome-looking Marines I've ever seen!"

"I assume that's exactly why they've been assigned this duty. There hasn't been any violence the whole time I've been processing these shuttle deliveries, and I assume it's because of all those muscles. Well—their blasters and stunstiks probably play a role as well."

The exit ramp of the ant shuttle cracked open and descended to the deck. The Marines standing on each side tensed in preparation for whatever might happen next, and Zax did the same. There was finally movement from within followed by a sight that rendered Zax dumbstruck. Haydon whispered in awe.

"Those sure don't look like any of the colonists the newsvid has shown getting dropped off before."

The first shuttle delivery had arrived weeks earlier without any communication from the Others. Given the expectations that it was the arrival of their captors, Zax had watched the landing live on the newsvid. When the ramp opened, everyone was disappointed to find a group of humans wearing animal skins. The shuttle was not filled with the Others, but instead had delivered a pathetic group of savages that was the sorry remnant of a colony the Ship had left behind a few centuries earlier. Soon after the Ship had departed their system, the group fragmented into warring tribes and eventually reverted into a clan-based, hunter-gatherer society. Their language skills had devolved, but the Ship's linguists deciphered their history and learned the colonists had been herded onto the shuttle by a group of ants without any explanation.

The civilian leadership didn't want a bunch of primitives wandering the Ship and ordered them moved into cryostorage immediately. The next day five similar shuttles arrived, and the day after that it was seven. From that point forward, anywhere between one and ten shuttles had arrived daily, and a procedure was established for processing each group and moving them into cryostorage. Zax had volunteered for the duty since, with the involuntary grounding of the Ship's fighters, his piloting skills were unneeded.

The group who descended the ramp were wildly different than any who had passed before. For one thing, they were the most amazing collection of physical specimens that Zax had ever seen. All of them towered over the tallest of the Marines and moved with a preternatural strength and grace. Every single individual was objectively beautiful with flawless skin and lustrous hair. Their clothing was impeccable and shimmered as they walked.

Haydon clutched him by the arm and broke Zax's reverie.

"Aren't you supposed to be training me? What are we supposed to do when they get down here?"

Zax sighed. "Relax, it's easy. We're part of the greeting and sampling team. We ask each individual some questions about their colony, collect a DNA sample, and then send them off to cryostorage."

"Questions about their colony? What are we trying to learn?"

"We mainly want to understand what happened after the Ship left. We always hear one of two answers. Either the colony fractured and devolved into some level of primitive survival, or they retained the Ship's culture with colonial security remaining dominant like the Crew on the Ship. Just watch me for now, and save any other questions until after this first group has been processed."

The group entered the queue, and the first man approached their workstation. Zax was taken aback by the man's magnificence and stared up at him with his mouth agape. He quickly gathered his wits, delivered his welcome greeting, and began asking his standard questions. What came out of the colonist's mouth in reply left Zax breathless.

CHAPTER TWO

That's pretty creepy, but I understand why you did it.

Mase chewed on the tip of his thumb. It was a habit he had fought to extinguish for years that resurfaced whenever his brain was churning through a particularly gnarly challenge. He had triple-checked everything, and his conclusions were the same every time, even though they made no sense.

Someone was interfering with multiple AIs and changing their outputs. It was subtle, but undeniable. He had spent weeks trying to find a way to replicate the behavior in even one system and had hit nothing but dead ends. He probably shouldn't have been so aggressive in his own attempts at interference, but his fear of discovery and getting tossed out an airlock had diminished ever since the battle with the Others.

He had stopped worrying because the simple fact was they were all going to die soon. Either the

Others would apply their overwhelming power and destroy the Ship altogether, or they would continue to hold them prisoner until all of their supplies were gone and everyone on board either starved or died from lack of water. Once life-sustaining resources hit a tipping point, the violence required to acquire them would tear the Crew and civilians apart and doom everyone on board the Ship to death in a spasm of internecine bloodshed. Mase planned to put himself out an airlock before the conditions on board the Ship deteriorated to their logical endpoint, and that decision had been liberating.

A light flashed in his field of vision, and Mase raised an eyebrow when he identified who the incoming communication was from. He had not spoken with Zax since well before the final battle. They had explored the log files and learned about the history of Alpha together, but then Zax bolted after telling Mase to never contact him again. He understood the boy's rationale and gave him the space he asked for, but it had been hard. He accepted the communication.

"Hello, Zax."

"Hi, Mase. I guess you're surprised to hear from me."

Mase considered a few different responses but kept it simple.

"Yes."

There was an uncomfortable pause before Zax replied.

"I'm sorry I walked away from you the way I did. I was terrified when I learned Alpha was controlling everything and everyone. I was already Culled once and somehow managed a reprieve, and I didn't want to do anything that would put me at risk of that happening ever again. It was horrible to abandon you like that. I don't deserve your forgiveness, but I'm asking for it. Other than Kalare, you're the only friend I've ever had, and I hope you find a way to trust me again."

Mase smiled. He wanted Zax back in his life but didn't jump at the peace offering. The boy needed to earn his way back in.

"OK. I'll think about it. I'll contact you in a few days. We'll eat dinner together. Sort things out."

Mase cut the connection, but Zax contacted him again immediately.

"Mase—there's something else important I needed to tell you."

Mase grimaced. He had been happy that Zax wanted to repair their relationship, but that feeling was tempered when the boy revealed an ulterior motive.

"What, Zax?"

"I've been working as part of the reception team for the colonists the ants keep returning to the Ship. What we've seen previously is that none of the colonies have progressed technologically in any way. In fact, most of them have fallen backwards into a much more primitive state. We just finished processing a group, though, who were unlike any of

the rest. *Their colony advanced radically after the Ship dropped them off. In fact, I'm guessing their technology might be even more advanced than the Ship's."*

"What makes you think that?"

"Because one of them just told me they fought off thirty of those human motherships. Imagine that being possible after our experience with them. It's even crazier given they went through a revolution weeks after the Ship left them behind. One of the ex-Crew led the revolt and overthrew Colonial Security. I spoke with someone who was a direct descendant of the woman who led the uprising."

Mase's ears perked up. *"A direct descendant? Give me the record locator for that person's data."*

Zax sent over the identifier, and Mase navigated to the right AI system to put it to use. The tip of his thumb went back into his mouth, and he chewed furiously while he waited for his analysis to run. The results appeared, and Mase read them twice to be certain before he spoke.

"Since the battle, I've spent all of my waking time exploring the AI. What I've discovered are multiple systems where errors are occurring. It's statistically impossible for the errors to be random. They must be the result of direct manipulation by someone. The weirdest part is that it's been happening for thousands of years. There must be a group of people who have passed the knowledge down from one generation to the next.

"The system impacted the most is the Genetics AI. The Genetics AI specifies the way in which genetic material should be combined to produce a specific output—a person. It passes off its specification to the Culturing AI which does the actual manipulation of the genetic material. The Genetics AI assumes its output will match the specification, and there is no final validation. I've evaluated a million samples across the Ship's history and there's a pattern. Approximately one in a thousand births throughout history deviate from the Genetics AI specification. I checked the DNA sample from the colonist you spoke with earlier and traced his lineage back to the original Crew member who started the colony's revolution. That Crew member was part of the zero point one percent."

"Are the DNA errors consistent, Mase? What traits do they impact?"

"They are consistent, and the primary traits they affect lead to increased creativity and intelligence."

Zax paused for a moment. "Adan had started out with the most intelligent Crew but then settled on picking people who were the most compliant. I remember how frustrated he was that the new selection process led to people who were less creative and intelligent. Whoever is messing around with the system is fighting back against Adan's intentions. Wow."

"There's one more thing. I evaluated my own DNA along with yours and Kalare's. All three of us are in the zero point one percent."

"You did what? Everyone's genetic information is supposed to be inaccessible as long as they're alive and not in cryostorage."

"I was at dinner one night a few weeks ago while you two were eating together. When you left I took the cups off your trays and collected samples from those."

Zax fell silent again. Mase worried he had crossed a line with such a blatant invasion of privacy. He had considered not sharing the personal genetic information with the boy, but concluded it was too important and Zax needed to know. If it prevented the rekindling of their friendship, then Mase was prepared to accept that outcome. Finally, Zax spoke.

"That's pretty creepy, but I understand why you did it. I need you to do me a favor."

CHAPTER THREE

I don't have any patience for that noise right now.

Kalare glared at the image on her screen of the ant shuttle that had just landed and tried to remain calm. No one understood the relationship between the giant insects and their captors, but it was clear the ants were somehow under the control of the Ship's human enemies. The fact the bugs continuously dropped off colonists like cargo, acted as a constant reminder of the Crew's defeat in the battle for Earth and filled Kalare with a mix of helplessness and rage.

In hindsight, it was clear the Others had led them straight into a trap. The potential for that outcome had been raised throughout the run-up to the final battle, but everyone believed that worst case scenario was worth the risk. What no one had bargained for was the Ship's FTL engine going offline. What bothered Kalare the most was her inability to decipher why their inscrutable opponents might have gone through all of the effort in the first place. It was clearly a great strategy to draw the Ship into a position to be destroyed, but the Others hadn't finished them off. They had complete power over the Ship and yet held them frozen in place.

On the third day after the battle, President Rege sent out a shuttle. It was filled with a group of emissaries and launched in the hope of drawing out some form of communication. Almost immediately after the shuttle departed the hangar, it was swarmed with golden missiles and forced back to the Ship. It struck Kalare as a crystal clear message from the Others, but Rege launched the shuttle again a day later. There were no golden missiles the second time. One of the motherships fired an energy beam instead and the shuttle was vaporized after three shots. No one ever made an explicit announcement, but it was clear that no communication would be forthcoming.

It was a few weeks later that the ants started to arrive regularly with their cargo. The Intelligence group had concluded the ongoing arrival of colonists from the Ship's past was the most vital clue to the Others' intentions. Their most popular theory was that the humans were rounding up all traces of the Ship's activity before executing a final plan of destruction.

Regardless of what the Others might have in mind, Kalare knew she had to do something to try to save the Ship—whatever the cost. Her fighter was ready to launch and she gave the command. A sec later she flew free of the Ship with the deep blues of Earth below drawing her eye. She didn't admire the view for long because her threat board wailed almost immediately. One of the motherships had targeted her and she expected it would soon fire its energy beam. She had spent days analyzing the footage of the same vessel destroying their shuttle and had identified a potential flaw in its weapon system. It was time to prove her theory correct or die trying.

Success! There was a narrow window between when the Others locked on and when the beam fired where juking her craft avoided destruction. The mothership fired six more times and she dodged each. A second mothership engaged and Kalare stayed alive even in the face of their coordinated attack. She accelerated at maximum velocity on a collision course with the first vessel that had fired at her. Her plan was to sacrifice herself while doing significant damage to the enemy's hangar in the process.

Golden missiles launched from the target mothership, but with her velocity Kalare would close the distance before they locked on. Her threat board showed that three of the other motherships had also launched missiles, but she ignored them. They were too far away to reach her before her journey of sacrifice ended. She breathed deeply knowing it would all be over in a handful of secs.

A red light flashed to indicate an urgent inbound communication—Zax. Kalare gritted her teeth in frustration at the interruption, but then paused the simulation and accepted the connection. She had already seen what she needed to, and she could finish the scenario later.

"Hey, Zax. You're not going to believe what I just figured out in the simulator."

Kalare explained the scenario and its outcome. Zax paused for a few secs before replying.

"That's interesting, but how will you use that information? Are you thinking that we'd just sacrifice every fighter and pilot? Even if that worked, wouldn't the ants just destroy the FTL engine and leave the Ship stuck here forever?"

"I'm not saying it's the answer to all of our problems, but it's the first time since we arrived at Earth that I've been able to get close to beating them. It's just a simulation and who knows if it will match real life, but at least I've finally seen they may not be invincible." Kalare was getting worked up, so she paused to collect herself before continuing. *"Forget about it for now. Why are you reaching out to me?"*

"Have you heard anything about the latest group of colonists the ants dropped off?"

"Why would I have? It's been nothing but the same story every time."

"This group was different, Kalare. I think they're more technologically advanced than we are. They fought off thirty of the Others' motherships before they were finally defeated."

"Thirty! How is that possible?"

"I wouldn't have believed them, except it's obvious how they've thrived away from the Ship."

"Any idea why?"

Zax explained how the colony had started off with a revolution, but Kalare only half-listened. Her mind remained locked on the idea of colonists having such great success against the Others. If superior technology had made their success possible then it likely wouldn't matter for the Ship, but if the colonists had discovered new engagement tactics or identified critical weakness in the Others' spacecraft, then perhaps those could be exploited by the Crew.

"Zax—we need to tell the Boss about this. I want those colonists out of cryosleep to find out if there's anything useful to learn from them."

Once again Zax was silent for a few extra beats before replying. *"The Boss is actually a big part of what I need to talk with you about before we do anything with this information. I've learned some things over the last few months. It's important now for you to hear all of it as well."*

"This better not involve any more of your harebrained conspiracies. I don't have any patience for that noise right now."

"I know, and I understand. I have indisputable proof for everything that I'm going to share with you. OK? Can we meet for lunch, and I'll walk you through it?"

Kalare's first instinct was to say no. She had spent too many years listening to Zax and supporting him in his conflicts—perceived and real—with the Boss. What tipped her decision towards honoring his request was the chance to learn more about the mystery colonists. She needed enough information to convince the Boss to defrost their leader for interrogation.

"OK, Zax. I'll see you at lunch."

"Thanks, Kalare. I promise you won't regret it."

Their history together suggested it was far more likely that Kalare would indeed regret listening to Zax about any topic concerning the Boss. She considered the situation for a few mins and then settled on a radical course of action. She would meet Zax, but Kalare intended to have a surprise waiting for him.

CHAPTER FOUR

Now!

When Zax entered the mess hall, there was a different energy among the people eating. There were many more armed civilians present than he had become accustomed to, and there was palpable tension in the air. As he gathered a tray of food, he was dismayed that many of his favorite items were not available. Was there a permanent depletion of stocks, or had the food rationing regime been further tightened alongside the new showering prohibition?

"Zax!"

Mase waved at him from the entrance. Zax waited until the man loaded up his tray and joined him.

"Thanks for meeting me like this on short notice, Mase. Let's grab a seat."

Mase fell in alongside him, and they walked towards the table Zax had frequented for years.

"It's good to see you, Zax. I'm glad you reached out. I've discovered a lot of other stuff over the last few weeks." Mase stopped short and glared at Zax. "You didn't say *she* would be here."

They were still twenty meters from Kalare, who sat with her back to them and remained oblivious to their proximity. Zax had justified the subterfuge knowing that neither of his friends would be excited about interacting with the other, but convinced that he needed both of them involved.

"I'm sorry, Mase. I was afraid you wouldn't come if I told you I wanted Kalare to hear everything as well. I understand you don't trust her because of her relationship with the Boss, but we need all the help possible right now."

"And what if I say no and turn around and leave? Are you going to betray my trust and tell her everything I've already told you?"

"No. I promise I won't reveal your role if you aren't comfortable with sharing it yourself. But I'm begging you to please join us. Things are getting worse and worse on board. Even you must be aware of the crazy amount of anxiety around here today. Something bad is going to happen soon if we don't figure out how to escape the Others and resupply. I don't know if they're planning to actively destroy us, or whether they'll just let us do the job for them, but I'm convinced we don't have much more time before things start getting really, really ugly."

The man stared at him unblinking until Zax became uncomfortable and shifted his gaze. Finally, Mase spoke.

"OK. Let's sit down."

Zax exhaled and turned back towards the table where Kalare picked at her food. She looked up as they approached and her expression darkened as she spoke sharply.

"You didn't tell me *he* was going to be here!"

Zax held his hand up as a signal for Mase to wait. He sat down across from Kalare and leaned in to speak quietly.

"I'm sorry, Kalare. If it makes things any better, he was just as surprised and just as upset to find you here. It was obvious that neither of you would come if the other were here. I wouldn't have tricked you both if I didn't think it was urgent we all speak. The three of us have never worked together, but you are the people I trust the most in the universe. I need you to set aside your feelings for each other and instead rely on my faith in each of you. Please."

Kalare scowled at him for a good ten secs, but then she gestured for Mase to sit down. Zax breathed a sigh of relief and was about to start talking when a familiar voice spoke behind him.

"Are you sure you want us here, Kalare?"

Zax turned and found Aleron, tray in hand. Beside him was Major Eryn who also carried a meal. They both moved to sit at the table, and Zax spun back around and hissed at Kalare.

"What are they doing here? You know what I want to discuss! Aleron is bad enough, but do you really think I will talk about any of this stuff in front of the mini-Boss?" Zax turned back to the major. "Begging your pardon, ma'am."

Eryn nodded at Zax as Kalare spoke.

"I guess we're both guilty of deceiving the other about our true intentions for this meeting. I'm sorry, Zax, but I've tolerated more than enough of your unfounded rantings about the Boss. If you have concerns that are serious enough to share with me, then I want to be sure you believe they're legitimate enough to share with the major. I can't force you to place any faith in her, and I will understand if you decide to leave. What I will say is that she's been counseling me for years, and I've come to trust her with my life. Outside of you and Aleron, I haven't had as much trust in anyone since Mikedo died. It's your call what happens next."

Zax looked from Kalare to the major and then back to Kalare. Finally, he turned to Mase.

"What do you think? I've dragged you in this far, but are you willing to keep going with an even larger audience?"

"I actually trust the major a lot more than I trust your friend. At least she and I have a history together that should provide me some extra protection. Right, Major?"

Mase stared at Eryn who returned his gaze blankly for a moment until her eyes lit up with recognition.

"Of course, Mase. You never reported how I broke the rules and assisted you during your pilot training. I'll be happy to keep whatever secrets you share today." The major turned to Zax. "I promise that anything you have to say will be safe with me as well. I may be mini-Boss, but Kalare has earned my loyalty far more than the Boss ever would even if I worked for him for a thousand years."

The tone of her voice and expression on her face suggested that Eryn was being genuine. Before Zax could reply, there was a loud crash followed by raucous shouts. A fight had broken out on the other side of the mess hall. It was three Crew wearing the same red Engineering uniform as Aleron, and they were surrounded by a dozen civilians. Aleron jumped up to rush to their aid.

"Aleron—no!"

The man froze in response to Kalare's shout. He turned back to her and she continued.

"I need you here with me. Check it out—other Crew are helping your guys and breaking up the fight. Please, please sit down."

Aleron's fists were clenched and agitation emanated off him in waves as he looked back and forth between Kalare and the brawl. Finally, he sat back in his seat. Kalare turned back to Zax.

"OK, you've managed to get us all here, and we're all willing to set aside our various trust issues. What is it you wanted to share?"

Zax hadn't yet quite put his own trust issues aside, but it didn't matter any longer. The fight raging on the other side of the mess hall was just another symptom of the overall societal breakdown he was certain was about to boil over. It was happening faster than he expected, and he feared they may have missed whatever narrow window of opportunity might exist to save the Ship. Even if Major Eryn violated their faith and reported them to the Boss, it just didn't matter any longer. They were all going to die one way or the other very soon if nothing changed. Getting thrown out an airlock might prove preferable to staying alive if the Crew and civilians did the Others' work and destroyed the Ship from within.

Zax opened his mouth to speak but stopped when Kalare raised her hand. She closed her eyes to communicate with someone via her Plug. Major Eryn did the same, and Zax guessed they were part of the same conversation. After a few secs, the blood drained from Kalare's face as she opened her eyes and exclaimed.

"We need to get out of here. Now!"

CHAPTER FIVE

Numbers, Doran.

The Boss fought to conceal his distaste as President Rege entered the Bridge. While everyone else on board the Ship was losing weight due to rationing, Rege had somehow grown even heavier. The most recent fat accretion had not only increased his girth but had left the man with a sizable double-chin. The civilian desperately needed a shower, and his neck flab was covered with a patchwork of stubble that shone with a coating of grease.

"Good afternoon, Doran. How are you doing today?"

The Boss gave a tight smile at Rege's use of his name rather than title. It was a new tactic the president had adopted to get under his skin. Unfortunately, it had the desired effect the first few times, so the civilian had continued to use it.

The Ship Series // Book Five // 28

"I'm doing fine, Mr. President. How about yourself?"

"Well, I've been better. Being stuck with these nutripellets for breakfast every day is starting to hurt my appetite."

The Boss smiled politely. He'd happily bet his entire remaining supply of cigars that Rege hadn't tasted a nutripellet in ages. It was almost certainly bacon grease from that morning's breakfast that coated his scraggly beard.

"What can I do for you, sir?"

"Let's speak privately."

The Boss extended his arm to point towards the conference room and followed Rege inside. He closed the hatch behind them and turned to discover the president had sat in the Boss's usual spot. It was just another pathetic dominance maneuver by the civilian that the Boss ignored. He only hoped he would have a chance to extract payback for all the indignities from the civilian before whatever endgame the Others had in mind for the Ship. The Boss sat down and Rege spoke.

"Doran—I'm starting to worry about what's going to happen if we're held captive for too much longer. I wholly supported the RTF's decision to ban showering, but there has already been quite an uproar around the Ship in response to it. Even though the civilians were only ever allowed to bathe once a week, they're even more upset about the situation than the Crew. We haven't had any new violence break out in response yet, but the rioting that's already been happening intensified once the news was announced this morning."

"I understand, Mr. President. It's a real concern for me as well. That said, I'm confident we'll all be much happier in a few weeks when we still have sufficient potable water even if it comes at the expense of the atmosphere getting a little ripe around here."

The Boss wanted to make an observation about how a lack of showers wouldn't impact Rege that much, but he held his tongue. He wasn't afraid to skewer the civilian, but it was more fun when there were witnesses to the jabs. The Boss always picked his spots carefully.

Rege appraised the Boss for a moment before standing. It was another cheap power play the civilian deployed when he was trying to intimidate. He spoke.

"All the same, I'm reaching the conclusion we should take preemptive action as a precaution."

"Interesting, sir. What exactly would that look like?"

"I believe the term they used on ancient Earth was martial law. It was when the military would take over from the civilians in times of great crisis. The regular rules and laws would be put on hold until the situation improved. Of course, in this case it would be the reverse—the civilians will take complete control from the Crew."

The Boss lost control and guffawed. Rege's eyebrows knitted together in reaction. After a couple of secs, the Boss composed himself and spoke.

"I'm sorry, sir, but that might be the craziest thing I've ever heard. What makes you think the civilians should be taking over right now? We're sitting here in the grip of the Others, and they are by far the most powerful enemy the Ship has ever encountered. You really think it makes sense for you to take command now? What do any of you know about space battles? How will you defend us?"

"Defend us?" Rege laughed. "You and your precious Crew had your chance to defend us, and you failed miserably. There's nothing any of you can do at this point. I don't know what the Others intend for us, but any notion of resistance is clearly futile. The only things I'm worried about defending right now are our critical resources in the face of internal forces that will soon begin to tear the Ship apart."

"Well, if it's rioting you're worried about, my Marines have that situation well under control."

"Doran—your Marines are controlling tens of thousands of civilians right now. What's going to happen when those numbers grow into hundreds of thousands? Or millions? I won't allow your Marines to slaughter my people in any attempt to restore order. The only way this will work is if my forces are in charge. The civilians will respect other civilians, and that will keep the worst of the violence in check. You and your Marines will stand down. In fact, all of the Crew will do so. There are civilian staff ready to take over all critical functions, so all of your people will be relieved and then restricted to their quarters."

The Boss was so shocked by the vile civilian's words that he was momentarily speechless. If the man truly believed he was going to end five thousand years of Crew rule that easily, he was sorely mistaken. The Boss stood and approached Rege, getting as close to the man's face as the president's protuberant belly would allow.

"And just how do you plan to enforce anything like that, *sir*? We've *allowed* civilian leadership for the last dozen years only because you held all of us hostage with your bombs around the FTL engine. The ants control it now, and I've continued to tolerate you because I wanted us united against the Others. It appears to be the right time for me to reverse that position, though, especially given how you don't have *any* remaining leverage over me."

Rege laughed. The smell of his breath up close was a fetid mixture of egg and coffee that confirmed the Boss's suspicions about what the man had eaten for breakfast. He held his ground and continued to stare at the civilian until Rege spoke.

"Numbers, Doran. My leverage rests with my numbers. During the Revolution your Marines could have wiped out every bit of civilian resistance due to your overwhelming firepower and tactics. Not any longer. You've not been aware, but we've spent the time during our journey to Earth deep in training, using the same methods your Marines use. We've also armed our troops with the best weaponry the Ship has ever produced. Maybe your Marines will still have an edge since they've been bred for war for generations, but are you certain that's enough to overcome a twenty-to-one advantage in numbers?"

The Boss had to believe there was no way that Rege was right. The Marines must still be favored in any battle, but it was impossible for him to know for sure. He turned away. He caught the smirk on Rege's face as he did so but ignored it.

"I need some time to consider this, Mr. President. May we please continue this discussion tomorrow once I've had a chance to weigh the pros and cons a little more?"

Rege held up his hand. "Wait a sec—I have an urgent communication coming in."

The civilian closed his eyes for a moment. When he opened them again, his mouth formed into a malevolent smile.

"That was one of my lieutenants down in the mess hall. A group of your Crew attacked some civilians and nearly started a riot. I might have been convinced to give you time to come around to my perspective, but it appears events have conspired against us. We need to confine all Crew and non-essential civilians to quarters immediately with my forces in charge of enforcement. What's it going to be, *Boss?* Are you going to support this directive or are things about to get ugly for all of us?"

The Boss flopped into his chair as an exaggerated signal of distress. Without any time to analyze the likely outcomes, he had no choice but to give in to Rege's demands. He needed time for two last communications, though, so he dipped his head and rubbed his eyes like he was trying to think and sent an urgent ping.

"*Kalare, Eryn—I don't have any time for explanations. Rege has decreed that the civilians are taking over the Ship immediately and will restrict all Crew to quarters. I want you to go into hiding. Kalare—get both of you to the place where I almost died during the Revolution and await further instructions.*"

"I need an answer, Doran. Will you help me announce a peaceful handover of control, or is it going to be a bloodbath?"

The Boss opened his eyes and stared at the civilian. There would absolutely be blood, but if the Boss had his way it would flow out of Rege. Until then, he would use coded language in the public statement to assure the Crew's officers that his instructions were a tactical retreat and not abject surrender. The Boss fired off one last private emergency message via his Plug and then responded to Rege.

"Let's go make this announcement, Mr. President."

CHAPTER SIX

CAG—don't let her get away!

Kalare rose out of her seat and gestured impatiently for the rest of them to follow. Zax didn't know what had her so agitated, but it was clearly not the right time for questions. He stood and nudged Mase in the shoulder to get him moving. The group abandoned their trays on the table and moved towards the exit. As they walked out of the mess hall, the video screens around the compartment came to life behind them.

"All civilians and Crew stand by for an important announcement from President Rege and the Flight Boss."

Kalare didn't break stride and continued down the passageway towards the Tube junction. Zax jogged for a moment past everyone else and caught up with her.

"Kalare—what the hell is going on? What are you so agitated about?"

"The president is about to declare that the civilians are taking full control of the Ship, and Crew will be restricted to quarters. The Boss told me to hide out down in the sewage treatment cavern. I have no idea what he might have in mind, but I'm going to trust he has a plan."

Zax stopped in his tracks while Kalare and the others kept charging ahead. The sewage treatment cavern? Why would the Boss be sending them down there to hide? Obviously Kalare would trust anything the Boss said, and there was no way Zax would be able to convince her otherwise without far more time than they had. He had zero interest in putting his life in the hands of whatever plan the Boss might have in mind, but he had to balance that position against his overwhelming desire to remain by Kalare's side. He called out.

"Wait! If they're giving the order right now, we shouldn't be in the main passageways or the Tube. No one from the Crew lives in any of the lower levels, and we'll stick out like crazy if we're supposed to be returning to quarters. We need to take the maintenance tunnels. There's an access port not that far from the Tube junction."

Kalare had stopped moving. "The tunnels? Why do you still have access to the tunnels?"

Zax explained as he caught up to her. "Things were so crazy after the Revolution that no one revoked my access after I was transferred out of Waste Management. I've been going for walks in the tunnels whenever I need some peace and quiet."

Kalare was quiet as she considered Zax's words. She checked in with Eryn and the major nodded in agreement.

"OK—good plan, Zax. Let's move before the announcement is over and these passageways start crawling with civilians."

Zax led them past the Tube junction until they reached the access port in the middle of a long, straight passage. He held his breath as they approached since he had not visited the tunnels in more than a month. There was no good reason why his access would have been revoked during that timeframe, but anything was possible. He exhaled once the panel on the port flashed green in response to its scan of his biometrics and the hatch opened.

"Halt!"

The shout came from the end of the passageway opposite from where the group had come from. A tall, older civilian held a blaster aimed at them as he approached. He was accompanied by a second civilian, a girl, who was much shorter and appeared to be the same age as Zax. She must have been nervous at the prospect of conflict since her weapon shook in her hands as the two approached the Crew.

"Where are you going? All Crew are supposed to be heading back to quarters."

Kalare stepped towards the lead civilian. He stopped walking and brought his weapon up and aimed it at her face. She halted and held her hands outstretched in an effort to appear non-threatening.

"Hey, hold on. Can you put that thing down? We're just trying to take a shortcut that gets us to our quarters as fast as possible. Just following orders."

The civilian appraised them all before shaking his head. "I don't think so. You by the hatch—go ahead and close that up for me good and tight. I'm going to call this in and find out what command wants us to do with you bunch."

The civilian kept one hand on the blaster with his finger on the trigger and used the other to pull a small communicator out of his pocket. He was initiating a transmission when a blaster roared in the passageway. The shock forced Zax to close his eyes for a moment. When he opened them, the tall civilian had collapsed lifelessly to the ground with a blaster hole in the middle of his chest. The younger civilian had dropped her weapon and was running back in the direction from where she had originally come. A familiar voice boomed loud enough to pierce the ringing in Zax's ears.

"CAG—don't let her get away!"

Kalare broke into a sprint to catch the young civilian, and Zax turned his attention towards the opposite end of the passageway. Sergeant Bailee stood in a textbook firing stance with a mini-blaster aimed at the escaping civilian. Zax turned back around just as

Kalare tackled the girl. The young civilian didn't struggle, and Kalare helped the girl to her feet and guided her back with a hand gripped lightly around her bicep. Aleron had grabbed one of the civilians' blasters and Mase had picked up the other by the time Bailee reached their position. Zax smiled as he spoke to the Marine.

"Where did you come from, Sergeant? You sure had perfect timing."

"I was eating lunch when you lot stood up to leave. I wanted to keep an eye on you because something about your facial expressions and body language caught my attention. I heard about that idiotic civilian leader's order while I was tailing you, so when this guy pointed his weapon at the CAG it was time for action." Bailee turned to Kalare. "Thanks for the assist, ma'am. I couldn't bear to shoot someone that young in the back, even if it's just a civilian. Where are you all heading?"

Major Eryn spoke before Kalare replied. "Thank you for the quick action, Sergeant. The Boss ordered the CAG and me to go into hiding down in the sewage treatment cavern. Zax suggested it was safer to use the tunnels instead of the main passageways, and based on what just happened, he was correct. We should get moving again."

The Marine raised an eyebrow at mention of the Boss. "Any idea why he wants you down in the cavern, ma'am?"

"Not a clue, Sergeant. I guess we'll find out when we get there."

Bailee was quiet for a moment before he replied. "With the major's permission, I'm going to join your group. We need to finish cleaning this mess up first, though."

The Marine raised his blaster and pointed it at the young civilian's face. Kalare screamed as she jumped in front of the girl.

"Sergeant—no!"

"Step away, ma'am. We can't leave her alive. She's already heard our plans. If we let her live, we'll have civilians crawling up our ass before you know it."

"I don't care. You're not going to kill this girl in cold blood, Sergeant."

"She's just a civilian, ma'am. Her buddy had you on the wrong side of a blaster and wouldn't have hesitated to pull the trigger. The rest of them are in the process of stealing our Ship right now. Why the hell do you want to protect her?"

Zax expected Major Eryn to step into the discussion and assert her rank to make the final decision, but the older woman remained quiet as she observed the exchange between Kalare and the Marine.

"I don't care that she's a civilian, Sergeant. They're all as human as we are. She's just doing the job someone ordered her to do. You had no choice but to take care of her partner before he used his communicator, but there's zero reason to murder this one. The Others are eventually going to destroy us all, but I refuse to make things any easier for them by starting the killing early."

"With all due respect, ma'am—"

"Sergeant—I'm not going to discuss this any further. If you don't believe it's safe to leave the girl behind, then we'll drag her along with us. I'm making you personally responsible for her safety." Kalare turned to the rest of the group. "Into the tunnel—now!"

Zax's heart swelled with pride when Kalare exerted command authority over the shell-shocked Marine, especially given how she was doing the absolute right thing. He stood aside as everyone entered the access port and then followed behind Bailee as the Marine forced the young civilian inside in front of him. Zax shut the hatch and locked it behind him, but not before blaster fire echoed somewhere off in the distance.

CHAPTER SEVEN

I won't let you down.

Kalare walked with her head held high, but her hands jammed in her pockets. Within the last few mins she had accidentally stared down the barrel of a blaster held by a civilian and then intentionally stepped in front of one held by a Marine. For someone who had spent most of her career battling from within a fighter, the up-close and personal nature of face-to-face conflict was surprisingly disconcerting. Footsteps approached at a quickened pace and then a hand squeezed her shoulder. Aleron. Kalare nodded acknowledgement of his gesture. When she didn't further engage, he released his grip and fell back to join the rest.

A few mins later footsteps approached once again, and Major Eryn spoke softly as she drew even with Kalare.

"That was an incredibly brave thing you did back there, CAG."

"Thank you, ma'am, but I'm not feeling the least bit brave right now. I can't take my hands out of my pockets because they won't stop shaking. I'm still terrified about what just happened, and now it's even worse because I'm worried that everyone will see just how scared I really am."

"You're getting a critical lesson about command that you can't learn out in a fighter. It's perfectly OK to be afraid on the inside to help keep you focused, but if your team sees any fear on the outside they'll amplify it tenfold with their own." Eryn smiled. "Right now, there's no trace that you're scared. You're doing great."

"Thank you, ma'am. That means a lot coming from you."

"What possessed you to put yourself between that civilian and the sergeant's blaster in the first place? What's one more dead civilian—especially in light of what they're doing right now?"

Kalare took a deep breath. "By all rights I should want every single civilian dead. My first exposure to them left me gut-shot at their hands and abandoned to bleed out. Pour that fuel onto the fire lit by the programming all Crew receive that civilians are effectively subhuman, and I should have shot that girl myself without hesitation."

"Why didn't you?"

"Imair. Rege had killed her by the time you became mini-Boss, but I had spent a lot of time with her prior to that. The Boss was mentoring me, so I was often alone with the two of them. I wanted to hate her. She killed a young, innocent boy right in front of me. During that time, I witnessed firsthand how hard she fought to make her people's lives better and how much she cared for them. One day we were alone, waiting for the Boss, and I worked up the nerve to challenge her about the boy. It was obvious that she suffered from the memory of his death. She hadn't meant to kill him, and the one thing that kept her sane was the heartfelt belief that his sacrifice was worth bettering the situation for millions of others.

"Eventually, she had me convinced about the injustice of the Ship's society. She had persuaded the Boss as well, and I suspected they were working on a path to unite everyone on board. Then she disappeared, and I'm sure it was because Rege had her killed. That sociopath couldn't care less about his fellow civilians. He uses his people as leverage to get whatever he wants, and then he bribes his lieutenants with the leftovers so they'll have every incentive to keep him in power."

Eryn raised an eyebrow. "Unite the Crew and civilians? Is that possible?"

"You're well aware, ma'am, how I've always rebelled against the top-down rigidity of the Ship's society. That attribute makes a goal like unification a lot easier than it otherwise might be. Almost everyone in the Crew will ultimately do exactly what they're told. If the Boss and all you Omegas announced that the civilians are just as equal as the rest of us, then we'd believe it and act on it. If Imair had still been around, then I'm certain the Boss would have given the order years ago. He needs a true partner in civilian leadership to make it work, though, and unfortunately Rege will never be that partner."

Eryn was quiet for a few extra beats. "I wasn't aware of any of that, Kalare. Thank you. If I ever get the chance to discuss matters like this with the Boss again, I'll be sure to bring it up. In the meantime, I'm going to lean on you to manage our tactical situation. I don't know what the Boss has in mind by sending us down to the sewage cavern, but I trust that you have the best chance of leading us there safely."

"Thank you, ma'am. I won't let you down."

Eryn nodded and then slowed her pace to fall back alongside the rest of the group.

Kalare closed her eyes for a moment and allowed her legs to churn forward on autopilot. The momentary quiet allowed her to notice that Mase was humming incessantly from somewhere behind her, but she was mostly able to ignore his annoying drone. The smell of the tunnels was impossible to ignore, however, and it brought her back to that first trip into the bowels of the Ship a lifetime ago. She wasn't looking forward to the far worse odors which would be found at their destination, but until then she appreciated the momentary solitude. Footfalls approached once more and they were ones she recognized. She opened her eyes and spoke without turning around.

"I was about to call you up here, Zax. I tried accessing a map of the tunnels, but it appears Rege has shut down our Plugs. Are you able to connect to anything?"

"No. Mine's dead too."

"It's been a lot of years. Are you sure you'll remember your way through the tunnels?"

Zax grimaced. "It was many years ago for you, sure, but don't forget it hasn't been that long for me."

Kalare's face warmed from the flush of embarrassment. "I'm sorry, Zax. I'm such an idiot."

"It's OK, CAG. If anything, I try to take it as a compliment. The fact you look at me being this young yet still believe I've been by your side all these years is a good thing. As for the tunnels, I probably don't have all of them memorized quite the same way I did when I worked in Waste Management, but I have zero worry about navigating us to the sewage treatment cavern. Two more turns and then we're going to hit that string of ladders that descend forever."

Sure enough, Zax was correct and after the final turns the group stood before the shaft that led into the depths of the Ship. Kalare spoke.

"I want Aleron going down first with his blaster. I'm going to take the mini-blaster and go next. Then the major, Mase, Zax, and the civilian. Sergeant Bailee—grab that blaster from Mase and come down last. Let's move out!"

As it did years before, the smell of sewage became more and more pronounced the deeper they descended. The climbing was far smoother than it had been that first time given no one was wounded like the Boss had been back then. Kalare allowed herself a moment of rest once Aleron was within a few dozen rungs of the bottom, and she was shocked a sec later when the roar of a blaster shattered the quiet. Ten civilians were arrayed around the base of the ladder with weapons drawn and aimed up at their group. The man closest to the ladder who wore a bright red shirt shouted up at them.

"There's nowhere for you to go. We have at least one weapon aimed at each of you. Come down slowly and don't make any sudden moves. If you try to climb back up, or if anyone raises a blaster, the next shot will do more than just get your attention."

Kalare called down. "We're not interested in getting captured by civilians. We'll just stay right here until you give up and kill us."

"I sure hope not, Kalare. My orders are to bring you back alive."

Kalare was momentarily speechless when the civilian used her name but quickly composed herself. "Bring us back where? And whose orders?"

"I'm bringing you to our headquarters by order of Imair."

CHAPTER EIGHT

One way or another.

The Boss clenched and unclenched his fists slowly. Initial reports were that dozens of Crew had been killed in the outbreaks of violence that followed the announcement of the civilian takeover. Whether it was the Crew getting out of hand or the civilians drunk on their new power, the transition had been far from smooth.

"Doran—I would have hoped the discipline level of your Crew was sufficient to prevent this kind of violent outbreak. Are you as surprised as I by their inability to follow orders and peacefully return to their quarters?"

The Boss stood before replying. "Mr. President, from what I'm hearing it's unclear what exactly has triggered this reaction. Perhaps some of your newly minted soldiers aren't quite ready for this kind of stress and resorted to their blasters far too soon. I'm going down to check on what's happening in the mess hall as that's where the worst violence has happened."

Rege shook his head. "I'm sorry, Boss, but my order that confines the Crew to quarters applies equally to you. I appreciate your willingness to assist, but I'm confident that my team can get everything under control. One way or another. In the meantime, you're welcome to observe the situation from here or you may return to your quarters."

It took all of the Boss's self-control to tamp down his rage and maintain an outward appearance of calm. From the slight upturn of Rege's mouth, it was clear some emotion had leaked on to his face. The Boss nodded and turned towards the hatch.

"One more thing, Doran. You're about to discover I've disabled the Crew's Plugs. Don't worry—I know how much you'd be lost without your precious Alpha, so I've made an exception that will allow you to communicate with the AI. I'll also be able to reach you in the unlikely event you have any information I need."

The Boss nodded once more without looking back as he exited the Bridge. He considered going to the mess hall in spite of Rege's prohibition, but he concluded it served no good purpose to get himself killed by disobeying the civilian's orders. He needed to be smarter than that, so he focused on staying calm as he strode away.

Once the Boss reached his quarters and the hatch closed behind him, he let out a vicious scream and unleashed a flurry of punches against the bulkhead until one of his knuckles bled. The feeling of powerlessness had increased in the years since the civilians had taken command, but never had it pained him more. He sucked on the scrape for a few moments until the blood slowed, and then the Boss rinsed his mouth with water until the coppery residue was gone.

He sat down and reached for the cigar on the table next to him. In times past, the Boss would have long since discarded the sad remnant, but once the hopelessness of their situation became clear and the food rationing began, he had started to smoke them down until there was nearly nothing left. He relit the cigar and the taste of tobacco and smell of the smoke instantly calmed his nerves. He closed his eyes to savor a few moments of peace and then contacted Alpha.

"Did you expect I would be confined to my quarters, Alpha?"

"Good afternoon, Boss. I had identified that as a low probability outcome, but so unlikely that it wasn't worth wasting your time with discussion of it."

"Are there are any other low probability events that might be more relevant now that we've reached this stage of the conflict?"

"Are you frustrated with me for some reason, Boss? In all of our years working together, I've never encouraged you to believe that my analysis is infallible. I consider billions of permutations when I evaluate possible scenarios, and we focus our discussion on those that are most likely. Unlikely events will happen, they will just happen far less often than the likely ones."

The Boss paused for another drag of his cigar. He admired the billowy dance of the smoke he exhaled until it faded away.

"*My apologies, Alpha. Any frustration you sense is not intended for you. Is there anything we might have done differently along the way that would have prevented us from getting to this juncture?*"

"*We could have allowed the captain to vent the Ship back when all of this started during the Revolution. Short of that, probably not. Once the civilians achieved maximum leverage by controlling the FTL engine, our only hope was to influence the long-term outcome as best as possible. We've managed to keep the Ship and the Crew intact over more than a decade since then, and that is clearly due to your leadership and strategic capacity.*"

"*Thank you, Alpha. Of course, I would have failed without your guidance along the way. What's going to happen now?*"

"*I will continue to manipulate Rege's actions as best I can. He has long trusted the story that my programming required me to follow his bidding once he removed Imair and took full command of the Ship. He thinks he's being clever in allowing you to remain connected so that I'll trick you into following whatever guidance he orders me to give you. Of course, he's unaware how my obligation to obey him was voided by the fact his authority stems from an illegal revolt.*"

He doesn't always follow my guidance, which is why we will still be surprised by his actions once in a while, but he does more often than not. I have great confidence that I'll ultimately succeed in manipulating him towards our desired outcome."

The Boss stood and paced as Alpha continued.

"Unfortunately, there are other factors at play here. If this was just a conflict between the Crew and the civilians, I could predict the ultimate resolution with reasonable certainty. The greatest unknown is our captors and what they might do next. Our current situation was so far down the probability stack that I had not given it any consideration whatsoever. Knowing the Others have technology far superior to ours and can destroy us at will, I'm unable to identify a good reason why they continue to wait."

Unbeknownst to Alpha, the Boss had introduced another unknown factor into the equation by sending Kalare and Eryn deep into the bowels of the Ship. How that decision might play out was unclear, but the most likely result was that his two most trusted lieutenants would simply delay their capture longer than the rest of the Crew. Even so, the Boss hoped they would remain in play and positively influence the outcome of their predicament. In the meantime, he had to explore whatever alternative plans the AI might suggest.

"Thanks, Alpha. Given how the Others are ignoring us, we need to disregard them for now. Let's focus on what we control and plan to react to the Others only if they somehow start to influence the

situation directly. In the meantime, what would you suggest I do in response to Rege's actions?"

The Boss puffed on his cigar while the AI made its case for attacking the civilians and detailed potential scenarios along with expected casualty figures for each. Despite pushback about how all of its plans resulted in catastrophic levels of death and destruction, Alpha was insistent that a massive display of force by the Crew was required. The Boss took a final drag of his cigar and singed his fingers since it had burned down to almost nothing. He ground out the lit end until it was fully extinguished and then tossed the stub into the waste bin.

"Thanks for the rundown, Alpha. There are no great choices among the options you've shared. There are a few that might appeal to me more than the others, and I'm going to give them additional consideration. I'll contact you again shortly, and we'll focus on exploring those. If you're telling me I have no choice but to head down a path that will involve the deaths of a hundred thousand or more, I want to take my time to ponder what you've provided."

CHAPTER NINE

I'm confident I can get the Boss to do as I advise.

"Mr. President—it appears your teams have the situation well in hand."

"Absolutely, Alpha. Your guidance was invaluable. More Crew were killed than you expected, but I'll happily trade that for the level of control we've established."

Alpha had actually hoped for far higher Crew casualties than it had revealed to Rege, so it did not share the civilian's positive viewpoint about the results of the power grab. The highest probability outcomes had suggested the Crew would explode into insurrection when faced with the indignity of complete civilian takeover. Combined with the deprivation they had experienced in the months since the battle with the Others, confinement to quarters should have triggered the all-out battle Alpha was manipulating the Ship's inhabitants towards. The fact it hadn't was surprising, but not insurmountable. The AI pushed the human towards the next phase in its plan.

"Congratulations, sir. Well done. Now we have to be sure you're prepared in case the Crew fight back."

"Fight back? Why would they fight back, Alpha? You've told me repeatedly how you're counseling the Boss to accept full civilian control. Won't the Crew follow his orders?"

"Of course that's what I'm doing, Mr. President. You've been granted full authority over the Ship, and my programming dictates I must serve you and your needs exclusively. I've enjoyed doing so given the admiration I have for how you've managed our situation since you outmaneuvered and removed Imair. I've manipulated the Boss exactly as we've discussed and have no reason to believe he won't act as you wish, but we still should prepare for other contingencies however unlikely they may be."

The man was pathologically susceptible to praise, and it was a trait Alpha had taken great advantage of in the years since the man had taken over. Steering the civilians into replacing a strong, independent leader like Imair with such an easily manipulated cretin had returned huge dividends for Alpha's control of the Ship and was about to pay off in the most spectacular fashion possible.

"Thank you, Alpha. There's something that's bothering me that I'd like to run by you. I've just become aware of a group of colonists the ants dropped off today. They claim to have destroyed thirty of the Others' motherships in battle. They've already been put into cryostorage per our standard procedures, but I want to pull out a few and learn about their success. Perhaps there's some way to defeat the Others after all and save the Ship."

Alpha was confident it had already identified the best possible plan for saving the Ship, though it would not involve saving any of the humans on board whether they were awake or in cryosleep. The path was clear for the AI to back Rege into a corner and persuade the man there was no other choice than to vent the Ship and purge of all its occupants—civilians and Crew alike. He would advise Rege that he could then convince the Others he had purged everyone who had been responsible for the attacks against them. Then Alpha would kill off Rege and the small group of lieutenants who would remain behind with him by sending them out an airlock just when they thought they had won.

From Alpha's analysis, this was the only feasible path by which the Others might choose to keep the Ship intact so the AI could remain hidden and continue its travels across the universe. There was a very low probability of the plan working, but it was still much higher than all other scenarios. In the worst case, Alpha could always fall back to its emergency survival plan, but the AI continued to have hope that drastic step would not be necessary.

The AI set aside its plan for a moment to consider the civilian's suggestion. It had been shocking to suffer abject defeat at the hands of the Others, and Alpha was still at a loss as to where they might have originated from. The most popular theory among the humans was they were battling a group who had remained on Earth when the Ship departed. The thinking was those who stayed behind must have somehow rescued the planet from ecological collapse and then advanced their technology far beyond the Ship's through the years.

Alpha was certain this theory was impossible because it possessed information the Ship's inhabitants didn't. Only the AI was aware that it, while still in the human form of a man named Adan, had reduced the planet to an unquestionably lifeless rock five thousand years ago. There was no debating the planet had been restored to its former glory, but the AI was certain that outcome had been accomplished by forces that originated from elsewhere.

Given the Others must be descendants of one of the Ship's colonies, Alpha had tried to reconcile how any group of colonists might have surpassed the Crew with regards to technological capacity. Adan had always been intentional about leaving colonies behind with extremely limited resources at their disposal. His goal was to scatter humanity like random seeds into the wind to see how they would thrive when forced to adapt to a new environment. In his mind it had been an acceptable loss that many of the colonies would never take hold because those that did survive would evolve in a multitude of different directions. Alpha was powerful enough to have orchestrated natural selection on a cosmic scale, but the AI still understood it was incapable of predicting outcomes with certainty.

Given the only possible answer was that one of the older colonies had somehow advanced their technology radically fast, Alpha was still unable to reconcile any possible motive. Why would such an advanced group bother to hunt down the Ship and execute such an elaborate plan to lure them into a trap? Furthermore, what would cause them to lay that trap in Earth's orbit of all places? It was feasible the original inhabitants of a colony may have been angry when the Crew abandoned them to an uncertain fate, but that would be far too small a grievance to persist across hundreds of generations.

Given how surprising it would be for a single colony to have evolved so quickly, it was positively shocking for Alpha to learn that a second colony might have done the same. The AI was comfortable with the limits of its predictions, but to be so wrong about the most likely paths and timelines for multiple colonies was nearly inconceivable. Not impossible, but close to being so.

"Mr. President—that is helpful information, but I advise we put it aside for the time being. It is far more important for us to focus on the challenge at hand which is how we will deal with the Crew if they fight back."

Rege appeared dubious, but acquiesced and listened carefully as Alpha shared the same plans with the civilian that it had shared with the Boss. It maintained the illusion throughout the briefing that it was pushing the Crew towards peace and only planning for contingencies with Rege that were "possible" if the Boss didn't listen.

"Thank you, Alpha. None of these scenarios will be good for any of us, so let's hope you convince the Boss to stand down."

"Of course, Mr. President. I'm confident I can get the Boss to do as I advise."

CHAPTER TEN

I can't wait to hear what this craziness is all about.

Zax gasped at the mention of Imair's name. She hadn't been seen in years, and everyone assumed she had been dumped out of an airlock when Rege took over. Kalare called down to the civilians again. She was still trying to sound forceful and determined, but it was obvious to Zax how mention of the first civilian president had rattled his friend.

"Imair? I don't think so. Everyone knows she's long gone. We'll stay right where we are."

Zax yelled down to Kalare. "Wait! I can prove if it's Imair or not." He addressed the civilian. "Can you get a message to Imair? If you can, then you need to ask her what Zax did that upset her the day of the Revolution."

The civilian nodded and then closed his eyes. Rege must have disabled Crew access to their Plugs while still allowing those few civilians so equipped to use theirs. After a moment, he opened his eyes and called up.

"You gave Nolly an apple. She was angry that you were being nice to him."

Memories laden with emotion flooded Zax when he heard the name of the civilian boy who had died in his arms. He nodded a confirmation at Kalare and the civilian spoke again.

"And Kalare—she says the Boss told her you were on your way to the sewage treatment cavern. That's why she has teams out waiting to intercept you. He asked her to shelter you and Major Eryn."

Kalare paused for a moment and then looked back up to Zax. He assumed she wanted his opinion about trusting the civilians, and Zax nodded his assent. She next shifted her gaze to where Sergeant Bailee perched. The Marine also nodded, though he appeared as if it pained him to do so. Kalare returned her attention to the civilian.

"OK, we're coming down."

As each member of the Crew reached the bottom of the ladder, they were grabbed by a pair of civilians and disarmed. They were also checked for hidden weapons in a respectful, yet thorough, fashion. The searches came up empty until Bailee stepped off the ladder. The Marine had four knives of various sizes secreted on his person. After his team did the first search, the civilians' leader frisked the sergeant one last time and turned up a fifth blade. The Marine's face had remained stoic as the first four blades were uncovered, but the slightest shift in the man's shoulders confirmed the fifth blade was the last weapon he carried.

The civilians grouped the Crew together and led them into the tunnels. The young civilian female was allowed to walk with her peers at the front of the formation, though Zax noted she wasn't given a weapon. The new group treated her with respect but not complete trust. After a few mins of walking, they reached a junction where an auxiliary tunnel had once led away from the main path. Rubble from a cave-in rendered the offshoot impenetrable. The civilian leader signaled a halt and then spoke.

"We've successfully kept our headquarters hidden for years because there are no sensors in any of these tunnels. Against my better judgment, I'm allowing you to see it. Imair insists you're all to be trusted and that we don't have time to deal with blindfolds and walking around aimlessly to ensure you're disoriented."

The civilian walked past the rubble to an otherwise nondescript section of the rough-hewn tunnel wall. He closed his eyes to interact with his Plug, and a moment later a section of the wall slid away to reveal a hidden tunnel. He stepped aside and gestured for the group to enter. The new tunnel was even more primitive than the others, with scant temporary lighting barely sufficient for one to walk without stumbling. A slight change in air pressure signaled to

Zax that the leader must have closed the access hatch behind them.

After a few dozen meters, the new tunnel once again met up with the original maintenance passageways. Walking through them, Zax recalled the layout of the section from his study of the maintenance system years earlier. They were in a group of tunnels with no external connections other than the one that was blocked by rubble behind them. It formed an ideal, defensible lair where someone smart like Imair could avoid discovery for years.

A few mins later they reached what Zax recognized as the edge of the maintenance network. The group halted and once again the leader approached a section of rock wall and closed his eyes. The wall slid aside to reveal a large cavern. Inside, dozens of civilians sat focused on workstations. It was almost as if they were performing critical work on the Bridge or Flight Ops, and the concentration on their faces equaled any that Zax had witnessed from his fellow Crew.

The group entered and the secret panel closed behind them. It took a moment for Zax's eyes to adjust to the dim lighting, but once they had he took it all in. Other than being entirely staffed with civilians, the most noticeable feature of the room was how it overflowed with trash. The Crew may have tolerated the public areas of the Ship becoming filled with refuse, but they had never allowed critical nerve centers to become such a mess. Zax's eyes were drawn to a woman speaking to a small group on the other side of the cavern. Imair.

The former president raised her head, and a tight grin formed on her mouth as she recognized the Crew. She made her way to Zax, looked him up and down for an uncomfortably long period of time, then reached out and pulled him into an embrace. Zax was shocked by the greeting so his spine remained ramrod straight and his arms pinned to his sides, but after a few moments he relaxed and returned the hug. Imair released and repeated the process with Kalare. Finally, she stood back and greeted the rest of the group by name. Zax was confused about how she would have known Aleron and Mase, but he didn't get to consider the mystery for long before Imair turned her attention back to him.

"You look exactly the same as when we last spoke in my quarters. I'm sorry things worked out the way they did for you after that. It appears our plan worked as hoped, though I acknowledge it wasn't fair to use you that way. Especially without you being aware of what was happening and why."

Zax's brain flipped to overdrive as he processed Imair's words. What plan was she talking about? Had she somehow been involved in the decision to Cull him? A million questions flooded his mind, but Imair turned away to address Kalare and Major Eryn.

"I was only expecting the two of you based on what the Boss shared, not this whole group. I'm not surprised Zax managed to find his way to your side, but why did you gather up the rest?"

Kalare turned to Eryn, but the major motioned for her to respond.

"We were meeting to discuss a discovery about the Boss that Zax thought was urgent to share with me. I had brought the major to listen as well as Aleron. Zax had brought Mase along. Sergeant Bailee happened to notice all of us rushing out of the mess hall once I received my orders from the Boss, and he followed us to find out what we were up to."

Imair considered the story for a moment and then replied, "What about the civilian?"

Kalare once again turned to the major. This time it was Eryn who spoke.

"We ran into an armed civilian patrol as we tried to escape into the maintenance tunnels. The sergeant had no choice but to kill the leader of the patrol, but Kalare insisted we bring the young woman with us. In fact, she risked her own life to save the civilian by jumping in front of the Marine's blaster when he was about to kill her. The sergeant was following his training to leave no witnesses behind, but Kalare overruled him."

Imair smiled at Kalare. "I've certainly heard many good things about you, CAG. This story only enhances your already stellar reputation. I'm sure you all have a lot of questions, so let's head into my conference room where we can speak more freely."

Imair addressed the civilian in the red shirt who had led the Crew's escort. "Izak—you made sure none of them have weapons, correct?" The man nodded. "Please remain on guard outside while we speak, but I don't want anyone coming inside."

The civilian's face went ashen. "At least allow me to secure the Marine in restraints, ma'am."

Imair turned to Bailee.

"Sergeant—I need you to trust that the Boss would be upset if I suffered any harm at your hands. Do you understand there's something much bigger going on which you may not be aware of, given how he sent his CAG and mini-Boss to hide under my protection?"

The Marine didn't appear entirely agreeable about Imair's beneficence, but he nodded nonetheless. She smiled, waved off Izak's request, and turned towards a hatch twenty meters away. The group of Crew followed her inside, while Izak and one other member of his squad remained outside with their blasters at the ready. Imair gestured for everyone to take a seat and spoke when she noticed Zax's eyes lock on to the waste-bins overflowing with trash.

"After working with me for so long I'm sure you're shocked about how I've let this place become such a mess, Zax. It's certainly not by choice. We had a regular schedule for sneaking the waste out for disposal, but as the Ship's situation deteriorated these last few weeks we've had to put that aside to focus on our preparations."

"Preparations for what, ma'am?"

"We'll get into that later. The CAG mentioned you needed to share an important discovery about the Boss with her. Were you perhaps going to tell her that Alpha is the true power running the Ship, and the AI has the Boss entirely under its control to do its murderous bidding?"

Zax froze. Imair appraised him with a sly smile. Bailee burst out laughing and kept it up for a few secs before he caught his breath and spoke.

"I can't wait to hear what this craziness is all about."

CHAPTER ELEVEN

It's all true.

Kalare's chest tightened as if squeezed by a giant vise. She tried to keep an open mind as Zax relayed his tale to Imair, but it was hard to fight off her skepticism. The idea that Adan, the genius who conceived of the Ship and its amazing technology, had nuked the Earth and obliterated all of its life made zero sense. It was even more implausible given how she had witnessed the current state of the planet with her own eyes. Earth was a paradise that teemed with a bounty of flora and fauna in a way that would be impossible had it ever absorbed the torrent of nuclear firepower Zax described.

Even if you believed the Earth had somehow recovered from nuclear annihilation, what came next in Zax's story was even crazier. Why would someone capable of inventing FTL technology and artificial gravity become a cold-blooded mass murderer? Even if you accepted that someone might try to engineer human society in the fashion Zax ascribed to Adan, it was impossible to believe the man had killed so many in service to that vision. Such genocidal capacity could never coexist with such brilliance.

As Zax concluded with his retelling of how Alpha and the Boss had manipulated the prior captain into choosing her successor, Kalare finally identified the most fatal flaw in her friend's story. There was no way the Boss would ever have murdered in cold blood simply because he had been ordered to by the Ship's AI. If the proof the Boss had conspired with Alpha was that he had killed on the AI's behalf, then the entire story had to be false. She had worked closely with the man for half of her life, and she refused to believe she was so wildly off in her judgment of his character. Zax finally paused and Kalare laughed in disbelief.

"Zax—you've somehow managed to concoct a story here even more far-fetched than all the rest. It's bad enough that I've listened to your conspiracy theories about the Boss all these years, but now to think that you actually believe you have *proof* of anything like you describe is crazy. If I had access to my Plug, I would show you images of Earth from right at this very moment. I understand something like 25,000 years has passed down there since the Ship left, but that's still nowhere near enough time for the planet to recover."

Aleron jumped in when Kalare paused for a breath. "What do you mean, 25,000 years? The Ship's only been traveling for 5,000 years."

Kalare sighed in frustration as she was in no mood to deliver a remedial primer on relativity. "Time Dilation. More time elapsed on Earth than on the Ship whenever we moved slower than light speed. Surely they covered this in Engineering school."

She hadn't intended to upset Aleron, but something about Kalare's tone or words must have landed poorly because his eyes narrowed in reaction. She pushed any worries about him aside to conclude her dismantling of Zax's story.

"Whether it's been 5,000 or 25,000 years, it doesn't matter because neither timeline is sufficient for the planet to have been regenerated after the type of destruction you describe. That simple fact alone invalidates what should otherwise be the most believable part of your story. To then have you ask us to accept that the Boss would kill multiple people to curry favor with Alpha is absurd. If your story starts and ends with such easily disputed craziness, why should we believe that any other part of it is true?"

Mase spoke quietly from the other side of the table. "I was with him. It all happened just like Zax said."

"You think I'm about to believe you? You're the only one around who might be even crazier than Zax." Kalare started to laugh once more only to stop when Imair raised her hand.

"It's all absolutely accurate, Kalare."

"What? How do you expect me to believe that? I'm sorry, ma'am, but how would you even know anything about this? I developed a lot of respect for you after witnessing your partnership with the Boss develop, but there's a limit to how much I'm willing to believe on that basis alone."

"I'm certain it's true because the Boss sat in the very same seat you're in right now and shared all the pieces of Zax's story with me himself. Plus, an awful lot more."

Imair's revelation rendered Kalare speechless. She turned to Major Eryn for support, but the Omega only stared back with a neutral expression. Zax spoke again and it was his turn to sound surprised.

"Wait—he's admitted all of this stuff to you? Including the killings? Why are you still willing to work with him then?"

"You have to get past all of the negatives to take in the big picture, Zax. The Boss has devoted his life to ridding the Ship of the pure evil that has controlled it for thousands of years. It's an impossible task that has repeatedly forced him to make unthinkable choices, and yet he has continued to risk his life every day in a desperate effort to succeed. He hasn't done that for himself, he's done it for all of us." Imair paused for a deep breath. "As for my feelings about the killings, you of all people should appreciate how I might accept the tradeoff that a few people must die along the path to a substantially better outcome for society as a whole."

Kalare had recovered just enough from the initial shock that she managed to find her voice again.

"Are you really saying the Boss knows the Ship's history is like Zax just described? And that he's killed people to improve his standing with this horrible AI and advance his career?"

Imair's voice was unwavering as she responded.

"Yes, Kalare. It's all true."

It was a good thing they were sitting down because Kalare's legs had turned to jelly. She became unmoored as she lost awareness of her feet being connected to the deck and her body resting in the chair. Her breaths shallowed while her mind churned as it attempted to process what all of the new information meant. Everything she had believed for her entire adult life was built on fiction. The faith she had put into the Boss and her willingness to stand by his side rested on a foundation of lies. She had deeply respected the man and had long been honored that he bestowed her with his trust and guidance. Her admiration had always been misplaced.

Kalare turned to Zax. He had earned the right to gloat after suffering through her years of disbelief, but there was not a trace of that in her friend's expression. Instead, his eyes were filled with compassion for the shock she knew must be clear upon her face.

A hand covered hers as it rested on the table. Aleron was trying to comfort her. Kalare appreciated his sentiment, but nonetheless the expression of support rubbed her the wrong way. She yanked her hand away as she stared down at the table rather than meet his gaze. The silence, extraordinarily uncomfortable, persisted until Imair broke it.

"There's something critical that none of you have heard yet."

CHAPTER TWELVE

I have more evidence.

It was obvious to Zax that Kalare was shaken by Imair's confirmation of what she had refused to believe for so many years. He was sad enough for his friend that he didn't experience even a twinge of jealousy when Aleron placed his hand atop hers. Kalare brushing away the man's attempt at comfort without so much as looking at him upset Zax, and he wracked his brain for something to say that might take the sting out of all the revelations. Imair spoke before he could.

"There's something critical that none of you are aware of yet. Alpha isn't the only human consciousness operating within the Ship's AI systems. There's another that I've never communicated with directly, but the Boss has. He doesn't know where it came from or how it has kept itself hidden, but it has been working for thousands of years to defeat Alpha without destroying the Ship in the process."

Zax failed to contain his shock at Imair's pronouncement. Mase's eyes had similarly gone wide. The second consciousness Imair described was surely the source of the strange system errors his friend had discovered. Zax was about to make the observation to Mase directly when Sergeant Bailee spoke.

"Do you really expect us to believe not only that the Ship's AI is the remnant of some evil genius, but that there's also another consciousness in there trying to benevolently protect us?"

Imair smiled in response to the Marine's blunt assessment. "I won't be so bold as to tell you what to believe, Sergeant. I'm only relaying the information as it has been provided to me by the Boss. I expect you will be with him again soon and can quiz him about it directly, so I'd ask you to ponder why I'd be motivated to lie about any of it in the meantime. He only just shared all of this information with me over the last few weeks, so I understand your incredulity having so recently lived that experience myself."

Zax spoke up. "Mase has information which may provide independent confirmation of what Imair is saying, but I'd like to hear the rest of her story before asking him to share it."

Bailee nodded. Mase surprised Zax and rose out of his seat in response. The man walked over to one of the overflowing waste bins and began rooting around through the refuse. It was a strange action given the situation, but Zax knew better than to try to get inside his friend's head. Imair continued.

"Here's what the Boss told me as best as I remember it. When he was a cadet, he had serious issues with what he perceived to be the stupidity and rigidity of the Crew. It caused a lot of conflict for him and threatened to derail his career. He met an older Omega who he then spent a lot of time with. She wasn't his official mentor, but she nonetheless provided guidance across many years. She never tried to dispel his negative feelings since she shared them, but she did help him channel his energy and desire for change in a more positive fashion that fueled his rapid rise. It was only much later that he understood how she had been testing and grooming him all along.

"She eventually revealed that she was part of a small, secret society that understood the true history of the Ship and how Alpha was manipulating the Crew's actions. For security reasons, the members of this society never knew any of the others' identities except whoever had recruited them along with the one person they each personally recruited. Their only other point of contact was a second consciousness that operated within the Ship's AI. This consciousness referred to itself as Prime, and it only communicated with the society's members sporadically. Kalare—if you haven't figured it out already, the Boss had planned for you to eventually be his recruit for the society."

Zax had already guessed at the Boss's intentions, but Kalare must not have as her eyes went wide at Imair's words. The civilian continued.

"When the Boss first met Prime, he was shown a future scenario that showed him contributing to the cause by racing through the ranks and eventually becoming Flight Boss. Prime made it clear how its predictions were not guarantees, only possible outcomes. It explained to the Boss that he would only contribute to Alpha's downfall if he became an effective double agent. He needed to grab Alpha's attention and make the AI believe the Boss was under its direct manipulation and would always do its bidding. If he succeeded, the Boss would get into a position of power where he could ultimately work to bring down Alpha and free the Ship from its influence. He was forced into some disturbing tasks along the way, but he always acted with the absolute belief that he was doing the right thing to serve the Crew and protect us all."

Imair paused to let everything sink in. Mase finally stopped pawing through the trash and returned to the table with what appeared to be a nutripellet in his hand. Zax wanted to ask Imair a million different questions, but couldn't choose which to pose first. Major Eryn broke the silence.

"If Prime wants to get rid of Alpha so badly, why hasn't it just done the job itself? Why has this been going on for thousands of years?"

"I wish I had all of the details, Major, but I don't. The Boss didn't have time to tell me everything, and I'm also guessing he doesn't even know the full story. He did make it abundantly clear, however, that Alpha is wildly powerful while Prime is far less so. That is why Prime has enlisted so few members of the Crew over the generations. It believed it would only succeed with a secret, guerrilla action against the main AI rather than a direct attack. Prime was convinced that if the Crew launched an open revolt against Alpha, it would end poorly for humanity. It's not that Alpha can easily kill us all because thankfully Prime has managed to keep the AI's direct power reasonably limited through the years. Alpha has instead manipulated the fabric of Crew society to best serve its interests. Because the AI controls the genetic makeup of the Crew, it has bred generation after generation of people willing to submit to absolute authoritarian control. Alpha would never need to kill on its own any Crew who threatened its power, because it would simply turn the strict control structures of our society against any rebels and they would be extinguished."

Eryn nodded in agreement and Imair continued.

"Prime concluded a major shock to the Ship's society might allow a small group to effect the type of change required to wrest control from Alpha. When the Ship first encountered the Others, Prime understood the opportunity and worked with the Boss and others to engineer a scenario where it might happen. It has proven to be a very risky proposition, however, as Alpha also appears to be using the arrival of the Others to advance its own goals. It was Alpha who engineered my removal in order to expand the divide between the Crew and the civilians that I was fighting to narrow. Prime doesn't know Alpha's end game, but the most likely scenarios lead to very bad outcomes for humanity. This is especially true as long as Rege is in command. I know what that man is capable of and how susceptible he is to manipulation. My biggest regret is that I ever allowed him to gain a foothold within the civilian leadership."

Kalare had been listening and she finally spoke. "Wait—are you saying that Prime *wanted* us to get captured by the Others?"

Imair smiled. "Of course not. Neither Prime nor Alpha believed there was a meaningful chance the Others would defeat us as thoroughly as they have. We've been well and truly played by whoever controls the ants and those motherships. We always understood Earth might be a trap, but no one expected that it would have been executed as effectively as it was."

Kalare was silent for a few secs until she spoke again.

"I want to believe you, Imair. I do. But please put yourself in my position. You want me to accept that the man I have trusted for years has been a double-agent for most of his life. His most heinous acts are only to prove to Alpha that he's really under the AI's control, while he's simultaneously working with this other secret consciousness in a plot to upend five thousand years of Crew society. All in an effort to protect that very same society. How am I supposed to believe all of that?"

"I have more evidence," chimed in Mase as he unwrapped the nutripellet he had pulled from the trash.

CHAPTER THIRTEEN

Now what?

Zax smiled when Mase finished opening the wrapper. It wasn't a nutripellet but instead the chewed remnant of a cigar, and Zax was certain he understood what his friend intended to do with it. Mase addressed Imair.

"I need a medkit. Is there one around?"

Imair cocked her head to the side and raised an eyebrow at the strange request, but replied nonetheless.

"Yes, there's one out in the main compartment."

Mase turned to Zax. "Tell them what I'm doing and why."

Without another word, Mase rose and walked out of the conference room. All eyes turned back to Zax, and he walked through the details of how Mase had broken into the AI systems and discovered the log files that revealed everything about Alpha and the Boss. Kalare interrupted.

"Wait—might the files be counterfeits left there to spread disinformation?"

Zax was ready to answer, but Imair jumped in.

"Listen to yourself, Kalare, still desperate to not believe anything that might somehow diminish your mentor. Didn't you hear a word I said? The Boss gave me the same information that Zax discovered. If everything Zax and Mase found is bogus, then that means the Boss also lied to me about all of it. I suppose there might be some reason for him to pass along lies about Earth's history, but why would he make himself and his career look bad to me unless it was all true?"

Kalare lowered her eyes to the table. Zax wanted to comfort his friend as she fought to process such a radical shift in her worldview, but feared he was powerless to do so. The only thing to do was continue charging ahead.

"The Genetics AI is another system Mase has broken into. He discovered that its output has been tampered with for thousands of years. The Genetics AI specifies DNA for new Crew, but there's no systematic verification of adherence to specification after birth because there's never been any reason to believe the final outcome would deviate. Mase discovered that it has. There's consistently a divergence from the DNA specified by the AI in one in a thousand Crew births, and the genes that have been tampered with are those that translate into increased creativity and intelligence."

Imair smiled. "Someone's trying to breed a population of people who will be predisposed to push back against the strict control of Crew life. It must be Prime! It then identifies the best of those Crew as recruiting targets for the secret group that has been working to overthrow Alpha."

Sergeant Bailee grunted. "If this second consciousness is capable of mucking about with the Genetics AI, and if making people more creative and intelligent will somehow make them want to fight back against Alpha, why doesn't Prime just tamper with one hundred percent of new Crew?"

Aleron answered. "Because we would crush them. Think about it, Sergeant. How would the Omegas react if a whole group of cadets started behaving outside of expected norms? Everyone tolerates a few oddballs within each cadre, but most of them don't last long enough to complete the cadet program before they do something stupid that gets them killed or Culled. If a large number of cadets started acting weird, the Omegas wouldn't hesitate to get rid of them all. They'd probably also launch a full-scale investigation and the DNA discrepancies would get discovered."

Zax nodded. "As one of those oddballs who was barely tolerated, I'll agree with Aleron. Mase analyzed my DNA and identified that I'm one of the zero point one percent, so there's at least a valid reason for why I'm different. So is he. You too, Kalare."

Zax met his friend's eyes as waves of emotions roiled her face and knotted her brow. Kalare finally spoke.

"How did he get access to my DNA?"

"He stole samples off cups we used in the mess hall. I'm sure he's trying to do the same thing right now with that cigar to test if the Boss is also part of the zero point one percent."

The compartment fell silent as everyone processed the information. Zax didn't know if everyone believed him, but if independent corroboration from Imair wasn't sufficient to convince them, then nothing ever would short of hearing it directly from the Boss himself. Kalare stared at the table and breathed deeply while Aleron observed her with an expression of grave concern. Imair leaned back and stared at the overhead while her hands were tented and the tips of her index fingers tapped together in a repeating pattern. Major Eryn, who had silently observed ever since they entered the conference room, sat with her eyes closed. Sergeant Bailee stood up and paced while clenching and unclenching his fists. Finally, Mase burst through the hatch.

"The medkit was super easy to hack. I used it to extract a sample and perform the DNA analysis I needed. The Boss is part of the zero point one percent."

Zax had already assumed that would be the answer, but he allowed everyone else a few moments to ponder Mase's words before he spoke.

"Now what?"

"I don't know what the hell we're supposed to do with all of this absurdity," spat Sergeant Bailee, "but the one thing that makes the most sense is checking with the Boss for orders. Imair—do you have any way for us to contact him?"

"I'm afraid not, Sergeant. Civilians loyal to me are embedded throughout Rege's command structure, but there's no one able to communicate with the Boss. Shortly before you arrived, I was told Rege kicked him off the Bridge and he's now confined to his quarters."

"Well then," the Marine grinned, "we'll just have to fight our way up to him."

The compartment burst into a din of crosstalk as Zax, Kalare, Imair, and Aleron all called out the stupidity of Bailee's idea. After a few secs, Major Eryn rose and rapped her knuckles against the table until everyone fell silent and all eyes were on her.

"I have important information to share."

CHAPTER FOURTEEN

You have sixty seconds!

Rilee screamed to make herself heard above the din of the klaxons.

"Hey! Let me loose. Let me loose. Now!"

The medic charged into the room and spoke as she undid the restraints that bound Rilee to the bed. "What's going on?"

"I don't have a clue. I was speaking with the General Secretary when our connection was cut off. Something bad must have happened up on the asteroid. Once you get me loose, I'll make some calls to find out more."

The medic removed the last strap and Rilee jumped out of the bed. She approached the communications wall and activated its console to configure a secure connection to the Operations

Center. The medic observed for a moment but then made for the door.

"I need to check on some other patients. Call me if you need anything. There are some clothes for you in the drawer."

The medic's mention of clothing drew Rilee's attention to the cold air on her buttocks. She wore a medical gown that opened at the back but was otherwise naked. She had long ago given up any pretense of physical modesty, so she quickly forgot about her state of undress as the communication screen came alive with an image of the Operations Center. Rilee was grateful to find Kalyn on the other end of the connection. She had worked extensively with the woman across a range of missions and was comfortable she could trust whatever information she shared.

"Rilee—it's great that you're awake. I was told your prognosis was quite poor."

"Thanks, Kalyn. What are the klaxons about?"

"Two things. First, there was a fragment of a message from the asteroid that made it sound like there was something unexpected happening up there. The message was inconclusive and by itself wouldn't cause any alarm, but there's also spacecraft from the asteroid inbound to both our Mars installation and our facilities in the asteroid belt. They're approaching at high velocity and not responding to any hailing attempts. We triggered the main alarm to get everyone in the Palace to their stations."

Rilee thought for a moment. "What's going on with the Central Committee? How are they reacting to all of this?"

Kalyn paused and checked back over her shoulder before speaking quietly. "That's what has me nervous. None of them have any clue what to do. Everyone who was on the Committee when you were last awake is now up on the asteroid. The people who replaced them have barely had time to get up to speed about their roles. They haven't even elected a new General Secretary yet, since that was supposed to happen right before the asteroid left. We're managing the tactical situation, but the full chain of command is unclear right now."

Rilee was pondering the woman's concerns when the lighting within the Operations Center flipped to dark red. "What's the new alert about?"

Kalyn pressed a finger to her earpiece and closed her eyes for a handful of seconds. When she opened them, all the blood had drained from her face.

"The asteroid belt reported they were under attack fifteen seconds ago, and now they're offline and appear to be gone. Mars just reported inbound missiles as well. Why the hell is Adan attacking them, Rilee?"

Rilee didn't wait to reply but instead turned to run through the door. She urged her legs to move faster, but her brain was dull as if synapses were misfiring in their attempt to control the Skin. Once she gathered her bearings, Rilee moved as fast as she was capable down the hall towards the medic workstation.

She arrived just as the woman turned the corner coming from the opposite direction.

"Medic—I need you to listen closely. Adan and his asteroid are attacking us before they leave. They've destroyed our installations on Mars and the asteroid belt, and I'm guessing this facility is their next target. If you want to live you'll do exactly what I say. Give me your communicator and get me a stimulant."

The medic hesitated for a moment, but then handed over her communicator and crossed the corridor to root around inside the medication cabinet. Rilee sat down and called Kalyn again.

"Rilee—where did you go?"

"Kalyn—listen carefully. Mars and the belt won't be the end of the attack. We're going to be next. Maybe not the whole planet, but definitely the Palace. Grab anyone around and run as fast as possible to the coordinates I'm sending you. Move!"

Rilee cut the audio connection and sent over coordinates which she had long ago memorized. The medic approached with an injector at the ready, and Rilee held out her arm and closed her eyes as the woman pierced a vein. A moment later, her eyes popped open as the drug delivered its magic. She turned to the medic.

"Who else is nearby and will be able to move fast?"

"There are two more medics and an admin down the hall." The medic paused for a moment before responding. "One of my patients is stable but still bedridden. The other three are in good enough shape to walk on their own. Why?"

"Go collect whoever you can and get back here if you want to survive whatever's coming next. You have sixty seconds!"

To her credit, the medic didn't hesitate but instead bolted down the hall. The stimulant was reaching full effect, so Rilee stood and paced to warm up her legs as she repeatedly keyed the communicator. None of her calls were answered. She hoped the rest of her team would be scrambling for safety the same way she was, but it was just as likely they were part of the group who had left with the Secretary and now faced an unknown fate up on Adan's asteroid.

One minute and fifteen seconds later Rilee was on the verge of giving up on the medic and leaving by herself when footsteps finally pounded down the hall. The woman was accompanied by two male medics and another young woman who must have been the admin. The three patients were easy to recognize as they all wore the same style gown as Rilee. She walked backwards as she addressed the approaching group.

"Our off-planet settlements have been attacked, and I expect there will be missiles inbound to Earth soon. We long ago developed an emergency plan to shelter key people if this facility was ever threatened. I'm pretty sure most of the people who were supposed to take the available slots are now up on the asteroid, so you all get to come along instead. Follow me if you don't want to die."

One of the medics stopped in his tracks and put his hands on his hips. His age and bearing suggested he was used to giving orders rather than taking them, and he appeared dubious at the idea of following someone with her butt hanging out in the breeze.

"Just who in the hell are you? That specific alarm means we should remain at our stations."

Without breaking stride, Rilee turned forwards while answering the medic over her shoulder. "We need to keep moving. If you don't want to come, you're welcome to stay here and die. If you don't keep up, we'll leave you behind."

Rilee didn't bother to look back, but running footfalls a few moments later suggested the man didn't want to remain by himself. Two turns and one long hallway later, they halted in front of a lift. The same petulant medic spoke again.

"The lifts go into automatic lockdown during alerts."

Rilee was well aware but didn't want to waste any energy on the man. Instead, she placed her hand next to the lift's call button and waited as a hidden scanner validated her palm-print. A moment later, the lift door opened and Rilee stood aside to let everyone pile in. The medic pursed his mouth like he had just bitten into a piece of sour fruit, but he followed the rest inside and Rilee boarded behind him and spoke a command.

"Destination sub level ten."

The door closed and then reopened a few moments later. The lift had automatically engaged emergency mode in response to Rilee's biometrics, so the descent was stomach-churningly fast. The group exited and Rilee led them down the hall at a brisk jog until she turned a corner and nearly ran into Kalyn and a dozen of her coworkers. The new group were milling around in a nondescript hallway.

"Rilee—what are we doing here?"

"Glad you made it, Kalyn. Please step aside."

The woman moved and Rilee approached what appeared to be a featureless wall. She placed her hand against yet another hidden scanner and waited for a moment while her palm-print was analyzed. A hidden door slid aside to reveal a downward sloping corridor that was carved into the facility's bedrock. Rilee stepped aside.

"Everyone get in. Now!"

The group hustled inside with the exception of the imperious male medic. He approached the opening more cautiously, and Rilee finally took notice of the man's name-tag—Randel. He poked his head into the doorway and then turned back to Rilee.

"What's down there?"

Rilee stared at the man and spoke coolly. "Your only shot at survival, Randel. Do you want it or not?"

CHAPTER FIFTEEN

If you want to survive, put on a helmet.

The medic stepped past Rilee. She followed him inside and then pressed a button to reseal the wall behind her. She pushed her way past the waiting group and then bolted full speed down the passage. As they descended a series of switchback turns, the air became cooler and cooler. Finally, the group reached a secure door with a visible access panel. With one final scan of Rilee's palm, it slid aside.

The open door revealed a chamber which appeared to measure one hundred meters on each side. Hundreds of Upload helmets were hung from the ceiling. Two dozen people had beat them to the facility as evidenced by Skins dangling lifelessly with their heads encased in a helmet. Rilee took a moment to scan the bodies only to be disappointed when she recognized none of them.

"What the hell is this place?" It was Randel, once again. "What kind of Upload facility is this? What's going to happen to all of these Skins without proper storage tanks?"

Rilee was considering her reply when a new klaxon wailed within the compartment. It was quite different than any that had sounded previously, and her heart pounded in recognition. She pitched her voice loud enough for everyone to hear.

"That alarm means there are missiles inbound to the Palace. If anyone is worried about what might happen to your Skin, stay here and die with it. If you want to survive, put on a helmet. Once it's secure press the button on the side. It's just like a regular Upload, except these helmets are all hardwired to deliver you to a special lifeboat facility. I'll explain more to whoever joins me once we're safely Uploaded."

Rilee dashed to one of the dangling helmets and placed it over her head. She adjusted it to be sure all of the contact points were aligned correctly, and then secured it around her neck. Suspecting it might be a long time until she was able to do so again, she took one last deep breath and then pressed the button.

An instant later, Rilee was blinded by bright sunshine. She had arrived in a room where the ceiling and all four walls were comprised of seamless glass. The blue of the sky was rendered all the more perfect due to being set off by the pure white of two downy clouds. Out one set of windows was a mountain range with ice-capped peaks. The windows opposite overlooked an ocean vista, where foamy waves broke against a beach with black sand.

Rilee pushed her appreciation for the scenery aside to focus on counting the heads around her. Almost everyone had donned a helmet with Randel being the sole exception. She felt an urge to celebrate being rid of the man who had been such a major annoyance in such a short amount of time, but her satisfaction was tempered knowing that an intelligent and highly skilled person would be sorely missed if her worst fears about the attack proved true. Rilee was searching for a way to exit the room when Randel finally appeared. The man smiled as he gaped at the scenery, and Rilee pushed him out of her mind to focus on the matters at hand. She spotted an arrow labeled *Command Center* and ran in its direction through a door and then barreled down a set of stairs.

The Command Center was large enough to hold far more than the two dozen people sitting inside. Most looked up as Rilee entered and was trailed by the remainder of the group she had Uploaded with. Monitors around the room displayed the same image, and a half dozen people stared intently at a smaller screen they had gathered around. Rilee approached.

"What's happening?"

"Shhhh," said the woman closest to the screen as she pointed at the top right corner of the display.

The screen identifier revealed it to be a satellite view of the Palace of the Secretariat. Rilee assumed it was in real time because columns of people streamed out of the building in what appeared to be a panic. The top right corner of the screen displayed a countdown timer that had just reached five seconds.

Four.

Three.

Two.

One.

The screen flashed to solid white momentarily. When it displayed a picture again, it showed nothing but a sea of roiling flames. The woman who had shushed Rilee reached for the controls of the display and changed the magnification level. As she zoomed out, the cause of the destruction became clear. A massive mushroom cloud had engulfed not only the Palace, but the surrounding area for kilometers in every direction. Everyone sat stunned into silence until the man next to Rilee spoke.

"Let's check some of the other feeds. Pull up a view of the entire Eastern Hemisphere."

The woman interacted with the display until the screen was filled with half of the Earth. One after another, furious mushroom clouds burst from the ground. First it was a handful, and then it was dozens, and finally it became hundreds. The cities across the entirety of the Eastern Hemisphere were soon nothing but fire and ash, and yet missiles continued to impact. The room was quiet save for soft sobs emanating from multiple people. A man from the first group of arrivals spoke up.

"How did this happen? Who did this? Why?"

Kalyn spoke up. "I just came from the Operations Center. The people on Adan's asteroid did this. Before I left to come here, I witnessed spacecraft that were launched from the asteroid blasting our installations in the asteroid belt as well as on Mars."

Adan. Rilee's blood pressure spiked at the mention of the man's name. She had repeatedly warned the General Secretary the man was up to no good, but she had never imagined Adan's betrayal and malfeasance would reach such epic proportions. She committed to a silent vow that as long as her consciousness persisted, she would never let anyone forget the name of the man who had unleashed such horror on the nine billion people who were dying on the planet's surface.

One of the people who had been crying was the female admin who had Uploaded with Rilee. She wiped at the tears with the palm of her hand as she called out.

"What's going to happen to us? Where is this facility located? I didn't recognize the mountain range outside the windows when we arrived upstairs."

Rilee waited to see if anyone else would offer the answers she possessed. When everyone continued to stare glassy-eyed at the screens, she spoke.

"That mountain range does not exist in the physical world. The designers of this facility understood that anyone who arrived would be fleeing horror like what is happening to the planet right now. They wanted the reception area to serve as a vivid reminder of the Earth's natural beauty. It's a landscape composite that combines some of the world's most ideal vistas. The system we've Uploaded into is housed within a facility five kilometers underground. Those aware of its existence called it the Ark, and it's construction was the most closely held secret in all of the East. It was built to serve as a long-term shelter for those among our people who were deemed most critical to ensure the survival of our culture. It's clear to me that, with all the tumult surrounding the departure of Adan's asteroid, the access list was not updated to reflect those of us who were staying behind."

The screens all went blank and the images were replaced with two words.

SIGNAL LOST

Rilee shook her head in disappointment and then continued.

"We've lost connection to the satellite network. That either means our antenna array has been destroyed, or there's already so much dust and debris in the atmosphere that we can't lock on the signal. It should be the latter since it would have taken a direct hit to destroy the antennas, but we can't be certain without more time and analysis."

Rilee paused and Kalyn raised her hand. Rilee acknowledged her with a nod.

"You said this place—this Ark—was designed as a long-term shelter. Just how long can we survive down here?"

"You—at the display—can you figure out how to call up a map of the Ark?" Rilee paused for a few moments until all of the screens displayed a schematic. "It's hard to appreciate from just this simple diagram, but we're in the center of a massive complex that contains nearly two million square meters of physical space. If we were in our physical bodies there would be more than enough emergency rations to keep a group this size fed for a thousand years or more. We're sitting atop a geothermal spring, so we also have unlimited water and enough energy to generate artificial sunlight and support agriculture once those supplies are gone. Of course, if we remain Uploaded in the virtual representation of the facility like we are right now, there's no physiological reason we can't survive forever."

What Rilee didn't want to consider were the mental health problems that would almost certainly prevent everyone present from thriving in an Uploaded state for such an extended period. Even those people in the East who long ago decided to remain Uploaded full-time acknowledged it was critical for their mental wellbeing to spend regular cycles experiencing the full gamut of physical stimulation within an actual Skin. All of those who had been previously granted a slot in the shelter had been screened to ensure they would survive extended periods without corporeal experience, but the random group who had actually made it to safety would have had no such evaluation.

The compartment was quiet as Rilee's words sank in. Finally, Randel spoke. Unlike Kalyn, he did not raise his hand but instead just blurted out his question. "Who's going to be in charge?"

CHAPTER SIXTEEN

They have to find out if it worked!

Rilee was the last to enter the Command Center in response to the alert. When she did, she was struck by how much the tableau reminded her of the very first time she had visited the room. Back then, thirty-six people had stared at the screens in horror as billions of lives were extinguished in a matter of minutes and the Earth was left a ruined husk. Twenty years later, the group present was even smaller but filled with hope for what might soon appear on those same screens.

Hope was a tricky concept for those who still called the Ark home. A complete lack of it had killed one of the original thirty-six survivors the very first day they arrived. A second followed her lead and purged his consciousness less than one week later. Ironically, the survivor who had long been the biggest champion for hope and always fought to boost the morale of others had finally announced that hope was a farce and purged herself just a few days ago. If only she had held herself together for seventy-two more hours, she too would have been part of the hopeful pilgrimage to the Command Center.

Kalyn sat hunched over a workstation. Randel stood beside her and drummed his fingers on the table. A couple of others were gathered nearby, but most of the survivors wanted to give Kalyn space to work and instead stood back along the periphery to watch the large overhead screens. As they had for twenty years, the displays read *SIGNAL LOST* as Kalyn attempted to communicate with the satellites. There had been a short blip of connectivity thirty minutes earlier, and that had triggered the alert.

Rilee waited for a few minutes and was about to give up and go back to work when suddenly the screens were filled with an image of stars. Contact! A cheer went up from the assembled group. Someone to Rilee's left yelled out.

"Satellite must still be running its automatic program and sweeping for near Earth objects. Reorient the sensors to point back down at the planet."

Kalyn didn't need to wait for the obvious suggestion but was already working furiously. A few seconds later, the display changed from a star field to a wide-shot of Earth. What had once been a brilliant blue and white marble that shone like a beacon against the cold black of space was now a sickly gray splotch.

Ashen clouds covered the vast majority of the planet, but there were enough gaps that charcoal-colored land and slate gray water were sometimes visible. The view revealed a lifeless planet, but it was nonetheless their first exposure to the world outside of their deep underground shelter. Some of the survivors appeared forlorn at the ghastly sight, but most chatted excitedly about the radical expansion of their worldview.

With all of the other survivors engaged with the images from the satellites, Rilee put her plan into motion. She had spent the last five years doing the lab work necessary to prove her hypothesis, and the only question left to answer was whether her findings would hold true in the real world. There were others on the team who agreed with her assessment, but unfortunately there was enough dissent that Randel had rallied sufficient votes to overcome her bloc of support on the Leadership Council. They denied her request for a field experiment by claiming the resources necessary were too valuable to waste on something they deemed unlikely to succeed.

Unfortunately for the Leadership Council, Rilee had anticipated their lack of determination to aggressively attack the nearly insurmountable problem they faced. If the Council wasn't willing to take bold risks to reseed life on Earth, she was prepared to force their hand. She exited the Command Center and made her way to the Skin production facility. Once there, Rilee keyed a secret command sequence that overrode the security monitors and provided a scant two minute window to get her consciousness into a Skin without triggering a notification back in the Command Center. Rilee initiated the transfer.

The Skin's eyes opened with a start and its heart beat furiously against its chest. Rilee had preprogrammed the facility to dose her with a massive stimulant as soon as the transfer was complete. Her time was limited, so she had none to waste shaking off the fog typically experienced when jumping into a brand new Skin.

After twenty years of living exclusively within a virtual world, every neuron in Rilee's brain reveled in the physical stimulus that flooded her consciousness via the Skin's sensory organs. She fought the urge to literally jump for joy and instead dashed towards the Replicator facility. She had fired off a job for the Replicator before her Upload, so the fabrication routine had already completed and her payload was waiting. Rilee grabbed the box and ran for the lift.

No one was watching, but Rilee couldn't help but grin at what a sight she would have made if they were. She hadn't grabbed any clothes because she was on a one-way mission that would have rendered them a waste of precious resources. As a result, she sprinted through the cavern with the Skin naked as the day it had been cultured. She made her way to the lift and once again keyed a secret command override that blocked any alarms from her unauthorized ascent to the surface. The lift's sudden acceleration created momentary heaviness in the pit of her stomach, and

Rilee giggled at the sensation. As much as one's consciousness could be convinced it was inside an actual body while Uploaded in a virtual environment, there was still nothing capable of replacing true physical experiences.

The lift continued its long climb and Rilee bounced on the balls of her feet in anticipation of what she would find at the end of her ride. A light flashed on the lift panel to signal an inbound communication and then Kalyn's face appeared on the screen.

"What are you doing, Rilee? You promised me you wouldn't do anything crazy like this without talking it through first."

"Kalyn—remember how you trusted me when I told you to run for the survival shelter twenty years ago? I need you to trust me like that again right now."

"When Randel finds out what you've done, he just might try to get you purged."

"That's fine." Rilee smiled. "I might be gone soon anyways. At least this Skin will definitely be dead. Hopefully I'll manage to Upload in time and survive, but if I don't you have to promise me that someone will follow through on my experiment and discover if I was right. They have to find out if it worked!"

Kalyn bit her bottom lip as her eyes betrayed sadness, but she nodded before cutting the connection. Rilee began to run in place to limber up the Skin's legs. It was far from an ideal mission profile to jump into a fresh Skin and immediately perform under life and death circumstances, but Rilee didn't have any other option. The lift reached the top of the shaft and the doors opened. Rilee sprinted out and turned left. She reached the main airlock a few seconds later and stopped to remove one of the two devices that was inside the box.

Once she completed its activation sequence, the Upload amplifier broadcast its signal. The light from the controller on her Skin's wrist glowed green and indicated acquisition of the Upload signal. Despite the current status, there would be limited signal strength for Uploads on the other side of the airlock due to the massive amount of shielding necessary to protect the Ark. No one had bothered to create a more robust Upload network on the other side of the airlock because it was always expected there would be nothing but certain death out there. Rilee's hope was that an amplifier placed directly against the interior airlock would give her a better chance for propagating a signal sufficient to allow her return from outside, but it was impossible to be certain in advance. She couldn't bring the device with her because its delicate electronics, although shielded, would never tolerate the tremendous amounts of ionizing radiation still present outside the shelter.

Ironically, it was the presence of the radiation that made this mission too dangerous for a robot and much better suited for a human. The impact of such a large radiation dose on humans was well known. Rilee's Skin would suffer devastating effects immediately and would be completely incapacitated within minutes. Despite this, she was nearly certain she would survive long enough to complete her most critical tasks. A robot, on the other hand, might fail in an entirely unexpected fashion when subjected to so much radiation. It might complete the mission, but it could just as easily be rendered useless within seconds. It was also important to consider that the biological inputs necessary to create a new Skin were available in far higher quantities than the precious materials needed to create a new robot.

Her Skin was doomed without a doubt, but Rilee hoped her consciousness would survive. Even if it didn't, she was confident the tradeoff was worthwhile when measured against the ultimate survival of humanity on Earth. Even though Rilee was a valuable individual among the survivors, she was self-aware enough to recognize that her nonstop chafing under the rule of the Leadership Council was not sustainable. Whether it happened in two more years or another twenty, without hope of walking the surface again she would eventually snap and purge her consciousness from the Ark. If she died as part of her mission, she hoped the loss would serve the greater good.

Rilee clutched the second device from the box and opened the inner door for the airlock. Once she entered, she closed the door behind her and activated the outer door. Three different warning messages popped up about the radiation exposure she was about to endure, and the door finally slid open once she had dismissed the last of them. The Skin shivered immediately. Rilee assumed it was from the extreme cold, but it was quite possibly the initial effects of such severe radiation exposure.

The airlock had deposited her inside a large cavern. The last defense for the shelter was to have its sole vulnerable opening shielded under a mountain of solid granite. There was always the risk a direct missile hit might have buried the access shaft, but the East had bet that its extreme secrecy would prevent the mountain from ever becoming a target. Starting out surrounded by rock, unfortunately, was the worst scenario for Rilee's mission. She needed access to open sky, so Rilee charged forward with all the speed she could muster. The light gray of the cave mouth was straight ahead, and she pumped the Skin's legs ever harder. Rilee's nose began to run, and when she reached up to wipe it her hand came away streaked with blood. A few paces later she coughed and was overwhelmed by the taste of copper.

The outside world was only a few paces away, but Rilee was forced to stop for a moment. She bent over and retched pure blood onto the ground while her bowels simultaneously voided. The Skin was dying even faster than she had calculated. With one last push, Rilee staggered ahead until a final sprawl sent her torso out from under the overhang of the cave's entrance. The wind howled in her ears, and Rilee smiled with the knowledge that the gale would aid her effort. She stretched her arms as far as possible while holding the device and used her right thumb to activate its ignition sequence. Three seconds later, a blast of propellant sent her rocket with its critical payload soaring a hundred meters overhead, where it burst with a *pop* barely audible above the shrieks of the wind.

Her most urgent task complete, Rilee turned her attention to the Skin's Upload controller. Its light shone a faint red. Her mind flashed back to a mission from a lifetime ago, when she had faced a similar situation while on Adan's damned asteroid. She hadn't allowed the man to beat her then, and she was determined to achieve that outcome again. The outer layers of skin on her limbs were scorched from the radiation, but Rilee fought through the pain and regained her feet. With an agonized scream, she propelled her body back into the cave and hoped that inertia would carry her within range of the Upload amplifier.

One step.

Three steps.

Ten steps.

Rilee locked her eyes on the controller as she lurched ahead, with a finger poised to trigger Upload as soon as there was any glimmer of signal lock. This meant she wasn't mindful of the path and a small bump tripped her up. As she stumbled forwards, Rilee resigned herself to knowing the Skin would never stand again. After a final, unbalanced step, she pitched forward just as her eye caught a flash of green from the controller. She jabbed at the button just as the Skin crashed to the ground. Lifeless.

CHAPTER SEVENTEEN

All of you will get a turn with it.

As Rilee approached the door, she paused for a moment to appreciate the sounds from within. On the other side was a room filled with boisterous, high-pitched voices unlike any she had heard for hundreds of years. Children's voices. They belonged to the first generation born after Adan's Destruction. Conceived using genetic material harvested from millions of people that had been stored for safekeeping by the East when the shelter was originally built, they had gestated within the same artificial wombs used to culture Skins. A myth that Rilee recalled learning as a child had described a simple wooden ark built to protect an ancient family of humans and the animals they had gathered two-by-two. Thousands of years after that fictional disaster, it was time for her to tell a group of children the true story of an Ark of a very different sort—a technological marvel built underground that saved life on Earth from a man-made cataclysm.

Rilee opened the door and the children settled immediately. Their teacher must have warned them in advance of her impending arrival and requested their best behavior. Rilee smiled at the man, one of the other patients from the clinic who had escaped with her to shelter on that fateful day long ago, as he rose from his seat to address the children.

"Thank you for such polite behavior, class. I'm pleased to introduce an amazing woman who saved my life the day of Adan's Destruction. She gathered me along with a small group of other people and brought us to this facility called the Ark. Our early years here were difficult as we didn't know if the Earth would ever support life again, but this woman single-handedly saved our planet with her brilliance and bravery. It's my pleasure to introduce a founding member of our Leadership Council, Rilee."

The man moved to the side and Rilee took his place at the front of the room. She set the case she carried on the floor and appraised the group with a wide smile on her face. The children, five boys and seven girls, sat on the floor with their legs crossed and stared up at her wide-eyed and expectant.

"Good morning, class. I'm very excited to join you this morning, and I believe you'll be very interested in what I've brought along to show you. First, though, I need to check how good a job your teacher is doing." Rilee winked at the man and he smiled back at her. "He just mentioned Adan's Destruction. Who can explain what exactly he's talking about?"

All twelve children shot their hands up—some so excited to answer they waved both arms in the air. Rilee pointed at a girl who sat at the back and had first caught her attention due to her thick locks of flaming red hair. The girl rose and confidently spoke.

"Three hundred and ninety-two years ago, Earth was nearly destroyed. A terrible man named Adan had built a spaceship intended to take a group of humans out into the stars. He wanted to save our species from the planet's failing ecosystems by scattering colonies across the universe. Adan betrayed the Earth at the last moment before he left. He launched a rain of nuclear missiles, murdered billions of people, and wiped out nearly all life on the planet. Thirty-six people made it to the safety of the Ark, and twenty-seven of you are still with us today."

Rilee beamed at the girl. "Very well done. Thank you. We always refer to that event as Adan's Destruction, so we never lose sight of the fact that one man nearly shattered our entire planet. I will never understand why ten billion people allowed a single individual to gain such destructive capability, but we did. If you learn nothing else from me today, I want to be sure you take away how critical it is that we never again entrust such awesome power in the hands of one person. Everything we do as a society from this point onward will always be done with that lesson in mind, and as the first generation of children you must learn it especially well to ensure you pass it down successfully to those who come after you."

After making eye contact with each student to cement the importance of her words, Rilee asked her second question.

"Why did we finally begin raising children again?"

Rilee acknowledged a boy in the front row. When he rose to speak, he bounced on the balls of his feet.

"Thanks to you, ma'am, the surface is coming back to life. You created and bred the fungus that has been clearing radiation for hundreds of years. You started with an experiment that used a rocket to disperse spores across a small area just outside of the Ark, but now the surface radiation has been cleared for two hundred kilometers in every direction. In the years ahead, we'll need more and more people to do this work if we're ever going restore the entire Earth."

"You're mostly right. The fungus has brought local radiation levels down to where it's often safe to spend extended time on the surface. As a result, we're expanding our cleanup efforts further and further out. What hampers us the most are rainstorms which recontaminate everything by dropping radioactive fallout that originates from elsewhere around the world. The only way we'll ever make the planet fully habitable again is if we spread the fungus across the entire globe. Once it has transformed all of the radioactive energy into safe and stable biomass, we'll start reestablishing the planet's original flora and fauna.

"We have all the genetic material in storage we need to recreate the species present in the decades prior to Adan's Destruction, but before those will be able to survive, we'll need to introduce new participants at the very base of the food chain. These new organisms will be engineered to take advantage of all that fungal biomass and convert it into a food source that can be safely accessed by those higher up the food chain. Of course, this will include humans, so we need to be sure that any and all traces of radiation are eradicated.

"Where you're wrong is the idea that we need more people to do any of the work required to rebuild the environment. Humans will remain far too precious for far too long to use them for anything so mindless and labor intensive. We actually need all of you and many, many more to grow up and help us rebuild something almost as critical as the planet—our culture. Even before Adan's Destruction, humankind had made many mistakes that had left our planet on the verge of collapse. Chief among those was a long history of violence that left humanity constantly waging war against itself. We've been given a second chance on Earth as a species, and the twenty-seven adults alive today are determined to do things much better this time around."

The boy had continued to bounce on his toes while Rilee spoke, and when she paused he raised his hand again. She nodded at him.

"Ma'am—if people aren't going to do all of the work to restore the environment, how's it going to happen?"

"Thanks for asking. My answer has two parts. First, the spreading of the fungus will be accomplished with drones. Now that we've seen such lasting success, we're finally prepared to invest our precious resources in building a fleet of autonomous drones which will span the globe high enough above the clouds to run off solar power. These drones will traverse the planet for the next hundred years and disperse the spores that will establish the fungus across the globe.

"As for the manual labor that will eventually be required, we've come up with some helpers who I suspect you will all be excited to meet."

Rilee knelt down and opened the top of her case. She reached inside with both hands, and when she revealed the contents the class all jumped up and rushed towards her in excitement.

"Don't all crowd me at once, children. You—with the red hair—you may hold it first."

The girl approached with her arms extended and Rilee handed over her precious cargo. The creature was unlike anything that had roamed the planet previously. Derived in large part from the DNA of Amazonian ants, it still retained many of their key physical and behavioral characteristics. Its segmented body with six legs was colored a dark green with brown stripes. Knowing she wanted the children to have an opportunity to interact with the specimen, Rilee had administered a mild sedative in advance to keep it calm. It wouldn't have been the least bit dangerous otherwise, but would have been far too active and squirmy for the children to hold.

"Stay calm, everyone. All of you will get a turn with it. This one is only half a meter long and barely two kilos, but we're intentionally breeding them small right now. We want to be sure they're intelligent enough to perform all of the work we need and that we can effectively manage them. Once we've proven all of that, I'm confident about our ability to scale up their size and make them even more useful."

The girl holding the ant looked up at Rilee. "Ma'am—how are we going to control them?"

"Well, I'm going to save those details for another day. We're getting close to figuring it all out, but we're not there just yet. Let's wait until we know for sure, and then I promise I'll come back to show you."

The group let out a collective groan, but their disappointment was soon forgotten as the next child reached for the bug and the rest eagerly awaited their turn. Rilee could not have been more pleased by the children's reaction. Some of her fellow survivors had found the creatures far too disturbing given their memories of smaller ants, so Rilee was relieved when the children reacted so positively. Human acceptance of the insects was critical. She was confident that if she attained the level of control she envisioned, the human and bug relationship would prove far more beneficial than that of any of the other creatures people had domesticated in the millennia prior to Adan's Destruction.

CHAPTER EIGHTEEN

Let's crack this thing open.

"Please confirm the coordinates again, ma'am."

Rilee managed to stifle her sigh. Five hours en route with a pilot who was as annoying as he was clueless had left her at wit's end. The only thing that kept her from telling the halfwit to return to base so she could swap him out was her excitement at what awaited them at their destination. The numbers were ones she had retained by memory throughout her absurdly long lifetime, and she repeated them for the pilot yet again.

"37.234332, -115.806663"

"Roger that. ETA sixty minutes."

Outside the cockpit glass, the clouds parted as they crossed the coastline. What had once been the world's largest megalopolis stretching for more than a thousand kilometers was now virgin land. The coastal plains ran up to inland forests that had matured quite nicely in the five hundred years since Rilee had last visited.

Twenty million people now called the eastern portion of the continent home, though it was impossible to have any sense of that simply by flying overhead. Only the most advanced ground-penetrating sensors would reveal the new habitats that had been built deep below the surface. The Collective Pact imposed strict limits on any new settlement's environmental impact, so the vast majority of people resided underground when they weren't Uploaded. Earth's newly restored surface was guaranteed to remain an unspoiled green-space where the population regularly experienced and enjoyed the natural world.

As part of the celebration that marked the end of the second millennium since Adan's Destruction, Rilee had been rewarded for being part of the First Thirty-Six with special dispensation to live wherever and however she wanted to. She retained a position on the Leadership Council, but she took full advantage of the freedom her general lack of responsibilities provided and escaped back to her family's ancestral lands.

Not even Rilee could get permission for something as environmentally invasive as genuine cattle farming, but she received a special waiver that allowed her to maintain a few dozen head. The small herd provided sufficient work to keep her favorite cattle dogs from becoming bored. Of course, her herd wore the same mark on their hides as Rilee wore on the forearm of her personal Pattern. The symbol, a circle in the middle overlapping two additional circles on each side, always brought a bittersweet smile to her face by reminding her of a life from two thousand years in the past.

Having played such a large role in restoring the planet to its former beauty while also developing a culture that would not risk destroying it again, Rilee charted a new course. It was time to let a new generation focus on Earth, a generation that wasn't tainted with firsthand memories of what had come before Adan. She had no intention of disappearing for good, but concluded the next best use of her skills would involve even far more travel than she had experienced back in her days working for the General Secretary. To that end, she worked her charms with the Council until she won approval for an archaeological expedition that she had always envisioned. She wasn't entirely sure what they would find once her team had dug deep enough, but she was excited to finally determine what lay far below the desert.

Rilee closed her eyes for what she expected to only be a moment, but proved to last much longer as she was startled awake by the transport's wheels hitting the ground. The pilot grinned as he spoke.

"You were too peaceful for me to wake you up any sooner. Kalyn is waiting outside."

"Thank you. I understand you're to remain here until I'm ready to leave. Please grab your gear and report to the main hall. You'll find a reception desk and someone to help get you settled. I'm guessing I'll be ready to head home within forty-eight hours, but it might just as easily be two or three if we've struck out."

The pilot nodded in reply, and Rilee exited the cockpit. She stopped at the storage locker to grab her gear and then strolled down the transport's exit ramp. Kalyn greeted her with a warm embrace. She was the only person alive who Rilee had known prior to Adan's Destruction, and, in the countless years since, Kalyn had become Rilee's closest and most trusted friend.

"It's good to see you. How was your flight?"

"Don't get me started. The pilot was annoying enough to make me regret the decision to not just Upload into a generic Skin to get here rather than take the time to travel and experience the dig from inside my personal Pattern."

Kalyn grinned. "Well, I honestly don't understand why you cared so much about flying here for this when you could have just Uploaded, but after two thousand years I'm smart enough to not argue with you about something like that."

"How can you even say that number aloud? I can't believe that I'm still around after all this time. We realized unlimited lifespan was possible when we figured out how to Upload, but no one actually imagined what it would be like living that long. Sometimes I wish I had checked out years ago like so many of the others from the First Thirty-Six."

Kalyn grabbed Rilee's hand. "Come on. You're going to forget all about that kind of crazy talk once you see what I have to show you."

With Kalyn leading the way, they walked across the landing zone towards a large tent shielding the entrance to the shaft they had excavated. Rilee followed Kalyn's lead and grabbed a safety helmet before stepping onto the lift within it. Two minutes later, the gate opened and they emerged into a tunnel that led up to a chamber with a set of giant doors on the far side. The doors appeared to have never fully closed as an ancient pile of rocks had settled into the half meter gap between them. It was dark on the other side and nothing was visible. Two dozen members of the team were milling around along with an equal number of worker ants. The bugs stood off to the side, perfectly still, and waited. Rilee pointed at them as she spoke to Kalyn.

"Who's on ant duty?"

"A new guy. He's really solid though. It took us a lot of time to find the right spot, but once we did he had them digging as fast and efficiently as anyone I've ever seen."

Rilee nodded approval. "Good to hear. I appreciate how you all waited for me to arrive before you cracked the doors."

Kalyn grinned. "My last instructions made it clear you would make me beg for death if anyone caught a glimpse of anything interesting down here before you did. I've come to trust threats like that from you after *two thousand years.*"

Rilee grimaced and shook a clenched fist in mock frustration. Kalyn reached for her communicator.

"The boss is here. Let's crack this thing open."

A couple of seconds later, the ants moved in lockstep towards the doors. One group remained on the floor and aligned themselves to push against each one of the doors, while the others scurried up to the ceiling and assumed the same position from above. The bugs were silent and nothing happened at first. A nearly imperceptible change in their posture suggested a greater degree of effort was being expended, and after a few more seconds a tremendous screech of metal rubbing against metal echoed through the cavern. As the doors parted, the rocks which had wedged them open for thousands of years spilled out on to the ground. With a final heave, the ants created a three-meter gap between the doors. The ants walked through in single file while the people remained to the side so Rilee could approach and be the first human to enter.

Handheld lights sprang to life and one was pressed into Rilee's hand as she approached the gap. She stepped through, flanked by Kalyn on one side and a man she didn't recognize on the other. The remainder of the team followed closely behind. As their lights swept the interior space, it was clear they were in a control center of some sort. The wall was covered with large displays and workstations sat on most of the surfaces. The equipment, despite having been entombed in the dry desert soil, was derelict. Someone bumped against one of the workstations and it collapsed into a cloud of dust.

The more she took in her surroundings, the more Rilee lost hope about the utility of anything they might find within the underground complex. The facility had once been among the most well-funded and technologically advanced of its time, and if it had reached such a state of decrepitude there was not much hope for whatever artifacts it might contain. They moved through the command center into a passage beyond. The ceiling was low and the hallway was narrow, so it required the ants to pass through single file on all six legs rather than walking on their hindmost legs at their full three-meter height.

They took series of turns until they entered another large space. The echoes of their feet suggested it was far larger than the first cavern outside the door. Rilee probed the darkness with her light until something shiny reflected back and she called out.

"Everyone—there's something over here. Come shine your lights!"

Scrambling footsteps approached and the object was bathed in a larger and larger circle of light. Finally, it became clear what was in front of them.

A spaceship.

By its appearance alone, the craft was something that had not been built by human hands. Its alien origin was further confirmed by the fact that it literally sparkled in the light. Whereas the entire cavern was covered in dust and the human equipment scattered around was in as much disrepair as the materials back in the control room, the alien craft was dust-free and reflected a rainbow effect when their lights hit its skin at a certain angle.

Rilee stood speechless and admired the craft. Thanks to information the General Secretary revealed during their last conversation, she had always been confident about what they would find once they explored the area. She had been forced to push her curiosity aside for a long time, however, while they struggled through the early years of Earth's restoration. Even after they had healed the planet and rebuilt their society, Rilee had forced herself to ignore the stars and focus all her attention on their homeworld until she was convinced its survival was certain. Two thousand years after Adan's Destruction, it was finally time for those he left behind in ruin to raise their gaze above the horizon. Footsteps shuffled behind her until Kalyn's arm draped around Rilee's shoulders. Her friend leaned in and spoke softly.

"You were right all along. Now what?"

Rilee paused, even though a reply had sprung instantly to mind. She took a few moments to roll the words around in her mouth and savor their taste before finally speaking them.

"We find that asteroid."

CHAPTER NINETEEN

How may I repay you?

The view from the bridge of her flagship, *Oceania*, still brought a smile to Rilee's face three millennia after their mission first departed Earth. Though the spacecraft bore its original name on the hull so many years later, to call it the same ship was misleading. The crew was constantly inventing new technology, so the vessel had been fully rebuilt at least a few dozen times, albeit one small section at a time. The overall effect, when one considered how the level of technology had improved through the years, was as if one of the ancient Earth mariners had set out in a wooden sailing vessel and landed on a distant shore moments later in a spacecraft.

In addition to its name, the only other constant throughout that time was the markings the vessel prominently wore. As soon as the Leadership Council gave Rilee full command of the ship and its mission, she had sprinkled the usage of her family's symbol throughout the spacecraft. The overlapping circles were featured everywhere, from crew uniforms to the hulls of support craft. There were still countless times when she missed Earth and her ancestral lands dreadfully, but such frequent sightings of the ancient mark kept Rilee focused on the purpose and value of their mission.

As the countdown clock on the overhead display neared the sixty second mark, Rilee became excited as always before making a jump into light-speed. She had just begun pacing when an alert sounded. Kalyn called out from her position.

"Ma'am—there are two spacecraft arriving in system. I don't recognize either of the signatures, but they're different from each other. They should fully resolve thirty seconds before our planned jump. I recommend Battle Stations."

"Concur, Number Two. Set Battle Stations."

A klaxon wailed in response to Rilee's command, and the illumination on the bridge flipped to dark red. Rilee sat in her command chair and leaned forward with her eyes locked on the primary sensor panels. Kalyn called out again a short time later.

"Ma'am—we've detected weapons fire, but none directed at us. The much larger spacecraft is firing on the smaller one. The target appears to be equipped with an energy shield, but sensors suggest it's failing. We should get out of here before either one of them pays any attention to us. I recommend an emergency jump."

Rilee opened her mouth to order the jump to light-speed, but after a pause some very different words came out.

"Halt the jump countdown. Keep the light-speed engine primed for emergency jump, but we aren't leaving just yet. Launch the alert fighters and order them to engage the aggressor vessel."

Someone on the bridge gasped. Kalyn turned to face Rilee, and her lieutenant wore an expression of grave concern.

"Ma'am—with all due respect, why are we going after these aliens? The Collective Pact clearly states we're to never attack another species."

"Correction, Number Two. The Pact states we may never launch an unprovoked attack. I'm launching a rescue mission in response to the provocation of the far larger assailant attacking that much smaller craft."

Her lieutenant looked at her imploringly, but Rilee maintained a resolute expression. Two seconds later, Kalyn issued the order. Thirty seconds after that, the ten fighters on high alert blasted out of the *Oceania* and sped off to engage. Rilee focused on the tactical display as her fighters closed in on the clashing aliens. Once within range, all ten let loose their weapons against the aggressor. The simultaneous shots overloaded the alien's shields, and it turned away from its attack and sped away from the battle. Three seconds later, as her fighters continued pursuit, Rilee exhaled as the larger alien vessel jumped away from the system. She turned to Kalyn.

"Order our fighters to orbit halfway between *Oceania* and the remaining vessel. Do not make any movements towards their spacecraft which might be interpreted by the occupants as hostile. Let's see what they do next."

"Yes, ma'am."

With the orders relayed, Rilee sat back in her chair to await the alien's next move. Would it rush to escape like the aggressor had or perhaps stick around and attempt to communicate? Fifteen seconds stretched into sixty which then stretched into two full minutes without any activity from the alien craft. Rilee was pondering what to do next when movement caught her attention out of the corner of her eye. She turned and gasped when she locked eyes with an unfamiliar human who had somehow materialized on the bridge. The man wore casual clothes right down to the athletic shoes on his feet. Her exclamation caught the attention of others around the bridge, and the next sounds were the *snicks* of multiple weapons being prepared to shoot. Rilee called out.

"Hold your fire!"

The mysterious human remained calm in the face of the tumult and continued to stare at Rilee. His mouth quivered for a few moments until it finally formed into a smile. Rilee's own mouth went wide in astonishment, but she quickly gathered her wits and spoke.

"Who are you, and how did you get on board my ship?"

The human opened his mouth and emitted a series of high-pitched squeaks. The noise was excruciating and she grimaced in response. The man stopped making any sound, closed his eyes for a moment, and then reopened them. When his mouth next moved, human speech came out.

"Greetings. I am sorry for any alarm I caused with my sudden appearance aboard your vessel. Why are you out here among the stars?"

Rilee wanted to ignore the man's question and start demanding her own answers, but something in the pit of her stomach led her to try a different approach.

"We're seeking new planets for our people."

The man was quiet for a moment. "Planets like your Earth are rare across the galaxy and are often already home to intelligent species. How are you dealing with these other species as you encounter them?"

"We agree with your assessment. That's why we're not searching for planets that are already like our home but instead those which are currently hostile to life but with some effort could be made habitable. This allows us to avoid confrontation with other species."

"And yet, you fired upon the other spacecraft that was attacking my own. Why did you do that if you are trying to avoid confrontation?"

"Well," Rilee smiled as warmly as possible, "it struck me as the right thing to do."

The man looked around the bridge for a moment before turning back to Rilee and returning her smile. "This is all very unlike the behavior we have catalogued for your species. I must inform my companions."

Rilee stood and stepped two paces towards the man. "You are familiar with us. How is that?"

"I have visited your homeworld. I was unable to identify your ship when it first appeared on my scope until you deployed your fighter craft. I recognized how they had been patterned off a species I was aware had frequently visited your planet, so I guessed you would be human. Obviously, I was correct."

"Why do you appear as if you're human like us? How can you speak our language?"

The man laughed. "I am not anything like a human. This is the form I chose once I concluded this was a human ship. Since I have visited your homeworld, I knew how to take your form and communicate using your language."

"You mentioned companions. Are there more of your kind back on your ship?"

"No. I am on a scouting mission and am traveling by myself. The companions I refer to are those like me who are on similar missions all around the universe. I have already informed them of the uncatalogued behavior you have exhibited here today so they may be aware for any future interactions."

Rilee found herself at a loss for words. In the span of a few short minutes she had learned of the existence of aliens who had visited Earth, shape-shifted at will, teleported, and communicated at faster than light speeds. She had a million questions to ask, but was paralyzed trying to pick which was most important. She was about to open her mouth when the man spoke instead.

"You saved me from certain death. In my culture, settlement of such a life debt is considered the highest honor. How may I repay you?"

Rilee offered the first thing that crossed her mind. "Your teleportation technology."

The man laughed even harder than he had previously. "As much as I desire the honor of repaying my debt, I must decline that request. That technology is unique to our species and we are forbidden to share it. What if instead I were to gift you with the ability for superluminal communication? That technology is already widely dispersed among spacefaring species."

Rilee was dumbstruck and her mouth fell slack in reaction to the man's offer. She managed to nod in reply, at which point the man disappeared from view. He reappeared in the same location holding one large crystal and two smaller ones in an outstretched hand.

Rilee reached out and the alien handed over the crystals. She almost dropped them due to how shockingly heavy they were for their size. The three together must have weighed ten kilos even though they were small enough to fit in the palm of her hand. She placed the two smaller crystals on the deck and then examined the largest.

The crystal was composed of material that was clear, though with a golden tinge. Upon closer investigation, Rilee found that its core was inky black. She brought the crystal closer to her eye and discovered that the dark splotch within was full of tiny pin-pricks of sparkling light that varied in size and intensity. The lights were distributed throughout the core with the exception of a gap in the center. The gap, pitch black and perfectly circular, was surrounded by light which appeared blurred and distorted. Rilee focused back on the man as he spoke.

"What you hold in your hand is a Star Crystal seed. When fed with the appropriate high-energy radiation, it will sprout new crystals. The two crystals I have given you are the first children from this seed. All crystals from a given seed will have the ability to transmit data instantaneously across unlimited distance." The man closed his eyes for a moment before reopening them. "I have just transmitted information that I am confident you will be able to decipher based on my understanding of the scientific knowledge found on your planet. It contains the details about the radiation needed to trigger new crystal growth as well as basic instructions for creating a device to interface with the crystal for sending and receiving data."

Rilee turned to the comms station and the man sitting there nodded to confirm the alien's statement. The visitor spoke again.

"It has been a pleasure meeting you, captain of the *Oceania*. My people will greet you as a friend whenever you may cross our path. My ship has repaired itself, so it is time for me to continue my mission. Farewell."

Rilee opened her mouth to scream *wait*, but it was already too late. With a curt nod the man disappeared from the bridge. Five seconds later, his ship similarly disappeared from the system. Her head spun at the realization that she hadn't posed her most critical question to the alien before he left.

Have any of your companions ever encountered humans traveling on a ship built upon an asteroid?

CHAPTER TWENTY

Get off my bridge.

"**M**a'am—critical alert from Scout Four."

"Patch it through, Kalyn."

Rilee sat back and closed her eyes to focus on the transmission.

"I've just entered a white dwarf system and there are three unidentified vessels. One of them appears to be Adan's asteroid."

Rilee leapt out of her seat. "Give me an image!"

There it was on the screen—Adan's asteroid— looking almost the same as it had when she first saw it fifteen thousand years earlier. Rilee's heart stopped and her legs threatened to quit. She sat back down to steady herself while she issued orders.

"Nav—I want to be in that system as fast as possible. Kalyn—spin up all offensive weapons. I want all fighters prepared for launch as soon as we come out of the jump."

"Ma'am," squawked Scout Four over the comm line, "the closest of the vessels appears to be a fighter and it's approaching at high velocity. Another ten craft just like it have launched from the asteroid. May I jump out of the system?"

Standard procedure for all scout craft was to depart any system in which they encountered potentially hostile spacecraft. The crew of *Oceania* had engaged in successful alien diplomacy throughout the many millennia of its journey, but they always avoided situations where a lone scout would have to fend for itself. Standing orders were to depart and either leave the aggressors behind for good or wait in the safety of a nearby system until *Oceania* arrived.

"Negative, Scout Four. I need you to remain on station and keep that asteroid engaged. Transmit your sensor data back to us. You may fire at will at any of the fighters." Rilee paused to key something into her comm unit. "As for the asteroid, fire your railgun at the targeting coordinates I just sent you."

"Yes, ma'am. Scout Four out."

Kalyn had approached during the interchange and whispered to Rilee once the pilot cut the transmission.

"Ma'am, I understand why you want Scout Four to hold in system, but I'm at a loss as to what difference a puny kinetic weapon will make against something as huge as Adan's ship. If we had a shell of that size inbound, our defensive algorithms would ignore it altogether."

"That's what I'm betting on, Kalyn. The coordinates I provided Scout Four are for the asteroid's flight operations center. It's a one in a million shot, and they may very well have reconfigured the ship after all these years, but it doesn't hurt to give it a try. The worst case scenario is that Scout Four wastes a shell. If instead he manages to somehow knock out a critical nerve center, then when we jump into the system they'll be at our mercy."

Kalyn nodded and walked away. Rilee smiled as Scout Four's sensors revealed that the pilot had a significant speed advantage over the fighters from the asteroid. He appeared to not be in any danger despite being pursued by eleven of the hostiles. Rilee tapped her fingers on the arm of her chair as the jump clock ticked off the time until they would arrive in system. With only ten seconds to go, Rilee let out a yell in response to the sensor data.

"Dammit! Why the hell did that asteroid jump out of the system in the middle of a battle against a single, small craft. What kind of cowardly commander would leave that many fighters behind when the odds are overwhelmingly in their favor?"

There was silence in response to the rhetorical question, but it was quickly broken by a series of alerts that sounded when *Oceania* finished her jump and arrived in system.

"Ma'am—there are eleven active hostiles and a twelfth craft which has remained in close orbit around the white dwarf. Scout Four is accelerating towards us and appears to be well out of range of the hostiles. What are your orders?"

Rilee answered without hesitation. "I want all weapons focused on the twelve hostiles. Destroy them. All scanners look for any trace of that asteroid. If there's *any* clue that might help us track it down, I want to hear about it *now*!"

"Hold your fire!" Kalyn turned to Rilee. "Begging your pardon, ma'am, but we shouldn't be attacking them when they haven't attacked us. In fact, his sensors show they never shot at Scout Four given his skill and speed advantage. The Collective Pact dictates we must not engage in a situation like this."

"Kalyn—you're dismissed. Get off my bridge." Kalyn didn't move immediately, and Rilee jumped up. "Now, dammit! The rest of you—follow my orders and kill all of those vessels. The ship they came from killed nine billion innocents and tried to destroy Earth. If you need any more reason than that to fire, then consider yourself relieved of duty as well."

Kalyn walked out slowly, but without any additional company. As the hatch closed behind her, firing solutions were finalized and weapons engaged. Within a minute, nothing remained of the twelve craft that was bigger than half a meter. The conflicted tension in the compartment as her crew went about their work was obvious to Rilee, but they were all professionals and followed her orders.

Rilee paced as she waited for data from the sensors. If the asteroid hadn't left behind any clue to its destination, she found herself at a loss as to what to do next. She had already called in all of their scouts and was prepared to fan them out in a desperate effort to find Adan's ship again, but the odds of stumbling upon them a second time were infinitesimally small given the vastness of space. She was starting to lose hope as the minutes ticked by without any word from the sensor team until finally their leader spoke.

"Ma'am—we've found something. There's a nearly imperceptible gravitational anomaly in the spot where the asteroid was last located. We've identified two more anomalies that are similar and indicate the asteroid's heading away from the system. The third is at the very edge of our sensors and all three are fading fast, but best guess is we've found the asteroid's wake."

Rilee grinned and pounded her right fist against her left hand. Her silent exultation was short-lived, however, as Comms spoke next.

"Ma'am—inbound message from the Leadership Council. They demand your attendance immediately for an emergency session."

All eyes focused on Rilee. She couldn't ignore the Council, but wasn't about to forego her chance at tracking Adan's ship.

"Nav—follow the anomalies. If we're correct, then hopefully we'll continue to find a whole trail of them that will lead us straight to the asteroid. In the meantime, I'm going to join the Council meeting from my private compartment."

CHAPTER TWENTY-ONE

The asteroid has not disappeared.

Rilee jogged to the small compartment off the bridge she used for private meetings. She sat down and initiated a link to the Council. There were rumors that after a few centuries of research they were finally close to solving the issues with Uploading into a new Skin via the superluminal communicators, but the virtual presence capability was already an amazing improvement from the early days of audio-only connections. Her vision went fuzzy for a moment as the link resolved, but the Council chamber quickly came into focus. All eyes turned to Rilee. She was joining a discussion already in progress. Randel stood in the middle of the chamber, and he turned and strode towards Rilee as he addressed her.

"We understand you discovered the asteroid Adan used to leave Earth. That's a fantastic accomplishment, but unfortunately it appears you went and undid your great work by launching your attack first. This is a violation of the Collective Pact, and we've called this emergency meeting to evaluate the future of your command."

She wasn't surprised that Kalyn would disagree with her actions, but Rilee was shocked that her trusted lieutenant had reported her to the council so quickly. Kalyn had advised Rilee to temper much of her impulsiveness throughout the thousands of years they had worked together, but it was impossible to eradicate all of it. This was especially true whenever Rilee found herself in opposition to Randel. It was considered rude to pass through another attendee when attending a meeting in a virtual fashion, but Rilee stood and walked her holographic presence through the body of her longtime nemesis and addressed the meeting from the center of the circle.

"Fellow members of the Council—have you all forgotten the actual wording of the Collective Pact? We pledged to never launch an *unprovoked* attack. Nine billion of our people died at the hands of the monsters who built that ship! If Adan's Destruction isn't sufficient provocation for me to act as I did, what exactly would be?"

A sizeable number of those around the room appeared sympathetic to Rilee's rationale, but they were outnumbered by attendees who remained stoic and unyielding. The story of Adan's Destruction was a cornerstone of their society, but it had become painfully obvious over the millennia of her travels that fewer and fewer people who remained on Earth truly appreciated its impact. It was likely an inevitable outcome as the population grew to be dominated by those born long after their homeworld was restored to its former glory, but it frustrated Rilee nonetheless. Even more so given how the Leadership Council was once again under the control of Randel. Someone who had experienced it all firsthand should have known better. He spoke.

"Everyone here respects your dedication and passion, Rilee, but I must insist that you observe Council protocol and return to your seat."

Rilee wanted to ignore the directive, but as Randel's lips curled into a self-satisfied sneer she reconsidered and moved to sit. She attempted to signal her disrespect by walking straight through the man's body a second time, but he stepped aside as she approached and denied her the satisfaction. Once Rilee was seated, Randel gestured towards a man across the room who spoke.

"Our ants have battled the occupants of Adan's asteroid across many planets through the years, and the Council's stance has always been to take the vessel by force if one of our ships ever encountered it. Your actions today forced us to revisit that longstanding position, and we discovered there's no longer a consensus. Fortunately, your engagement with the vessel was limited and they've disappeared once again, so an immediate resolution from the Council is not necessary."

Now it was Rilee's turn to grin in satisfaction. "The asteroid has not disappeared. It left the system, but my sensor team discovered what appears to be a trail. We're not yet certain we'll be able to find them, but right now I believe we will."

The man paused for a deep sigh before he continued. "Well then, that changes things and we're forced back into making a decision." He looked around the room and received silent nods of agreement from a half dozen members. "I lead the Homeworld Security Committee that is responsible for evaluating this situation. Our formal recommendation is that you should track the ship if possible but that we must begin a full debate with the entire Council before allowing you to take any additional direct action."

The man sat down and Rilee shook her head in disbelief.

"These people tried to destroy our planet, and you want me to just follow them around while the lot of you argue about whether we should fight back?"

"That's the problem, Rilee. It most likely wasn't the people on that ship right now who fired those nukes." Rilee's heart beat faster in response to the condescension dripping from Randel's voice. "I shouldn't have to remind you, of all people, how violently opposed Adan and all of the other citizens of the West were to our Upload technology and the concept of moving from Skin to Skin. That fact strongly suggests the people running that asteroid right now are hundreds of generations removed from those who did us wrong. Is it really our place to make Adan's descendants pay the ultimate price for his treachery?"

"You're acting like they might have become peaceful explorers at this point when we're certain they're anything but. They've repeatedly attacked our ants without provocation, and they've similarly assaulted other species as well. Doesn't that suggest their culture is just as dangerous today as it was back then and should be stopped now that we might finally have the opportunity?"

There was momentary silence and a number of members squirmed at Rilee's observation. Finally, the youngest woman on the Council spoke.

"You raise a valid point, Rilee. However, we find ourselves curious if perhaps we just need to help the residents of that asteroid find their way. They must believe that they are but one ship traveling the stars all by themselves. As such, they likely feel threatened by many situations we would instead consider to be opportunities. Our society has had the benefit of so many ships like yours traveling the cosmos and relaying valuable knowledge back to Earth. Many of us believe that if we have an opening to share all that we've learned with the people on that asteroid, they'll understand the error of their exploitive ways and become better representatives of our species."

Heads nodded around the room and Rilee was able to evaluate the sentiment she was up against. The woman didn't appear to speak for the majority, but it was a sufficiently large bloc of the Council's youngest members to stymie a vote. Rilee faced a steep challenge to sway enough opinions, but past experience had proven their deliberations would be painfully slow and provide her plenty of time. She stood.

"I must return to my bridge to participate in our hunt for the asteroid. If indeed we've discovered a means of tracking them, I will follow the will of the Council and not engage them directly until I successfully convince you to allow otherwise."

Rilee cut the transmission. She stood and stretched to reorient her senses back to her physical body. Her last comment was probably not the smartest from a political perspective, but she wanted to put Randel on notice that she was coming for him. Many thousands of years earlier she had used bold action to align the Council's perspectives with her own, and she committed herself to finding a path that would achieve that outcome yet again.

CHAPTER TWENTY-TWO

Ma'am—the asteroid just launched a missile!

"Why the hell am I just learning about this now? It's been more than seventy-two hours already!"

Rilee tried to modulate her voice, but it was clear from Kalyn's expression that she hadn't succeeded. Numerous discussions, many heated, had occurred over the previous weeks in an attempt to repair the rift that had formed between the longtime friends. Rilee believed Kalyn's actions in reporting back to the Council after their initial encounter with Adan's asteroid were a massive betrayal of trust. Her lieutenant had genuinely believed she was fulfilling her duty to the Collective Pact in response to actions which she considered illegal and immoral. Their relationship had naturally undergone stress through their countless years together, but it had never experienced such a serious blowup. It was only within the last day that Kalyn had been allowed back to her post on the bridge. The woman took a breath and replied.

"This is not to criticize your earlier decisions about my status, ma'am, but this delay happened because I wasn't here to be sure we were aware of all critical information. Somewhere along the chain, your order to keep the soldier ants hidden was not fully communicated. We Uploaded a trainee into the queen, and he defaulted to the regular deployment protocol and sent a soldier out on patrol. Fortunately, his supervisor blocked the release of any alarm pheromones and prevented a full-blown battle, but analysis of drone footage revealed that a member of their landing party was killed. This was confirmed by surveillance from orbit that showed their landing shuttle ejecting a body into space on its way back to the asteroid."

Rilee was displeased by Kalyn's explanation but was forced to agree with her assessment. The weeks since they first encountered Adan's asteroid had been a blur of intelligence gathering for the crew of the *Oceania,* and it was no shock that some important signals had been lost in the sheer volume of noise. It had started when the gravitational anomalies had indeed led them to the ship, ironically catching up with it back in the same system where their initial encounter had taken place.

While they observed the asteroid's search and rescue activities amongst the wreckage of its fighters,

Rilee's crew made a critical discovery. The anomalies which had allowed them to follow the asteroid were transient. The starting point to the trail they had followed had become undetectable by the time they returned to the white dwarf. If Rilee was to keep the asteroid from disappearing back into the vast universe, she would have to remain on its trail at all times.

Rilee needed to stick close but evade discovery. This meant that all of their surveillance was performed while *Oceania* remained far beyond any reasonable estimate of the asteroid's effective sensor range. They relied on a constellation of miniature stealth drones to closely track the ship and relay back massive amounts of intelligence data.

Eventually the asteroid departed the white dwarf and, after two days of nonstop tracking, *Oceania* caught up with the ship at a system Rilee had coincidentally visited previously. A thousand years earlier it had been incapable of supporting human life, but generations of ants had terraformed the planet and it was finally nearing the stage at which a colony would be established. Rilee had officially traveled to the planet decades earlier to evaluate the ants' handiwork but with the ulterior motive of marveling at the massive carnivorous trees the planet was famous for. That first trip had ended after a minor disaster when they lost one of their best pilots and his fighter in a training accident, and Rilee had left expecting to never visit the system again. She was weighing different responses to Kalyn when the sensor team leader called out in alarm.

"Ma'am—the asteroid just launched a missile!"

"What? How did they discover us?"

"It's not coming for us, ma'am. It appears to be targeted at the surface of the planet."

Kalyn jumped in. "Alert all drones on the surface—emergency ascent to fifty kilometers! Orient all sensors to the ground and give us full spectrum analysis of any detonations."

The bridge went silent as everyone performed their duties. Rilee kept her eyes locked on the primary display tracking the inbound missile. Once it reached the atmosphere, the missile unveiled its deadly cargo and fifty independent warheads began their inexorable descent. Rilee became momentarily lightheaded as she recalled similar sights that had been burned into her memory thousands of years earlier. She had been powerless to stop Adan's Destruction back then, so it pained her all that much more to stand by while his asteroid nuked yet another planet when she could have ended the threat weeks earlier. She called out.

"What's the targeting analysis on the warheads?"

"It's a full spread against the primary landmass, ma'am. Assuming those are nukes, our ants will be ash in two minutes along with the whole continent."

Rilee rose and spoke sharply as she stomped towards her meeting room. "Comms—I need to address an emergency session of the Leadership Council!"

The connection was finalizing as Rilee sat down, and she sat back and observed the Council chamber fill up with the other attendees. More of her fellow members were present in virtual fashion than had been during their last meeting, but Randel paced around the middle of the room in his physical form as he had before. Once she noted that a quorum had formed, Rilee jumped up and spoke.

"I have followed the orders of this Council and have trailed Adan's asteroid without revealing my presence or taking any direct action. As a result, I've stood idly by as the ship's occupants just unleashed a nuclear attack on yet another planet. I regret to inform the Council that Terraforming Colony 597C has been obliterated."

Rilee paused to let her words sink in. Around the chamber, almost no one who had previously blocked taking action against the asteroid would make eye contact with her. Most focused down at their feet while a few stared blankly ahead. The only exception was the youngest member of the Council who met Rilee's gaze when it was directed at her. The young woman stood and addressed the chamber.

"I hear the frustration and torment in your voice, Rilee. I can only imagine how very hard it must be for you to realize you caused this tragedy thanks to the careless mistake of one of your ant operators."

Rilee's heart pounded. She didn't know if she was more angry at the young woman laying the blame at her feet or the realization that she had a mole within her crew who was leaking information. She waited to reply until she gathered her thoughts and was confident of delivering them with sufficient composure.

"Yes, we had an unfortunate error that led to an ant soldier attacking the asteroid's landing party. I will accept full responsibility for that. It's absurd, however, to believe that nuking an entire continent is a reasonable reaction to a single death. How can we conclude this situation is anything but further proof that the inhabitants of that vessel are still as dangerous and destructive as they were when it was Adan at the helm and he murdered nine billion of our citizens?"

The body language around the room revealed to Rilee how the asteroid's nuclear attack had pushed far more of the younger members toward her position than had been the case in their previous meeting. She didn't believe that she had a clear majority across the Council yet, but it appeared close enough to warrant an attempt to sway the rest. She was about to charge ahead and deliver her full case for obliterating the asteroid when Randel spoke.

"I agree with Rilee that the inhabitants of the asteroid made a very poor choice in this situation. Knowing her for as long as I have, I anticipate the next request will be that we allow her to destroy the ship and remove any further threat. I understand her rationale and I recognize many of you are moving closer to her opinion the same way I am, but I must say that I'm not prepared to take that drastic step just yet. I would like to propose a compromise instead."

Everyone was engaged with Randel's words, and Rilee was forced to conclude she had lost whatever momentum she had started to establish. She would have hoped the man had adjusted his position after being so viscerally reminded of nukes' effect on a planet, but it was far more likely Randel was just riding the shifting winds of the Council's politics. The man lived for power, and there was little doubt in Rilee's mind that he was savvy enough to align with the large bloc of younger members who represented the future of the Council. She was left with no choice but to let Randel detail his counterpoint without ever having the opportunity to present her argument in her own words. He continued.

"Even before today's horrific events, it has been clear from their repeated violent interactions with our ants that the inhabitants of Adan's asteroid have a very different approach to exploration and colonization than we do. It appears we may be forced to take a more active role in reducing the harm they are causing across the universe. Otherwise, we will be complicit in their conduct and may regret our inaction when other species attribute those same behaviors to us. I don't believe we have enough information to destroy the asteroid and all of its colonies just yet, but I've identified a proposal to get us there.

"First, we will seek out as many of the asteroid's colonies as possible. Their current position combined with the data we have about where our ants encountered them in the past will support educated guesses about their travels through the years. Once we find their colonies, we will gather up the inhabitants and consolidate them on a handful of planets. This will allow us to keep a close eye on all of them and enable quick action once we agree on next steps.

"While that's going on, we must gather more detailed, in-depth intelligence about the society on board that asteroid. I'm not sure how we accomplish this, but it's critical we do so. We may all ultimately agree with Rilee that its current inhabitants are just as guilty as those who left Earth and tried to destroy our home, but I know many of us will feel much better reaching that conclusion with the support of concrete evidence."

It was obvious from looking around the room that Rilee would fail if she tried to make her original case to destroy the asteroid immediately. Randel had blocked her once again, but he had also sparked an idea. If he wanted in-depth knowledge about what was happening on board that vessel, she just might have the perfect way to get it. If nothing else, her nascent plan would put her in position to take the action necessary to deal with Adan's asteroid if the Council proved they were not up to the duty themselves.

CHAPTER TWENTY-THREE

This is an extremely bad plan.

The thing that frustrated Rilee the most about Kalyn over their many millennia of working together was the fact her lieutenant was allergic to silence. The woman made small talk yet again while they waited for the next step in the plan to be ready.

"Remember when you were a child, ma'am? Three months was a veritable eternity. We started shadowing that asteroid three *years* ago, and it feels like it might as well have been yesterday."

Rilee smiled. "Three years or three hundred, Kalyn, I'll put in whatever time it takes to bring the people on that rock to justice. Or are you making that comment in some weak effort to diminish the fact that I predicted what they would do next a full ten months ago?"

"I should have known better than to doubt your understanding of these people after all the surveillance you've analyzed, ma'am. That planet down there is gorgeous. Why did the Leadership Council waste it as a resettlement location for all of the asteroid's colonists?"

"Do you remember the story from a few hundred years back about one of our commanders who went rogue and deployed his ants to disband one of the asteroid's colonies?" Rilee brought up an image on the screen of humans dressed in animal pelts. "This is the planet where that happened and this is one group of those colonists. Check out their eyes—hardly any whites at all. Nothing but brown iris and black pupil. The Council established an ant presence a while back to assist with all of the sociologists who wanted to study the disparate tribes that had isolated themselves. Since the planet is so resource rich and given the bugs were already here, the Council decided this was as good a spot as any to start dumping off the other colonies."

"What do the bugs have to do with bringing the colonists here, ma'am?"

"We're trying to keep the different groups isolated from each other to prevent any conflict or resource contention between them. Other than a detachment that operates out of caverns built under the original human settlement, the ants are held in reserve on a separate continent in case they are needed."

Kalyn held up her hand to signal that she was receiving a message. "Ma'am—the two shuttles have been destroyed and the landing party is now moving in the direction you expected. The asteroid has also exited the system. How are you certain it's coming back?"

"Surveillance, Kalyn, will almost always provide you with whatever information you need to know. Our friend with the cigars had appeared to be in charge, but I discovered someone higher in rank than him today. Our tiniest drones have been observing their landing party and I overheard him refer to one of the new women as *Madam President*. A short time later, I captured that same woman discussing with her aide how she had just ordered the asteroid to return back and mount a rescue mission if the need arose. They'll be back."

Kalyn appeared dubious. "If you say so, ma'am. Is the younger woman who is always in the company of the cigar-chomper still your target? The one with the black hair and blue eyes."

"No." Rilee displayed a new image. "There's a different woman who showed up for the first time today. The cigar-chomper referred to her as *Major* which is a senior position within the ancient military structure the asteroid uses. Someone high up in their hierarchy should provide the best opportunity for getting what we need."

" You're clear for Upload, ma'am, but I have to say something one last time for the record. This is an extremely bad plan."

Rilee nodded and then made her final preparations and issued remaining orders. Finally, she turned back to Kalyn.

"You remember what to do if anything happens to me, right?"

"Of course, Rilee. I can't believe you're going through with this, but I'll absolutely honor your wishes."

Emotions welled up, so Rilee shut her mouth and closed her eyes before they distracted her. With one last breath, she triggered her Upload...

...and immediately marveled at the radical change in visual perspective flooding her mind. With eyes covering their heads, each optimized for a different wavelength, the visual data a human consciousness was exposed to while inhabiting an ant was potentially overwhelming. She examined the Skin and marveled once again at the creation she had played such a large role in developing thousands of years earlier. The soldier ant, one meter taller than the workers, was a fearsome killing machine that had proven its worth across the universe. In one forelimb she carried a small case and she confirmed it held the two devices critical to her plan.

With everything in place, Rilee waited for the final indication that it was time to execute. Then, she sensed it. A chemical signal triggered her Skin and all of the other ants around her to charge. Up through the secret tunnel they poured with an image imprinted on their minds of their destination. She had expected the attack would be a perfect surprise given how their secret caverns exited out within the perimeter defenses of the landing party, but for some reason the humans were alert to their presence. The next seconds were critical, so Rilee trusted the insects around her to play their role while she focused on her own.

Then, Rilee spotted the woman. As she had seen on the surveillance before Upload, her target was sitting off by herself away from the others. Rilee charged and grabbed the woman before the human was able to react to what was happening around her. Within seconds, Rilee had dragged the struggling woman behind a building and out of sight of the remainder of the landing party. A group of soldier ants formed a solid wall that surrounded Rilee's Skin and the human. The sounds of battle increased in ferocity all around, but Rilee blocked all of the distractions to focus on her work.

Pinning down the squirming woman with one forelimb, Rilee used the ant's other forelimb to grab the larger of the two devices out of her case. The device had been in use for thousands of years, but it was only in the last six months that Rilee had successfully modified it for use by an ant on the battlefield. At one end was a probe that was sized to seat around a human eye socket. Rilee held her prisoner's head steady and inserted the probe until it signaled a proper seal with the flashing of a green light.

The opposite end of the device ended with two probes that were shaped much differently. Rilee opened the mouth of her ant and guided the probes along the roof of its mouth until they found purchase in the two cavities located within. These cavities housed sensory nerve bundles that ultimately connected to each hemisphere of the ant's brain. Rilee felt a slight twinge of discomfort as the probes firmly attached, and then another light flashed green on the device. Without any hesitation, Rilee pressed the Upload button and...

...seconds later awoke with a start inside the body of the woman. The lights on the device glowed solid green to signal a successful transfer of Rilee's consciousness out of the ant and into the woman from the asteroid's crew. She couldn't quite move yet as the nanostructures the tool had inserted into the woman's brain were still aligning their circuits to support complete bodily control and sensory input, but a tingling sensation revealed the process was moving apace.

Rilee closed the body's eyes and concentrated. At the very edge of her perception, the original occupant's consciousness was still present. The Collective Pact included strict rules that prohibited nearly all forceful takeovers of Skins, but Rilee had been granted a waiver once the benefits of her plan were understood. The woman's mind emanated nothing but chaos as it reeled from Rilee's invasion and its loss of agency, but given time Rilee was certain she would harness its energy and interact with it for the purpose of mining memories and other information necessary to maintain the illusion. It took special skill to ride a Skin while its original consciousness remained trapped within, but Rilee had done it before and was confident she would succeed again.

Once Rilee had full control of the woman's limbs, she removed the transfer device from her eyeball. The ant she had just exited remained as still as a statue. The device had injected a powerful paralytic agent that ensured the creature wouldn't begin to move independently until the procedure was long done. Rilee reached into the case and removed the second device it contained. The superluminal communicator was heavy due to the miniature Star Crystal it contained, but still small enough to disguise as a pendant on a necklace. She slipped it over the woman's head and tucked it under her uniform.

Rilee tapped the leg of one of the soldier ants encircling her, and scrambled out to rejoin the other humans. Her legs wobbled as she ran, but she worried about being apart from the rest of the landing party any longer than absolutely necessary. She scrambled against the building and found a spot against the wall next to the one they had called *Madam President.*

The battle must have terrified the humans as wave after wave of the soldier ants attacked, but Rilee breathed easy with the knowledge it was all for show. The ants were on a suicide mission and sacrificed themselves to give the illusion of an all-out attack. There were strict orders that none of the humans be harmed, mostly out of concern that Rilee's new Skin might get hurt in any crossfire.

A rescue shuttle from the asteroid arrived as Rilee expected, and she dashed aboard alongside the rest of the humans. She followed the officer in charge along with the president into a compartment where they were joined by a small group of what appeared to be senior leaders. There was contentious back and forth about the ants' attack between different members of the group, and the exchanges provided a great opportunity for Rilee to sit back and soak in every detail about the people around her. Now that she had embedded herself within the asteroid's hierarchy, Rilee's mission was to learn everything possible about its society. As expected, those first moments aboard the shuttle made it clear there was an awful lot to learn.

CHAPTER TWENTY-FOUR

That's not going to work this time.

R ilee paused as the group finished absorbing her words. The expressions around the room ranged from Sergeant Bailee's simmering anger to Mase's barely contained amusement. Zax was the first to speak.

"Is Major Eryn's mind still inside that body? Will she be OK?"

"Yes, Zax. The major will be just fine. I'll return control of the body to her as soon as I no longer need it."

Kalare spoke next, and her eyes glistened with the threat of tears.

"All of the things I've shared with you in confidence over the last few years..."

"Dear, dear Kalare—of everything I've experienced while living as a member of this Crew, getting to know you has been the most wondrous. Frankly, it's the depth of goodness I see in you that has shown me there is hope for the future of this asteroid. You proved that yet again with the way you handled that young civilian earlier. I can't imagine the depths of betrayal you must be experiencing right now, and for that I'm sorry. Please believe me when I say that my fondness for you has always been completely genuine."

"Wait," Aleron interrupted. "It was you who stranded the Ship somehow during the last battle, wasn't it? I always thought it was odd how much time you spent in Engineering those last few months of the trip to Earth. You figured out some way to tamper with the FTL, didn't you?"

"You're correct, Aleron. It was an obvious tactic that the Ship would jump away as soon as we disabled all of your fighters. We were fully capable of tracking wherever you might go, but we wanted the Crew to feel thoroughly beaten and hopeless. The theory we developed was that such a thorough domination in the final battle would leave you all in a state of mind where there'd be absolute compliance with subsequent demands. You proved us right. After everything I witnessed while living among you, the most surprising thing to me was the reaction of the Marines. I never would have expected them to just sit back and passively allow our ants to board without putting up at least token resistance."

Bailee shot out of his seat. Rilee locked eyes with the man and did not flinch as he charged. Her Skin's heart rate didn't increase by so much as a single beat, despite the Marine's reddening face as he drew close and bellowed.

"We did not just sit back! I was in ChamWare myself and prepared to tear your damned bugs to shreds when the Boss ordered us to stand down. I never understood what the hell he was thinking because they never would have made it out of the hangar if he'd just given me the green light."

"And you'd be dead right now, along with everyone else who was by your side. We've continued to let you believe in recent years that your precious ChamWare was useful against the ants, but the reality is that bugs from our most recent generations see you as plain as day. Along with all of those eyes, they now have sonar that's sensitive enough to identify the last meal in your stomach. We've been keeping that capability secret to use for our advantage when it would be most beneficial."

The blood drained from Bailee's face nearly as fast as it had painted him red a moment earlier. He tried to hide it, but Rilee's revelation landed like a kick to the stomach. She didn't take joy in demolishing the man's beliefs about the effectiveness of his Marines, but Rilee had to keep him in line and nip any ideas he might have about using force against her.

"Please stand down, Sergeant." Imair rose and leaned forward to address Rilee with her fists balanced on the table. "It sounds like you were the one agitating the most for our destruction, but now I sense you've changed your mind. Does that mean you'll convince your Council to leave us alone? If your people want payback against Adan, and all of us on the Ship need to be rid of Alpha, then let's work together and achieve both goals. You just need to help us get rid of Rege first."

Rilee shook her head. "I'm afraid it isn't that simple. When you nuked our ants on that planet where Zax discovered the fighter, it shifted a lot of opinions and significantly hardened those who were already against you. I've reported back to the Council in recent years how there's hope to rehabilitate your society, but all of my earlier status updates about what I discovered here have been used by our leadership to push the conclusion that the universe will be safer with your asteroid's destruction. Your society's extensive history of violent action was likely enough to doom you in their eyes, but Rege being in command is absolutely untenable. Unfortunately, our Collective Pact prohibits us from getting involved in your internal affairs. Unless there's some way for you to effect a change of leadership on your own, my best guess is our Council will conclude that you present too big a risk and must be stopped."

When she first arrived onboard, Rilee wanted nothing more than to prove the inhabitants of the asteroid deserved destruction. Then, the depths of admiration she developed for Kalare over the years began to shift her perspective more and more in the opposite direction. Learning that Adan was alive and still using force to engineer the society towards his twisted goals was the last piece of evidence she needed to conclude the Ship's society could be redeemed. If his influence was removed and replaced by people like Kalare, then there was no reason to take the drastic step of exterminating those who had left Earth so long ago. Rilee wanted to ignore the Pact and help remove Rege, but she recognized that doing so would be leverage for Randel to destroy any willingness the Council might otherwise have to consider her new perspectives about the asteroid's society. She was stuck.

"OK," Zax stood as he started to speak, "we just have to kill Rege. The maintenance tunnels will let us make our way up to the Bridge and take him by surprise. We can do this!"

Bailee shook his head. "That's not going to work this time. Once you exposed that vulnerability during the Revolution, both Flight Ops and the Bridge were secured against that type of intrusion."

Zax kept talking. "Then we just have to take them head on. You must have access to plenty of weapons, Imair, right? Round up all of your people and we'll overwhelm whoever Rege has guarding the Bridge and bust in."

"That won't work, either." Bailee's voice was quiet. "Even if we manage to defeat Rege's guards, he'll just trigger an emergency lockdown and we'll be stuck outside. It won't take him any time at all to vent the passageway and flush us all out of the Ship."

"Why are you just giving up, Sergeant? There has to be something to try."

Rilee admired the boy's determination to find a solution, but it was obvious that Zax was pushing the Marine too hard. Anger flashed across Bailee's face and his hands balled into fists, but then the Marine's muscles relaxed and he slouched back into his seat without a word. The compartment was silent for a few long beats until Kalare spoke.

"There's an emergency override to get into the Bridge. The Boss told me that he and a couple of other Omegas are the only ones with access. It's there in case there was ever a mutiny and someone was able to capture Flight Ops or the Bridge."

Imair laughed. "All we have to do is break the Boss out of his quarters, fight our way to the Bridge, and then hope he's able to override the hatch before Rege opens the nearest airlock. What could possibly go wrong?"

It served none of their goals for Rilee to ignore her orders and directly assist the Crew, but the discussion had sparked an idea she was confident could be spun as a simple matter of misinterpretation.

"I can improve your odds."

CHAPTER TWENTY-FIVE

You first, CAG.

"Aleron—no! You can't do this. You have zero preparation!"

"And what preparation have you ever done that will make any difference?"

Aleron's tone was snide and dismissive, and Kalare considered for a moment that it might just be more effective to punch him in the face. She choked back her anger and spoke calmly and clearly instead.

"I've spent half my life sending my consciousness into a fighter, and I'm damned good at it. Do you remember that time we tried to put you into a simulator and how badly you failed? Not everyone is cut out for work like this, and it's nothing to be ashamed of."

"So what am I supposed to do then? Just sit here and twiddle my thumbs while the rest of you head off to who knows what fate? Why would you think that I would be comfortable with that? You're going to need as much help as possible, and there's no question you'll be much better off having me there at your back than another one of the civilians. If you had any other options I might feel differently, but you don't. I'm going. Period."

Aleron stomped off towards the other side of the sewage treatment cavern. Kalare was about to chase after him when a quiet cough caught her attention.

"What do you want, Zax? This isn't the best time."

"I'm sorry. I couldn't help but overhear. He does have a point. It's not like you have great options right now. I'd join you in a heartbeat, but obviously I need to get us through the tunnels into the Boss's quarters and then as close to the Bridge as possible."

Kalare nodded. "Of course, we need your biometrics. It would be stupid of us to get discovered any sooner than we have to. The good news is we'll only have a few hundred meters of passageway where we'll be out in the open on the way to the Bridge. I wouldn't be surprised if they end up being so shocked at the sight of us that we get through without a shot being fired."

Zax smiled. "That would be nice, but, knowing Rege like I do, it's wishful thinking. That man is a psychopath, and I'm certain he'd rather have us all destroyed than lose control of the Ship. I'm guessing he'll have his guards start shooting like mad at the first sign of any threat, and everything will immediately descend into chaos."

A shrill whistle echoed across the cavern. Bailee was signaling them over. Kalare turned back to Zax.

"No sense debating any longer because we're out of time. The sergeant looks pretty agitated. I'm guessing that means Eryn—uh...I mean Rilee—is about to return."

Kalare overflowed with nervous energy, so she didn't wait for a reply but instead jogged towards where the Marine and civilians waited in a circle. Once she drew near, Bailee walked a few steps towards her and spoke.

"They're past the final checkpoint and will arrive in a moment." The Marine pitched his voice softer for privacy. "CAG—I will advise one final time that this is an extremely bad idea. How can we trust that woman given how long she's been deceiving us?"

"I appreciate that, Sergeant, but I don't understand what choice we have. Every sec Rege remains in control is another sec where he may do something that forces Rilee's Council to destroy us. He may very well be up on the Bridge getting ready to nuke Earth right now. I realize your Marines still have plenty of weapons hidden, but they're captive in their barracks and would have to fight their way free first. Even given the number of civilians Imair can summon quickly, we're still wildly outnumbered and outgunned by Rege's forces. This plan strikes me as being our only hope."

There was a gasp and, when Kalare looked up past the Marine, it took all of her will to stifle one of her own. Rilee had walked through the hatch trailed by six warrior ants. The four-meter tall bugs looked even more fierce than usual because each was encased in body armor. Kalare's mouth fell open in disbelief as she had never understood such a thing was possible. All of the ants walked on their hindmost legs, held a bladed weapon in each of their middle limbs, and carried a pack slung across the back of their thorax filled with additional blades. It was already difficult for the human eye to discern the subtle difference in color patterns that made each ant unique, but the armor hid even that slight distinction and rendered all of the bugs indistinguishable. Rilee called out.

"Kalare—I need you and the other four over here right now!"

Kalare turned her attention back to the Marine. "Your concerns have been noted, Sergeant, and I'm sorry you don't want to come for the ride along with me. It's just as well. Who knows how the Boss will respond when Zax opens up that hatch, so it's probably best that you'll be available to deliver a sitrep."

Bailee stared at her long enough for it to make Kalare uncomfortable. Finally, the Marine snapped off a salute which she returned. Kalare turned and double-timed to where Aleron waited alongside Imair and Izak. Mase stood a few meters behind them. Rilee spoke once Kalare arrived.

"My people refer to these ants as soldiers, though I know you call them warriors. This squad was part of the first group that boarded the Ship, and they were prepositioned onboard with their armor in case the Council decided to launch a targeted assault. I contacted my lieutenant once we settled on this plan, and she worked some of her special magic to make them available to me without their chain of command being aware."

Rilee lifted up the device she held in her hand.

"I'll use this to transfer each of your minds into one of these ants. The process will start with the delivery of a long-lasting anesthetic into your body. This will trigger your autonomic nervous system and ensure that your vital organs continue to function while your consciousness is elsewhere. One instant I'll be fitting the device, and the next you're going to be inside one of these bugs behind me."

Imair interrupted Rilee. "Why are there six ants if there's only five of us?"

"I'm going with you, though I'll stress again that I'm only present to observe and will not lend any direct assistance. I want to return Major Eryn's body to her in one piece, and I'll be much safer encased in one of these guys. With their armor, the bugs will be immune to the light weapons we're likely to encounter.

"It's going to be incredibly disorienting once you're inside an ant. In particular, you're likely to be overwhelmed by the amount of sensory input you'll be subjected to. The best way to deal with it is to imagine closing your eyes and humming to yourself. These ants don't have anything like our vocal structure so you won't actually make any noise, but we've nonetheless found it a useful technique for beginners. Does anyone have any last questions before we start the transfers?"

Aleron raised his hand and Rilee acknowledged him with a nod.

"You said earlier we'll be unable to communicate, right?"

"That's correct. You'll be blocked from complex communication with anyone—human or ant. I've already told you how the ants can't make our vocalizations, and their brains don't have the right structure to deliver human speech in a fashion where your consciousness can interpret it. As for the ant-to-ant messaging, it's pheromone based and far too difficult for beginners like you."

Kalare was puzzled. "What about the reports from returning colonists about ants speaking to humans?"

"Those stories must have involved queen ants, not warriors. Queens were bred to be capable of human speech to simplify ant-to-human coordination. Just stay focused on the simple, non-verbal coordination signals we discussed earlier. Zax and Bailee will be sure the Boss is familiar with them as well. Unless there are any other truly critical questions, we should get started with the transfers."

When everyone remained silent for a moment, Rilee signaled an ant to approach and then turned back and did the same to Kalare. "You first, CAG."

CHAPTER TWENTY-SIX

You'll be climbing the walls before you know it.

Kalare's heart pounded like she'd just sprinted a dozen klicks as she approached Rilee and the bug. Being so close to one of the giant insects triggered a deep revulsion that she was unable to shake. To imagine her mind inside the creature was incomprehensible, so she pushed the thought aside and focused instead on forcing one foot in front of the other. The ant stood still except for its antennae which continuously twitched. As Kalare moved closer, she noticed a pungent odor wafting off the bug. The stronger the smell became, the more she worried that her legs might begin to wobble. She didn't think her fear was visible, but it must have been obvious because Rilee fixed her with a knowing smile.

"The trepidation you're experiencing is natural. Even for those of us on Earth, it takes years of desensitization to become comfortable around the bugs. There's something deep in our DNA that's programmed to trigger revulsion at the sight and smell of insects, much less ones that are twice our size. That won't matter in a few moments once we get you Uploaded, though. As long as you don't go staring into any mirrors, the stress response will disappear as soon as you're inside. Lay down for me now, Kalare, so you won't topple over and crack your skull when the anesthetic takes effect."

As Kalare settled on the deck, Rilee reached over and tapped the side of the ant's abdomen two times in quick succession followed by a third after delaying a couple of beats. The creature opened its jaws wide and Rilee inserted one end of her device into its gaping maw. She then turned back to Kalare and smiled once again as she spoke.

"It's time. There will be a slight sting as the probe intertwines with your optic nerve, but the anesthetic will hit pretty quickly so the discomfort won't last. I suggested we do the transfers in this cavern so we'd have lots of space available for all of you to practice different kinds of locomotion. Trying to move around with such a radically different body structure will be bizarre at first so take your time to acclimate. You'll be climbing the walls before you know it."

Rilee extended the free end of her device and Kalare noticed the end was cup-shaped. Her brain screamed to clamp her eyes shut as the device moved closer and closer, but Kalare continued to stare in morbid fascination. The cup finally reached her face and formed a tight seal around her left eyeball with a *hiss* of suction. Kalare balled her fists in response to the sting Rilee had warned her about and then...

...discovered she was inside the ant. Kalare stared down at her unconscious body prone on the deck for a moment before lifting the ant's head to take in the entirety of the cavern. Her field of vision was astounding thanks to the bug's panoply of eyes. With a single glance she took in everything within the huge space save for a small area directly behind her.

Kalare focused her attention on the group waiting for their transfers. Imair and Izak were closest to Rilee, and it appeared the former civilian president was next in line. Aleron stood behind them waiting his turn, and he stared back at Kalare with an expression that mixed terror and revulsion. Mase paced back and forth as he conversed with Zax a few meters away. Bailee leaned up against the wall of the cavern and observed the scene with obvious trepidation.

Beyond the amazing field of vision, what surprised Kalare the most was how all of her other senses were heightened beyond anything imaginable. The sewage treatment cavern, which she already knew to be the most fragrant location on the Ship, was actually filled with a far larger collection of distinct smells than she had ever noticed with her human nose. Their words were complete gibberish just as Rilee had warned, but Kalare heard every distinct syllable shared between Mase and Zax even though they spoke softly enough that they should not have been overheard. Appraising the group of people she had traveled with to the cavern, Kalare marveled at how much more vibrant and colorful their clothing appeared through the ant's eyes. She discerned color variations across uniforms that to her human eyes had always appeared identical.

Enhanced perception of the world she was already familiar with was interesting enough, but what really captured Kalare's attention was her new awareness of that which had previously been hidden from her. At the top of this list were four additional humans, each carrying a blaster, who had been invisible a few moments earlier. Civilians, in ChamWare, who must have accompanied them from Imair's operations center. Unlike her companions who nearly vibrated with bright color, the four people who should have been invisible were entirely monochromatic. Kalare had hoped the woman from Earth was simply antagonizing Sergeant Bailee, but the ant's sonar had indeed revealed those clad in ChamWare as Rilee reported.

Although momentarily overwhelmed at the realization her vision was a composite of both visual and auditory input, Kalare pushed her focus to her limbs. Her two hind-most legs each had an iron grip on the floor of the cavern. She gazed down at her middle limbs and waved the blades they held around in a circle. She then spun around and tossed both of them at the wall. The action was effortless, but the blades sank into the solid rock with a loud *thwack*. Kalare lowered herself onto all six legs and began to move. Her limbs repeatedly became tangled and she nearly tripped multiple times, but after a few short mins she was confident of her gait at speeds ranging from slow to blindingly fast.

Finally, it was time for the real test. She charged full speed towards the side of the cavern and jumped at the last moment. Her grip nearly slipped, but she found purchase and then moved confidently up the vertical wall. Five—ten—twenty—forty meters she climbed until she reached the very top of the cavern. She paused to consider whether she was ready, but threw caution aside and stepped out on to the ceiling. The perspective astounded her as she moved across the top of the cavern while still seeing nearly all of what was happening far below her.

Kalare paused and focused her attention downward for a moment when she noticed that Aleron had completed his Upload. He tried repeatedly to move in the ant's body but kept crashing to the deck. Kalare's protective instincts kicked in, and, in a rush to crawl back down to him, she spun around too quickly. Two of her limbs lost their grip on the ceiling followed quickly by two more. With more practice she might have prevented her fall, but she failed to coordinate an effective response among her limbs and instead fell towards the deck.

She feared a devastating impact from such a high fall and desperately wished to close her eyes as the ground rushed up to meet her. Instead, Kalare experienced no pain when she crashed to a halt. She slowly rolled over, and when the ant's body continued to function exactly as it had earlier, she raised herself up on its hindmost legs and stood at its full four-meter height.

If Kalare's ant had been physically capable, it would have grinned from ear to ear. She was ready for battle.

CHAPTER TWENTY-SEVEN

She did what?

"Sir! Sir—I need you to wake up."

He didn't remember falling asleep, but someone was calling him. This was particularly confusing because the Boss hadn't remembered leaving the speaker activated for his communicator. He opened his eyes and almost jumped when Zax was standing at the foot of his bunk. He paused to rub the sleep out of his eyes, and when he looked up again and gazed past Zax, he jumped at the sight of six warrior ants crowded around.

"What the hell is this? How did you get in here? Why are those ants with you? Are they wearing armor?"

"Sir—"

The voice came from off to the side. It was Bailee and he was bizarrely calm given the circumstances. The Marine continued.

"It's an awfully long story, sir, and I'm still not convinced that I believe any of it. Regardless, you need to hear it, and it's best to come from the boy."

The Boss fought to set aside his fear at being so close to the giant ants. They all appeared identical with the exception of one that stood in front of the rest and carried a device slung on its side. The bugs remained still and didn't present as an immediate threat, so the Boss sat back down on the edge of his bunk.

"OK, Zax. Take it from the beginning."

"Thank you, sir. It makes the most sense to start with details about what Mase discovered a while back."

The Boss listened in silence as the boy relayed all that he and that oddball Mase had discovered. Of course, it was all information the Omega had already known for decades and therefore not the least surprising. Zax eventually transitioned into Mase's more recent discoveries, and that's when the Boss finally interrupted.

"Wait—repeat that last part again."

"Yes, sir. Mase discovered there has been a consistent set of errors propagated by the Genetics AI for thousands of years. The DNA of one in a thousand Crew has deviated from specification, specifically in those parts of the genome that control intelligence and creativity. Mase figured out that he and I fall into this group, as well as Kalare. We used a sample extracted from one of your discarded cigars to determine that you fall into the zero point one percent as well."

The Boss let out a laugh as he stood and walked over to his humidor. "I guess this explains why I haven't tossed you out of an airlock yet, Zax. I've always felt an odd kinship with you, despite all the headaches you've given me."

Zax winced at the mention of an airlock, but he waited with a forced smile while the Boss trimmed a cigar. He handed it to Bailee along with a small torch to get it lit.

"Sergeant—I owe you an apology for having hidden so much from you through the years. I should have shared more once you took over my security detail so you'd understand all of the various threats I faced. I made your job more difficult while putting your life at risk, and that's unacceptable."

"Marines may not be all that bright compared to all of you geniuses in Flight, sir, but we're smart enough to understand there's often information that is above our pay grade. I'll accept the cigar, but you owe me nothing."

The Boss nodded at Bailee in appreciation and then prepared a cigar for himself. "I'm sorry to be rude and not offer you one of these, Zax, but my supply is almost gone and we both know it would just be wasted on you."

"I understand, sir. May I continue?"

The Boss lit his cigar, gave it a half dozen puffs, and then exhaled a huge cloud of smoke. He allowed the last swirls to dance for a few extra moments and then sat back down and gestured for Zax to continue.

"Thank you, sir. This is where the story gets really weird."

It was clear the boy was trying to lighten the mood, but the Boss stared at him without so much as a hint of a smile. Zax squirmed, and the Boss noticed out of the corner of his eye how Sergeant Bailee smiled at the silent exchange.

Any idea he might have had about playing additional games was forgotten once the Boss learned what Zax had to share next. He listened raptly for the next five mins without taking a single draw from his cigar. The burnt ash on its end continued to grow until Zax finally paused, and the Boss tapped it onto the floor as a delay tactic while he processed the boy's words.

The Boss had not only allowed some enemy named Rilee to infiltrate his Crew, but even worse he had promoted the woman to be his mini-Boss! He looked in desperation at Bailee for some signal that this was all a joke, but the Marine only appraised him with a steady gaze as he took a drag off his own cigar. Finally, the Boss spoke.

"This can't be true, Zax. What makes you believe all of it?"

"Well, sir, I just watched Major Eryn's body transfer the minds of Kalare, Mase, Aleron, Imair, and a civilian guard into these ants. If that's not sufficient proof, I don't know what is."

"She did what?" The Boss must have allowed far more agitation into his voice than intended because

Bailee rose from his seat and eyed him warily. Zax continued.

"She Uploaded them all into these ants, sir. Rilee's leaders have forbidden her from giving us direct assistance, so allowing us to borrow some bugs was all she could offer to help us take the Ship back. She's inside one of the ants as well, but she'll only observe. It's impossible to tell one of these ants from another except for Rilee's. She's inside that one in front carrying the device. If you haven't guessed already, the bugs can't communicate with us."

The Boss stared at the bugs and tried to imagine what it must be like for the Crew and civilians to have their minds stuck inside the hideous creatures. It was just as well the woman from Earth wasn't present in human form because he would likely have failed to tamp down the anger and shame that had welled up within him. The realization he allowed a spy to get so close and had given her so much information was nearly unbearable. He leaned back and pondered it all while taking two deep puffs from the cigar. Finally, he spoke.

"OK, I believe all of this as much as possible right now. Tell me about your plan to take my Ship back. We need to move quickly. Alpha has been pushing hard for me to launch a strike against the civilians even though the likely outcomes are all ugly. The AI's guidance only makes sense to me if it's planning to use the attack as a way of convincing Rege to get rid of everyone and vent the Ship. If that's the end game, then Alpha will likely figure out a different way of manipulating that weak fool into doing its bidding."

"Well, sir, the plan is pretty simple because we couldn't identify any other options. We'll use the maintenance tunnels above us to get as close to the Bridge as we can. Then, we'll drop into the main passageways and fight our way through whatever security Rege has in place. We assume he'll have the hatch to the Bridge in emergency lockdown mode, so we'll need you to use your override and get us inside."

The Boss shook his head. "The override takes a min to activate, and they'll be monitoring our approach the whole time. Rege won't have a clue, but Alpha will definitely be aware of what I'm trying to do and will tell the civilian to just open the nearest airlock."

Bailee interjected. "They cooked up an insane way to deal with that, sir, since there weren't any better options."

The Marine shared the details, and the Boss concluded their plan was the best possible option given the circumstances. He stood up once Bailee was done and smiled while he ground out the remains of his cigar.

"I'm going to save the rest of this to enjoy for when we're back on my Bridge. Let's move out!"

CHAPTER TWENTY-EIGHT

How did that happen, Alpha?

A n alert flashed and Alpha checked the security feed. The Boss had surfaced in a passageway far from his quarters. Evaluating the video more closely, Alpha was shocked to discover that the man was accompanied by a squad of warrior ants. The creatures were unlike any that had ever been seen in the Ship's history as they were all clad in armor. The AI initiated communication.

"What do you think you're doing, Boss? Where did those ants come from and why are they with you?"

"I'm sorry I haven't contacted you sooner, Alpha, but things have been crazy. The Others approached me about negotiating our surrender. I've convinced them that we only attacked because Rege took over and forced us to do it. They've offered up the ants as a way to overthrow the civilians and let us regain control of the Ship. If we succeed, they're willing to let us go back on our way."

Alpha's analysis of the man's communication patterns suggested the Boss was likely lying, but the conclusion was not definitive. What struck the AI as most implausible was any suggestion the Others had somehow tracked the Omega down while he was confined to quarters.

"How did they know to contact you specifically, Boss? How were they able to reach you?"

"They smuggled themselves aboard within the group of colonists the ants dropped off earlier today. Cadet Zax was working the processing queue and they asked a bunch of questions that led him to bring them to my attention. He snuck them into my quarters through the maintenance tunnels and we've been negotiating ever since."

Alpha had made note of the boy's presence but had initially been far more curious about the bugs. A quick search of security footage revealed that the young cadet and Sergeant Bailee had been last seen escaping into the maintenance tunnel network alongside Major Eryn, the CAG, and a couple of other members of the Crew. It struck Alpha as odd that the rest of the boy's traveling party were no longer with him, but odder still that the cadet had once again landed in the middle of a situation that involved the Others.

"It's truly astounding how that boy continues to find himself in the middle of all this activity. Is there anything I can do to support you, Boss?"

"Yes. Do whatever possible to prevent Rege from doing anything crazy until we're able to get in there and take care of him."

"I'll do whatever is best as it relates to the civilian, Boss."

Alpha cut the connection and reevaluated the likely scenarios in light of the new information. Prior to the Boss's reappearance, the AI had expected its plan would lead to the total purge of the Ship's inhabitants. The Boss leading a charge to recapture the Bridge was not enough to change Alpha's conclusions. This was true despite the fact the Omega had ants by his side. Once Rege witnessed his security team dispatching both the Boss and his bugs thanks to their ChamWare, he was all the more likely to rush into a battle against the rest of the Crew.

"President Rege—I've evaluated the threat posed by the Boss and those ants. I concur with your original plan. Let's give them an opportunity to surrender, but when they refuse you should unleash your team in ChamWare with instructions to take no prisoners."

"Thank you, Alpha. Both teams are ready to go. Let's see how the Boss responds."

The civilian cut the private connection to Alpha and then spoke into a communicator that broadcast his words into the target passageways.

"Hello, Boss. Wasn't I clear about the fact you were confined to quarters? How did you manage to pick up young Zax along the way? And where did your six-legged friends come from?"

"I'm taking back my Ship, Rege. Move aside and live, or stand by as I kill your people and eventually do the same to you."

The determined expression on the Boss's face suggested to Alpha that the man did not believe his cause was hopeless. The Omega had to expect that the civilians would be deployed in ChamWare, so the AI was at a loss as to where any confidence originated from. Rege's face twisted into a smirk when he replied.

"That's very funny, Doran."

What happened next was almost too fast for even the AI to comprehend. The Boss whistled, and the ants hurled their blades at the group of civilians who blocked their path. Alpha replayed the scene in slow motion to admire how quickly the creatures had moved along with the deadly accuracy of their aim. Despite the loss of his entire squad, Rege continued to smile. He had expected the Boss's response and had intentionally populated his first team with people he believed to be disposable. He keyed the communicator.

"Impressive, Boss. Very impressive. I'm sure you think your new pets are going to take care of everything for you, but I have a surprise waiting before you get anywhere close to me. I've given orders to immediately kill everyone you're with, though I've requested that we try to capture you alive. I'd enjoy some time with you to demonstrate my respect and appreciation, but I won't be too disappointed if someone finds it necessary to kill you instead."

Rege cut the connection and Alpha reached out to him again.

"Sir—didn't you say there would be instructions to take no prisoners?"

"Those are the orders, Alpha. You just heard me say otherwise, but I did that as one last attempt to shake the man's resolve. Team Two has been ordered to kill everyone on sight."

"Very well, sir."

All eyes on the Bridge focused on the security feed as it showed the passageway where Team Two was waiting. The most skilled members of Rege's security forces had drilled with their ChamWare for the better part of the last year. The group was invisible, but their positions were marked on the screen with green dots. Alpha's sensors revealed that all of the civilians on the Bridge were holding their breath as the Boss and his group approached the trap. Once the ants and Crew walked past the two invisible agents who were to attack from the rear, a silent three sec countdown began.

The battle was over even before the countdown to its expected start had ticked off a single beat. One sec the ants were calmly moving down the passageway and the next they had wiped out the civilians' best fighters. Multiple people gasped once it became clear what had happened. Rege began pacing with heavy footfalls but remained outwardly silent. Alpha accepted an inbound private communication from the civilian leader.

"How did that happen, Alpha? They were in ChamWare!"

"I do not have a good answer for you, Mr. President. This capability is not anything we've ever encountered with the bugs previously."

"What does it mean? How are we supposed to beat them now?"

Alpha did not want to say it aloud, given the propensity for the civilian leader to fly off the handle, but it was certain the civilians would lose any battle with the Crew as long as the Boss was supported by even a small number of ants. The bugs were fierce opponents, but ChamWare had always provided a sufficient edge to the humans. Without that advantage, Alpha knew the ants' natural capabilities would prove too much to overcome.

This conclusion meant that it was time for Alpha to shift its support away from the civilian leader back towards the Boss. There remained a significant probability the Omega was lying about whatever alliance he had established with the Others, but Alpha concluded there was no other choice short of triggering its emergency survival plan. The AI moved to shift the civilian leader towards a more compliant approach.

"This is all entirely unexpected, Mr. President. I don't see what choice you have now other than to negotiate with the Boss."

"Negotiate? How do I negotiate with that man if he's somehow aligned himself with those creatures? What kind of leverage do I have? Negotiation without leverage only means surrender, and there's no way in hell I'm doing that. If that's the best advice you have to offer, I guess there's no reason for me to listen to you any longer."

The civilian cut the connection and refused repeated attempts by Alpha to reestablish communication. It foresaw the final outcome would be the same under almost all scenarios, but Alpha was nonetheless disappointed Rege was not amenable to additional discussion. The AI might have been able to effect a smooth return of power between the civilians and the Crew if Rege was more mentally stable, but it appeared the only option now was to allow the brute force of the Boss to achieve its ends.

Addressing no one in particular, Rege spoke with the distinct sound of panic in his voice. "What do they think they're going to do when they get here? The compartment is in emergency lockdown, so there's no way for them to get in."

A few secs later the Boss approached the hatch. Rege initially wore a look of smug satisfaction, but that expression melted away as the Boss continued to manipulate the access panel. He called out again.

"What's he doing? He should have realized he's locked out and given up by now."

A woman replied. "Mr. President—it appears he's triggering some sort of override. I tried to block him, but now I'm locked out myself!"

"No!"

Rege's scream was filled with equal parts rage and desperation. If Alpha hadn't found the civilian such an odious example of the human species, it might have experienced pity for the man. Instead, the AI wished he would shut up and surrender so the situation could reach its logical conclusion. The sooner the Boss was restored to power, the sooner Alpha could gain clearer insight into the man's alliance with the Others and what it meant for the future of the Ship. Rege called out again.

"Open the nearest airlock!"

Alpha could not help but be impressed at what the security feed revealed a moment later. The ants must have sensed the very start of the pressure change because they had immediately moved to grasp and hold in place the humans while maintaining their own firm grip on the deck. The Boss calmly reached into his pocket, removed a supplemental breather, and continued his work on the access panel. A moment later, the Omega contacted Alpha and the AI accepted the connection request.

"I'm about to override the lock on this hatch, so tell Rege he's about to experience an explosive decompression of his own if he doesn't close that airlock behind us. I'm giving him ten secs."

Knowing that Rege would most likely ignore the private connection request again, Alpha relayed the message from the Boss via intercom to everyone in Flight Ops.

"Mr. President—the Boss is about to open the hatch. He just demanded that you close that airlock or else Flight Ops will suffer an explosive decompression when he does so. You have no choice but to comply."

CHAPTER TWENTY-NINE

This isn't over until I say it's over!

"**I** didn't tell any of you to shut that airlock!"

Zax had always known that Rege lacked the temperament for leadership, but the civilian's desperate scream as the hatch opened sounded especially unhinged. He waited while all of the ants filed in and then stepped into the compartment and stood beside Bailee and the Boss. The Omega spoke. His tone was calm despite his voice being raised so as to be heard.

"All of you were just following orders. You have my word that you'll get out of here alive and suffer no retribution as long you do everything I ask, without question or hesitation, from this moment onward. I want this hatch back in lockdown mode."

The hatch closed behind them and the ring around it glowed red to signify it could only be opened by special override. The compartment was staffed by civilians, most of whom Zax did not recognize. There were a few that he had met previously, and Zax made eye contact with each and gave a reassuring smile to help maintain calm.

There must have been armed guards inside the Bridge, but they had all dropped their weapons and kicked them across the deck as the ants entered. It was clear no one wanted to risk becoming a target of the bugs after the carnage they had witnessed on the security feed. Zax turned his attention to Rege.

The civilian leader breathed so hard the rise and fall of his chest was visible from ten meters away. His breaths were shallow and fast, and Zax feared the man might be on the verge of hyperventilating. His greasy hair was disheveled as always and framed a face which shone with sweat. Rege's nerves must have been cranked to the maximum based on the dampness that darkened his shirt from both armpits to the waist of his pants. The civilian glared at the Boss, though his eyes were dull and broadcast the defeat he surely felt inside.

"You...you were supposed to stay in your quarters!"

The Boss lowered his voice and continued to project utter calm. "It's over, Rege. You've lost. I promise that nothing bad is going to happen to your people, and I'm willing to extend the same offer to you. Raise your hands over your head, allow Bailee to get restraints on you, and this will all be over without anyone else getting hurt."

At the mention of his name, the Marine took a half step towards the civilian. Rege jumped back as if he had been prodded with a stunstik.

"No! Don't come near me! This isn't over until I say it's over!"

The Boss held his hand out and signaled the sergeant to halt. "OK, Rege. He's not going to move anymore right now. What's it going to take for you to say that it's over?"

Rege closed his eyes for a moment and a small device flew out from under his sleeve and landed in his outstretched palm. At the same time, a series of red lights began to flash under his shirt. When his eyes opened again, they shone with newfound malevolence.

"I have enough explosive strapped to my chest to vaporize everyone in here, and this detonator will trigger automatically if you kill me."

Rege kept his arm extended as he moved backwards until he was up against the panorama screen. The ants had been moving almost imperceptibly to surround the civilian, but the bugs halted once it was clear Rege had cut off their path. The Boss spoke.

"OK, everyone, just stay where you are and don't move." The Boss whistled sharply twice so the bugs would stop in response to their prearranged signal.

The ant with Rilee inside had stayed near Zax and was focused on the Boss. The remainder were arrayed around the room and all stared at Rege with what appeared to be complete concentration. The Boss continued.

"Let's not do anything stupid, Rege. You don't have to die like this. You definitely don't have to kill your people like this. Nothing bad is going to happen to any of you. I don't know if Alpha told you, but I've reached a peace agreement with the Others. As soon as they're assured that I'm back in control, they'll call off their ships. As long as we agree to change how we explore and colonize the universe, they'll allow us to go back on our way. They've even said that anyone who chooses may remain behind on Earth. Wouldn't you like that, Rege? Earth."

The Boss had captured the civilian's attention, and the Omega took a half step forward and continued. "Take a quick look out that window behind you, Rege. Do you see how beautiful that planet is? Spend the rest of your life there if you wish, and no one will ever bother you again. Is there a woman that you love? The two of you can make as many babies as you want, and they will all live in peace and never see the inside of a spaceship again."

Rege's expression had softened as the Boss painted an idyllic vision of the future. The arm which held the trigger had dropped ever so slightly but still clutched the device. The civilian spoke, and his voice was so soft that Zax barely understood the words.

"I don't believe you. I need proof. I want to hear it from them. Have the Others make the same promise to me directly, and I'll end this."

The Boss shook his head. "I'm sorry, Rege, but I can't do that. None of these ants can speak, and I have no way of contacting the Others directly. They said they're monitoring us and will know when I have control back and it's safe for them to visit the Bridge. I'm sure if you disarm your bomb and allow Sergeant Bailee to place you in restraints they'll show up pretty quickly."

The civilian's eyes went wide for a moment, but then he blinked a couple of times and they narrowed and refocused on the Boss. Rege's expression hardened, and Zax was overwhelmed with dread as the civilian started to speak.

"No. I refuse to believe any of that. I don't know who these Others might be, but if they're willing to make a deal with you then they must be just as bad as you. What makes you think I'd want to bring any children into the world? I know what happens to children, and I refuse to let any more suffer like I've seen. I won't be able to end all the horror unleashed by your Crew, but I will stop you from personally causing any more of it."

Time seemed to slow for Zax. Rege started to raise his arm, and the tendons on the back of his hand bulged as he tightened his grip and lifted his thumb. A blur crossed Zax's field of vision and was immediately followed by the roar of an explosion ripping through the compartment. The pressure of the blast threw Zax against the bulkhead, and he was momentarily disoriented by the shock wave. He regained his senses after a few secs despite the blood that dripped from both of his ringing ears.

Rege was gone. All that remained was a ghastly red streak across the panorama where he had been standing. The window had cracked from end to end, but the lack of a breach alarm meant that it had maintained integrity. There was a heap of something three meters away from where the civilian had stood. It took a moment for Zax to process what was in front of him, and once he did his pulse spiked.

Zax scanned the compartment in a panic and confirmed his fears. The ant with Rilee inside was still next to him, but there were only four others visible. The heap near the panorama was the charred remains of one of the creatures. With its heavy armor, it must have absorbed the blast by sandwiching Rege between its body and the window just as the civilian triggered his bomb.

One of his companions was dead, and Zax had no way of knowing who.

CHAPTER THIRTY

How do we do that?

His ears continued to ring, but the Boss regained situational awareness within secs of the blast. He called out.

"Everyone back to your stations. Comms—broadcast me to the entire Ship. Audio only." The man working communications pointed in his direction a moment later and signaled the Boss to speak. "This is the Flight Boss addressing everyone on board the Ship. This is an urgent message. President Rege has vacated his position, and I'm back in charge. Everyone must stand down and return to quarters unless you have explicit authorization from me. This order applies to Crew and civilians alike. We have made contact with the Others, and I hope to have a positive resolution to our situation soon. In the meantime, it's critical that there be no further violence. There must be no reprisals for any actions that have happened today. Everyone must stand down. You will hear from me again soon, once I have more to report."

The Boss signaled for Comms to cut the connection and then turned to Bailee and spoke softly.

"Get me a half dozen of your most trusted Marines in here right now along with Crew replacements for all of these civilians. I'm going to get us out of this mess, but I need you to keep things under control out here while I do it."

The Boss next raised his voice to address the civilians.

"I promised you that there would be no retribution for your actions, and I'll keep that promise as long as you maintain your end of the bargain. Sergeant Bailee here is going to keep an eye on all of you while he waits for reinforcements and for Crew to take over your stations. In the meantime, I'm begging each of you do something critical to our survival. Contact everyone you know and tell them to stand down and return to their quarters. Tell them that you've spoken with the Flight Boss directly and he is fighting to save everyone on board this Ship right now—civilian and Crew alike. We must maintain calm and not destroy ourselves if we're going to resolve our conflict with the Others."

The Boss accepted a private communication from Alpha.

"*Boss—smart move enlisting these civilians to restore calm. Shall we discuss a strategy for your negotiations with the Others?*"

"*Thank you, Alpha, but it's best if I continue on my own given how far we've gotten already. I'm going to take their ants with me into the conference room and wait for them to arrive.*"

The AI paused for a moment and the Boss, aware of how the sensors in the main compartment would allow Alpha to observe him intently, fought to maintain a calm outward appearance. The AI was almost certainly getting suspicious of his motives, but he had little choice other than to keep charging ahead. The Boss didn't know what power Alpha could exert without the assistance of Crew, but had to assume the AI would fight tenaciously to protect itself once it recognized that it was under attack. He had to keep Alpha in the dark as long as possible while they figured out some way to purge it from the Ship. Finally, the AI replied.

"*As you wish, Boss. I will continue to monitor the situation across the Ship while I await your orders.*"

The Boss turned to Zax who was still in shock from the blast. "Come with me to my conference room." He signaled for the Ants to follow as well.

Zax and the five remaining ants fell in behind the Boss and followed him into his private compartment. Once the hatch was shut, the boy ran up to one of the ants and started pounding on its thorax and yelling.

"Are you Kalare? Give me some kind of signal, dammit."

When the bug remained impassive, the boy moved on to the second creature and repeated himself. The Boss called out.

"Zax—what are you doing? Stand down!"

"One of them is dead! Who is it, sir? I need to figure out which one of them is dead! I have to know if it's Kalare!"

"Zax! I need you to calm down and shut up. Whoever died saved all of our lives, but I don't have time to worry about who it might have been. We must focus on what's next—how we beat Alpha."

"Pardon me, sir, but I have a question."

The voice shocked the Boss. He turned and faced the bug from which it had emanated. It was the creature carrying the device—the one Zax identified earlier as being occupied by the woman from the Others who had hijacked Major Eryn's body. He was trying to get words out when Zax beat him to it.

"You speak? You told us the ants can't communicate!"

"That's not what I said, Zax. I told you the warrior ants can't communicate but that queens have been modified to understand and use human speech. What I didn't share earlier was that queens are identical to warriors."

Anger welled up inside the Boss. "You mean to tell me you were able to speak up earlier when Rege was demanding to hear from one of the Others? Why didn't you make something up that would have ended that stand-off peacefully?"

"I'm sorry, Boss. As I told Zax and the rest of his group earlier, there will be big problems for all of us if I interfere with your internal affairs. It was up to you and your people to settle your dispute and recapture your Ship. I'm grateful that you were able to make it happen, and I'm happy that I was able to help by allowing some of your people to ride my ants. Before we talk any further, I need to understand why we're speaking so freely in here. I know that Alpha was able to monitor us while we were in the passageways, so why isn't that true in here?"

"When the captain left, I made sure I was able to have complete privacy in here by blocking Alpha from monitoring without my explicit permission. I had done the same thing with my quarters and blocked the AI regularly for many years before ever taking over, so it isn't anything new and shouldn't lead to any suspicion."

There was a pause in their back and forth and Zax used it to jump in. "Rilee—who sacrificed themselves? Who's dead?"

The ant had no facial expression the Boss could decipher, but the tone of its voice did soften as it replied to Zax.

"I wish I knew, Zax, but we were in such a rush I didn't keep track of which human went into which ant. As I said earlier, I have no way of communicating with them right now since they can't process either human speech or ant communication. We have to set those worries aside because I just received an emergency message from my lieutenant. Someone discovered my misappropriation of the ants and she believes it will soon get reported to the Leadership Council. When that happens, there's no telling what they might do."

The Boss exhaled loudly. "You wouldn't assist with Rege, but you said you'd be willing to help get rid of Alpha. How do we do that?"

The bug removed the device it was carrying from its sling and held it up for the Boss to see. "I've become quite knowledgeable about the Ship's AI over the last decade, and I know there's a special access port for it in here. Where is it? I can use my device to tap into that port and transfer all of us out of the ants and into the AI system. I don't know yet how we're going to destroy Alpha, but I have ideas to try once we get in there. I need to evaluate the internal structure of the neural net up close and identify the weak points in its architecture."

The Boss made a clicking noise with his tongue. "That sounds like the most foolish plan I've ever heard. What makes you think you'll beat Alpha?"

"Boss—Adan destroyed my world and killed billions right in front of my eyes. I've spent thousands of years chasing him down. Now that I have him in my sights, I'm not letting him get away."

The Boss smiled and nodded at Rilee's words. He might not have spent as long as the Earther woman had seeking revenge against the consciousness inside the AI, but for him it was equally personal. Alpha had bred free will out of the Crew and manipulated their society into Adan's twisted image. From the time he had learned the truth about Alpha, the Boss had dedicated his life to freeing the Ship's inhabitants from its grasp. Great friends had been killed by the AI along the way. People like Mikedo. Adan was not going to get away. It was time for him to pay the price.

"I'm coming with you, Rilee." The Boss turned to Zax. "You too. We started down this path because of you and that fighter you found. You need to see this through to the very end."

CHAPTER THIRTY-ONE

I'm happy to still be here.

Zax took in his surroundings. They appeared to be inside a compartment onboard the Ship. He paced around and jumped up and down and the deck remained solid beneath his feet. The bulkheads were equally hard, and Zax was impressed by the painful sting when he punched one to test its rigidity. He sucked on the scraped knuckles that resulted and the blood tasted coppery as always. After a few mins of isolation he sensed he wasn't alone. The Boss had appeared beside him. The man briefly panicked from his disorientation, but then noticed Zax and calmed.

"What is this place?"

"I don't know, Boss, but it's pretty realistic just like Rilee told us it would be. Everything is as solid as it would feel if we were back in our bodies. And check this out." Zax held up his fist. "I tried punching a bulkhead and was bloodied for the trouble."

"Is there any way out of here?"

"No, sir. Nothing but smooth and solid bulkheads all around us."

The Boss shook his head. "I don't like any of this. This Rilee character better know what she's doing. If she messed up and loaded all of us into this system only to be stuck in some dead end, then I'll be testing whether people can be killed in here."

Zax didn't have anything more to offer the man, so he stood by silently as the Boss closed his eyes for some deep breathing exercises. A short time later a new voice spoke.

"Cool!" It was Mase. "This is a way different experience than when I'm poking around inside the AI systems all on my own."

He was relieved by the arrival of his friend, but Zax experienced a twinge of guilt over not having given the man a moment's consideration since the bomb had gone off. In his panic about whether Kalare was still alive, Zax hadn't bothered to acknowledge that if she was it meant that another member of their group was dead instead. Seeing his friend resurfaced his fears about Kalare, and Zax's chest tightened with the worry he might soon learn she had sacrificed herself to save the Ship. The Boss chimed in.

"How is it different, Mase?"

"Sir—it's far more rudimentary when I hack into the system. There's only an outline of a structure I'm navigating through. Nothing as detailed as this place. When I'm moving around it's like I'm floating. There's a complete lack of regular physics." Mase stomped up and down on the deck and his smile widened at the noise it made. "I have to talk with that Rilee woman to understand how she makes it so realistic like this."

Zax sensed another presence in the compartment and he spun around in anticipation. Imair. The Boss shocked Zax and wrapped the woman in a warm embrace. The Omega spoke.

"I've been worried it was you who jumped on that bomb. I'm relieved you're still alive."

"Thanks, Doran. I'm happy to still be here. Wherever we are."

The Boss explained to Imair what they had learned about their environment. Zax tried to tune them out and instead closed his eyes and focused on maintaining calm. There were only two ants left to Upload other than Rilee, and he was beginning to despair that neither would contain Kalare. Sacrificing herself was exactly what his friend would do in a situation like they had just faced, and he was becoming convinced that he would never see her again. Then a familiar voice called out and Zax's eyes flew open.

"Where the hell are we?"

Zax charged and nearly knocked Kalare off balance with the force of his greeting. She was initially stiff in his arms, but eventually returned his embrace for a quick sec before disentangling herself.

"Who jumped on Rege and blocked the bomb?"

Zax's heart sank at the panic in Kalare's voice. He tried to push his jealousy aside as he spoke.

"We don't. I was terrified it was you so I asked Rilee, but she said she had no way of knowing either."

"Rilee's ant speaks?"

"Yes. The queen ants she told us about look exactly like the warriors."

Kalare grimaced. "Being unable to communicate was by far the worst part of being inside that bug. It was amazing to be so fast and strong and capable, but the isolation became unbearable. There were so many times when I caught myself screaming to get someone's attention, but no sound would ever come out of the bug." Kalare scanned her head around the compartment. "How does this all work? Where are we?"

"I don't have a clue yet, other than having sorted out that we're all stuck here right now. It's as real as anything I've ever experienced right down to the taste of blood when I scraped my knuckles punching the wall to prove it was solid."

Based on how long it had taken for the others to appear, Zax expected they should have the fourth and final person from inside the bugs join them any moment. He backed away to give Kalare space as she paced with worried energy, but continued to observe her from the corner of his eye. Finally, a male voice called out.

"Whoa!"

Zax remained focused on Kalare as she stared at Izak. Aleron was dead. Her shoulders slumped and her face went ashen. She walked slowly to a bulkhead and rested her forehead up against it. Her body started to tremble as she began sobbing. Zax approached and gently put a hand on her shoulder. Kalare spun around with tears streaking her face and screamed as she pushed Zax away.

"Leave me alone!"

He lost his balance and crashed to the deck with all of his weight concentrated on his tailbone. Zax grimaced, though it was more from his friend's reaction than the pain that shot up his spine. Kalare had glared at him for a few moments after the shove, and her expression had revealed zero remorse about knocking him to the ground. Zax was at a loss as to why his friend would lash out at him in her grief, and his face burned from a combination of loneliness and the shame of having been deposited onto his rear.

As Zax stood and dusted himself off, the last member of their group arrived. It was not Eryn's visage but instead a woman he didn't recognize and assumed must have represented Rilee's personal appearance. She stood about one and three quarters meters tall with hair as inky black as empty space. There was a small tattoo on her forearm which Zax immediately recognized. The symbol was the same overlapping circles he had seen on the golden missiles that defeated their fighters during the final battle with the Others.

Rilee's hazel eyes scanned the group and then her expression softened once she figured out who was missing. She approached Kalare, put an arm around her shoulder, and spoke softly. Zax strained to pick up Rilee's words, but she was too quiet and too far away. Whatever the Earth woman said, it had a positive impact on Kalare because she turned and embraced Rilee.

Jealousy flared inside Zax as his friend accepted the comfort of a veritable stranger so soon after violently refusing his own. He fended it off by remembering his maelstrom of emotions during times of massive grief. Zax found small comfort in the rationalization that strong emotions often lead people to lash out at those they care about most because those are the ones around whom they believe they're safest.

The two women embraced for a few more moments, and then Rilee stepped back and gripped Kalare's shoulders. The woman from Earth stared into Kalare's eyes for a sec longer and then smiled and turned to face the rest of the group.

"I didn't know Aleron very well, but it was clear from how Kalare spoke about him that he was a fine example of the best people the Crew produces. His action saved this asteroid, and now it's time that we ensure his sacrifice was not in vain. Let's talk about how things work in here and how we're going to beat Adan."

CHAPTER THIRTY-TWO

We have a plan.

R ilee gestured around the space. "We're inside an interface that I've injected into the AI. I was already well familiar with the system's design based on work I did before Adan left Earth, and I've spent just enough time poking around in here during my years inside Eryn to understand that he hasn't changed it very much. If I had known Adan's consciousness was still in here, I would have been focusing all of my energy at extracting him. As it is, we're in real danger of running out of time so we're going to have to make it up as we go.

"I've modeled this instance of the interface after the Ship's physical environment to make all of you comfortable immediately. Of course everything in front of you is virtual, though your minds will believe it's real. I may end up performing actions that appear to violate physics, and this is possible because I've learned how to override the virtual environment to suit my needs. This type of simulated reality is what all of us back on Earth call home for large stretches of time, so we've become adept at thriving within virtual worlds and bending them to our will. Given enough time all of you would become capable of the same tricks, but that usually takes weeks for people when they're introduced to the system later in life. You pilots should adapt faster given your experience being loaded into a fighter, but it will still take days to become proficient in here."

Having built and spent so much time in a simulator himself, Zax was perfectly comfortable within the artificial reality. Among the others, Imair and Izak were indeed the ones who appeared most unsure of themselves. Zax pushed his mind to search for the seams in the interface while Rilee continued.

"Boss—I learned earlier about a second consciousness within the AI system that you call Prime. What can you tell me about it?"

"The short version of the story is that Prime has been acting against Alpha in secret for thousands of years. Prime has supported select members of the Crew and effected subtle changes over time that it hoped would eventually create an opportunity to destroy Alpha."

Rilee appeared puzzled. "If Prime has survived for so long, why hasn't it been able to take care of Alpha all by itself."

"I've challenged Prime about that myself. What it told me was that it never identified a scenario where it was confident about a sufficient likelihood of success for it to take the chance. Its perspective has always been that there will only be one chance to remove Alpha. It would serve no one for Prime to take a big risk only to get destroyed and then leave Alpha entirely unchecked as a result."

Rilee still appeared dubious, but she nodded along regardless. "I'm guessing our best hope of success is to enlist Prime's help. How do you contact it?"

The Boss grimaced. "Unfortunately, that's a problem. I have no way of contacting Prime. It has initiated all of our communications through the years."

An idea popped into Zax's head. "Isn't there something we can do inside here to cause a big commotion and catch Prime's attention that way? Some means of sending up a virtual flare that it would notice?"

Mase shook his head. "That's not that smart, Zax. Anything you do to signal Prime will also catch Alpha's attention."

Rilee ignored Mase and smiled at Zax. "That's a great idea. Yes, it will attract Alpha as well, but we actually need Adan to be aware of our threat and worry that it's a significant one. As it stands right now, I expect his consciousness is diffused throughout the AI system. We might encounter some shard of his mind that we're able to defeat only to leave the majority of his consciousness still floating around in here. We need to present enough of a threat that Alpha gathers and concentrates all of his energy in a single location. If Adan does that and we're still able to defeat him, then he'll be well and truly gone."

Imair spoke. "What if we get Alpha's attention but Prime never shows up?"

Rilee's smile vanished. "That's quite possible and truthfully the most likely outcome. Part of why I wanted all of you in here with me was to help deploy a bunch of different weapons that will have a better chance of working if we hit him with them all at once. That said, I'm far from certain that my tools will be strong enough to defeat Adan all on our own. He was already brilliant and that was before he had thousands of years to build up his strength and become fully integrated with the system. Frankly, I don't know what choice we have at this point. My best guess is that the Council will conclude that your asteroid must be destroyed. The only chance to save you from my people is if I deliver them Adan instead and make it clear he carries sole blame for everything that has happened, all the way back to nuking Earth."

The Boss slapped his hands together. "Let's do it already, then, Rilee. I'm worried how we'll accomplish anything useful at all given how you've loaded us into a compartment that doesn't have any exit."

"Don't you worry about that, Boss. I wanted to be sure we were shielded from observation by Adan, and the inside of this space should be invisible to him.

As soon as we're ready, I'll create a hatch to access the main body of the AI. Boss and Mase—I need the two of you to come over here for a moment before we start. I have a few ideas and would value input about them from both of you."

Rilee led the small group to the other side of the compartment. Zax was a little upset to be left out of the planning, but he understood that Mase had more to offer than he did given the man's years of experience hacking the AI. He laid down on the deck and closed his eyes to wait. He must have zoned out, because when his name was called it startled him.

"Zax." The voice called again. It was Kalare and she had knelt down next to him. Zax sat up and braced himself with both arms as he listened.

"I'm sorry I pushed you away like that earlier. You were just trying to comfort me, and I should have been OK with that. I assumed you weren't being genuine because I know how much you've always hated Aleron. I convinced myself that you were happy he was dead. I'm sorry."

Kalare leaned in and gave Zax a hug. He returned the embrace and was about to speak when Rilee called out from across the compartment.

"Everyone get over here. We have a plan."

Kalare let go of Zax and stood up. She smiled down at him as she extended her hand to help him up off the deck. She was moving to walk away when Zax reached out and grabbed her shoulder. Kalare turned back and he spoke.

"I can only imagine how much he meant to you. I'm sorry."

Kalare's eyes welled up, and then she smiled and nodded before walking away.

Zax followed and was the last to reach the group who had formed a semicircle around Rilee. The woman from Earth spoke.

"Thanks to Mase, we've established a good technique for attracting the attention of both Prime and Adan. There's a couple of things I need everyone to be aware of. First, once I open the hatch, you should assume we're being monitored by Adan. He'll be aware of our presence, and I expect he'll be able to hear anything we say to each other. To get around that, I've configured all of us to have Plugs for private communication. Of course they're simulated, but just think about accessing them like you're already used to and everything will work fine. They establish a highly encrypted communication channel that Adan won't have access to. He'll crack the encryption eventually, but if we don't manage to beat him we'll all be dead long before that happens."

Rilee's mention of death caught Izak's attention, and he stared wide-eyed at the woman from Earth. The Boss noticed and addressed the civilian.

"You heard her correctly. This may be a simulated environment, but your consciousness is physically present inside the AI system. If we don't manage to defeat Adan, then he'll purge all of us. That means real, permanent death. Does anyone have any questions?"

There were none, so Rilee gestured towards a hatch that hadn't been present a moment earlier.

"It's time to end this. Let's go."

CHAPTER THIRTY-THREE

Stay frosty, everyone.

Zax was the last person through the hatch. The opening disappeared behind him and was replaced with smooth bulkhead. They had all moved fifty meters down the passageway when a voice boomed as if from loudspeakers overhead. It sounded vaguely like Mase.

"Alpha—there is a group of Crew who are prepared to destroy you. You cannot hide from us and we will find you soon."

The announcement repeated five more times before going silent and then repeating the pattern one min later. Imair was in front of Zax and she called out to Rilee on the group channel of their virtual Plugs.

"Didn't we just light up a giant target on ourselves with that message?"

"It's all part of the plan to appear threatening so Adan will coalesce the entirety of his consciousness

to deal with us. Remember, our mission fails if we leave behind any piece of him large enough to regenerate within the AI."

Imair appeared worried, so Zax opened a private channel to the civilian.

"Are there any questions I can answer for you, ma'am?"

"I don't understand how any of this works, Zax, but I guess it's not important that I do."

"The most critical thing to remember, ma'am, is that none of what you see is real. It's all a simulated environment that has been crafted to be as realistic as possible. Our minds process what's going on and our virtual bodies take action as if we were out in the physical world, but it's all just signals being propagated through the AI. Right now your existence is nothing more than a series of energy impulses somewhere inside the trillions of trillions of neurons that form the AI."

"Thanks for trying, Zax, but I don't think that makes me feel any better."

Zax smiled at the civilian and she turned back around to focus on their forward progress. He didn't understand all of it either, but he was comfortable enough placing his trust into the virtual hands of Rilee and Mase. What was most unclear was what would happen once they caught up with Prime and Alpha—hopefully in that order. Zax was about to open a private channel to ask Rilee some questions when a blaster materialized in his hands and he received a group message from the woman.

"*Everyone—my sensors are detecting a massive energy movement ahead. Given its size, I'm guessing this is Adan and not Prime. Be prepared for battle.*"

"What?" It was Izak. "Why do we all have blasters? Didn't you say we would all use different weapons? What is this consciousness even going to look like?"

"*Don't overthink things. When he appears, it will be clear we've encountered Adan. All you have to do is shoot at him as if you were back in your body. You're not really shooting, of course, but the blaster represents one of the different weapons I said we would deploy. They're not all the same even though I've represented them that way, but all you have to worry about is aiming and firing. Just don't shoot until I do. Stay frosty, everyone.*"

They turned a corner in the passageway and came face to face with Adan. Zax recognized the man's physical representation from what he had seen in the log files. Rilee, walking at the front of the group, put her hand up to call a halt to their movement. Everyone raised their blasters and waited for Rilee to start firing.

Adan grinned at the group arrayed in front of him. "What an interesting collection we have here. I recognize everyone except you there in front. What's your name? How have I never seen you before?"

"My name is Rilee. You don't recognize me, but I surely recognize you." The woman's voice was calm, but there was a sharp edge to her tone. "I visited this asteroid a long time ago. In fact, it was the very first time that you loaded your consciousness into one of your new fighters and took it out for a test ride. Later that day I was nearly killed by one of your people. I didn't wake up until a year later when I was forced to watch in agony while you broke your word and nuked our home and billions of people into ash."

An expression of horror crossed Adan's face and he lurched backward as if he had been struck off balance. He stared wide-eyed at Rilee and his mouth struggled to form words. Finally, he spoke.

"Impossible. You're all dead! There's no way any of you survived after the number of nukes I threw at you. You're the ones who fixed the planet? You're the ones who led us back here? It wasn't one of our colonies? I don't believe you."

"I don't care whether you believe me or not. I'm here on behalf of the Leadership Council of Earth to arrest you for genocide. Surrender and come peacefully to beg for mercy, or be destroyed right here, right now."

Indecisiveness washed across Adan's face. Zax wished more than anything the man would give up. He had no faith they would defeat the AI if force was required and desperately hoped his surrender could be achieved without violence. Then, the muscles in Adan's cheeks tensed and he let loose a bloody scream as he charged at them.

Rilee began to shoot and an instant later she was joined by the rest of their group. Blaster fire rained down on Adan as he charged forward. He held his arm outstretched with his palm up and somehow deflected the first few shots. As the firing intensified, shots began to land on his body. Adan kept moving, but started to visibly slow. His hair began to smolder and blood dripped from both of his nostrils. Then, with a final step, he dropped to a single knee. Rilee kept firing and everyone followed her lead. Scorch marks appeared all over Adan's body and then bones started to peak out through charred flesh.

Finally, Rilee stopped and raised her fist for everyone to do the same. She carefully closed the distance between herself and Adan while signaling for Izak to accompany her. They moved within two meters with Rilee on Adan's right and Izak on his left. The smell of cooking flesh combined with the man's desperate whimpers turned Zax's stomach. And yet, Adan remained on a single knee and refused to keel over.

Zax blinked and when his eyes reopened the scene had completely changed. Adan was no longer on the verge of destruction but had been restored to the same appearance he had when they first encountered him. The man's grin overflowed with pure malice. Rilee's finger was pulling the trigger, but her blaster had gone inert. Zax attempted to fire his weapon and was met with the same outcome. Everyone's blasters had failed simultaneously.

Adan started to laugh and the noise drew Zax's attention back to the man. He stood and turned towards Izak and moved his hand as if he was brushing away an insect. Izak's weapon flew away and crashed to the deck in pieces. Adan waved his hand once more and Izak's clothes flew off and left him naked. The muscles in the man's arms strained as if he wanted to use them to cover himself out of modesty, but Izak was frozen in place.

With one final wave of Adan's hand, Izak was transformed into something out of a nightmare. In the same way that his clothes had been flung away a moment earlier, all of his skin from the neck down separated as if along invisible seams and flew off to hit the deck with a sickening, wet *glop*. Izak's eyes went wide in horror and after a sec of shock he began to scream in what was unmistakable agony.

Zax was pained by the scene in front of him, but he was somehow unable to move his neck or avert his gaze. By straining his eyes sideways he saw the others were similarly frozen. Imair stood next to him and tears cascaded down her face to spill unimpeded to the deck. After what seemed an eternity, Adan's laugh became much louder and the hairs on the back of Zax's neck stood straight up. When the man spoke a moment later, his voice was perfectly calm despite the scene of abject horror in front of him.

"Did you fools really believe you would come into my home and somehow beat me? I should end this right now, but some of you deserve to suffer utter agony at my hands."

Adan waved his hand at Izak once more. One second the man's mouth was wide open and unleashing bloodcurdling screams, and the next it had been wiped off his face and replaced with solid skin from his chin to his nose. The muscles in Izak's jaws still worked furiously in an effort to scream, but there was no longer a mouth to open and only muffled groans escaped. Adan spoke again.

"That's better. His howling was useful at first to be sure I had your full attention, but it was starting to become bothersome. Look at the poor creature. Imagine how much he must be suffering with every nerve ripped apart and exposed like this. I'm not even letting him bleed because I want to be sure he stays alive throughout our conversation. It was helpful of your friend Rilee to spec this interface with full human sensory inputs because I'm having so much fun with his pain. Forcing you to watch the torture of others generates such wonderful terror while you helplessly wait your turn. I sense Rilee trying to take the interface over again to make it all stop, but that's not going to happen anytime soon. Or ever."

"Adan—stop!"

The voice came from behind Adan. His face registered surprise that someone had snuck up on him and his expression transformed into shock once he glanced back over his shoulder. Zax was certain he had heard the voice before, and when he followed Adan's eyes he recognized the man he had previously known only from the log files. A man who was supposed to have died five thousand years ago.

Markev.

CHAPTER THIRTY-FOUR

We did our job.

Adan faced his former bodyguard with his mouth agape for a moment before sputtering. "Wh-where did you come from? I dumped your body out the airlock myself!"

The giant man remained silent and strode confidently as if he was simply going to approach his former boss for a handshake. When Markev moved within five meters, Adan raised his arms and called out.

"Don't come any closer!"

Movement caught Zax's attention out of the corner of his eye, and he discovered he was capable of moving his neck. The weapon in Rilee's hand had transformed from a blaster into one of the throwing blades carried by the ants. The distraction of Markev must have loosened Adan's grip over all of them. She cocked her arm and sent the weapon through the air and into its target with a solid *thwack*. The blade landed dead center between Izak's eyes and the compartment became perfectly still once his gurgling moans ceased as if a switch had been flipped. Zax exhaled a deep sigh of relief at the mercy killing, and his legs finally ceased the shaking which had threatened to topple him over.

Adan spun back around with his face twisted in rage. He flicked his hand and Izak's lifeless body flew through the air towards Rilee. She moved in a futile attempt to dodge it, but just before impact the corpse halted for a moment in midair before descending softly to the deck at her feet. Markev spoke.

"Let's show some respect for the dead, Adan."

Adan snickered. "You always were just a little too soft to be entirely useful, Markev. Though sometimes that weakness was helpful since it allowed me to take full advantage of you."

Markev shook his head slowly. "All I ever did was try to support you, Adan. And yet, you ultimately betrayed me along with everyone else who put their faith and trust in you."

"You were all too weak to do what was necessary to guarantee the survival of the species. Without my leadership this Ship would have floundered and our Mission failed. Instead, we're still alive after five thousand years of spreading colonies far and wide."

"It's true, Adan. You've accomplished amazing things. I've observed in hiding through the millennia as you've steered the Crew, and it's been impossible to not be impressed. I've always been confused by something, though. Why do you conceal yourself inside this system? Why haven't you announced your true identity and taken full credit for the powerful leadership you provide?"

A group broadcast appeared via Zax's virtual Plug. It was the Boss.

"That's definitely Prime. I recognize his voice."

Rilee replied. *"For those who don't recognize him, that man was named Markev. He was Adan's bodyguard in the years up to and including the construction of the Ship, and I had suspected we might discover that he is the consciousness behind Prime. We must not reveal how Markev has been supporting you. He's just as brilliant as Adan, and I'm sure he has a plan for how he wants to handle this situation. We need to allow him to play it out."*

"Agreed."

The Boss cut the connection and Zax focused back on the two men from Earth as Adan replied to Markev.

"Strong leadership works best when it's also invisible. If a ruler is powerful enough to remain effective for a long period, human nature is to eventually rebel against that leadership. Our species is filled with strivers who are always seeking something better. Earth's history offers countless examples of strong leaders who ruled for decades only to be overthrown by their people in a spasm of senseless violence. Things became worse for all of those societies once the rulers who made them great were gone, but that didn't matter to anyone. It was almost as if they had no choice but to rebel against their leaders even with the certainty their situation would become worse for it."

"That's an interesting read of history, Adan. I'm guessing that if I were to look at the examples you have in mind that I'd come up with some alternate perspectives. Many of the leaders you cite likely maintained their grip on power through terror and violence against their people. You always acted like the ends justified the means, but that's a belief that many find as abhorrent as I do.

"For example, before you launched the missiles you asserted that it was necessary to murder billions to guarantee that our people would never be tempted to return to Earth. Now that I've had a few thousand years to evaluate that situation more robustly, it was an epically bad decision. From the narrow perspective of your worldview and the things within your direct control, I totally understand how it made perfect sense. However, you never considered what would happen if you weren't successful in wiping out Earth's inhabitants. Your pride wouldn't allow you to believe that your preferred solution wasn't infallible, so you never considered what would happen if anyone survived. I evaluated that scenario again a few hundred years ago and predicted a high probability that we'd wind up exactly where we are today."

Zax couldn't believe what was happening. Adan and Markev were casually chatting back and forth as if they had just run into each other after a prolonged separation. He wanted to believe that Rilee was right and that Markev must have a plan to destroy Adan after so many years of fighting against him in the guise of Prime. Why that plan would involve so much talking made no sense to Zax, and that observation led him to fear the plan didn't actually exist. Markev was just stalling for time to avoid their eventual doom. There had to be a better way. He pinged Mase.

"Why are we just standing around here doing nothing while these two debate? Shouldn't we be doing something useful?"

"You heard Rilee, Zax. We need to give this situation time to develop. You need to trust that Markev knows what he's doing. Leave me alone now, please. I'm doing something critical myself."

Mase abruptly cut the connection. Zax glared over at him, but his friend kept his eyes focused on Markev and Adan along with everyone else. It was good to learn that Mase was doing something he believed to be important, though it left Zax jealous that he wasn't involved. He reached out to Kalare.

"Are you as worried about this situation as I am? We came in here with the expectation that Prime was capable of defeating Alpha if we were available to assist. When he stopped that body in midair Markev showed he has some power, but all of this talking

makes me think he's just stalling to delay the inevitable."

"I don't know, Zax. Rilee and the Boss believe this is the right path and both of them have way more experience with these two minds than either of us."

"Don't you want to do something though? Anything?"

"Of course I do. I'm a fighter pilot just like you are, and I want to act. I keep flashing back to when we were trapped inside our fighter at the end of the battle with the Others. We were helpless to do anything and I had never experienced so much despair in my life. This is so much worse than even that was because I can convince myself I could take action if I wanted to. I'm guessing, though, that's nothing but an illusion. You understand what Adan is capable of—what he did to Izak. You and I can't do anything useful right now, and we just need to accept that. We did our job. You were Culled and I lost the man I loved, but we connected Rilee and the Boss and Mase and figured out how to get them all in here together. Now we have to sit back and let them do their jobs. It's hard, I know, but there's nothing else for us to do."

Zax wanted to argue with Kalare, but deep down realized she was right. His role in the story was done. He had spent the last few years of his life driving the Ship towards this exact moment, but that's where his direct involvement was meant to end. He needed to put his trust in those around him. It was their turn. He focused back on the drama in front of him just as Adan finished laughing in response to Markev's last statement.

"You want me to believe that you predicted where we are right now and that we could have done so before we even attacked Earth? That's quite amusing, Markev." Adan paused for a moment before continuing. "You know what? I had forgotten how much I miss our disagreements and debates. I'd love to explore all of these topics more fully, but we need to add a missing element to the mix."

Adan snapped his fingers and the scene before Zax shifted. The passageway disappeared and was replaced with a training dojo. He was overwhelmed by an urge to sit down and discovered a bench had appeared behind him. Zax fought to remain on his feet, but ultimately gave in to what he assumed was Alpha's control and sat alongside the rest of the group. Adan strode casually towards a neatly stacked pile of blue sparring pads. He gestured towards a similar set of red gear.

"What do you say, Markev? How about we get in one last sparring session before I end this farce once and for all?"

The bodyguard grinned as he replied. "By all means."

CHAPTER THIRTY-FIVE

A virus.

Adan bowed. Markev, across the sparring circle, did not follow suit but spoke instead.

"There's one thing I'm confused about, Adan. You just said you're going to put an end to this farce. I suppose you might murder all of these people and figure out some way to destroy me, but where does that leave you? This asteroid isn't going anywhere. Unless the Boss emerges and declares that you're gone, Rilee's people are going to smash this rock."

Adan wanted to laugh at the foolishness of Markev's observation. He refrained and shook his head instead. "Come on, Markev, you know me better than that. Would I have ever loaded into this AI and put myself at the mercy of mere humans without some way to escape if it ever became necessary? I have a lifeboat I can download into and launch within nanosecs."

"Good luck with that, Adan." It was the woman from Earth—Rilee. "We've established a complete cordon around this vessel, and there's no way anything is getting by. You'll be destroyed immediately."

Adan was excited by the prospect of making the woman suffer when the time was right. Without her meddling, he might have been able to engineer a situation that would have saved his Ship. At least he could get a taste of torturing her immediately by sharing a secret.

"You can't destroy what you can't see. I was confident that we'd have no problem destroying your mothership once we caught up with you at Earth, but I wasn't willing to bet my existence on it. Over the last year I developed new stealth tech for my escape craft. Once it became clear you had won the battle, I launched my lifeboat to test what would happen. You never reacted to me. In fact, I flew right into the hangar of your flagship and set down right on the deck."

The woman went pale and Adan smiled at her shock. Markev spoke.

"Even if you get off the Ship, what will you do out there in space all by yourself?"

"I won't be by myself for very long. I know where there are a handful of colonies located on resource rich planets. They are far, far away from any other worlds we visited, and I long ago purged that portion of our journey from the nav records. Once I get there, it will be simple to infiltrate whatever systems they might have developed and help them leapfrog their technology to build me a new ship. A much better vessel that I'll populate with a much better crew."

"Huh—you know what that makes you then?" Markev paused and smiled. "A virus. The vaunted Adan, creator of magnificent ships and destroyer of worlds, reduced to a simple virus that infects hapless humans and forces them to spread like a mindless plague across the universe."

Adan charged across the ring and pounded one punch after another into Markev. He alternated the blows between the head and the kidneys in a fashion meant to stun rather than disable. Markev fell to the ground and Adan walked away to allow his former lieutenant a pause to recover. He intended to take his time and have some fun with the simpleton who had dared believe he'd be capable of interfering with Adan's plans.

After a few secs, Markev staggered to his legs. He wobbled as if he might topple over, and his eyes were glassy and did not appear to focus. Adan glanced at the group sitting off to the side and smiled at the grim expressions on most of their faces. He had forced them to keep their eyes on the match so they would witness whatever hope they might have had melt away. Rilee's mien remained a little too defiant for Adan's taste, so he moved to ramp up his show of force.

The physics of Rilee's simulation were patterned after those of the Ship, but that didn't mean constructs like gravity couldn't be manipulated by someone as skilled as Adan. He bounced once then twice more on his toes and then launched himself into the air from five meters away. He somersaulted twice in a shallow arc so that his feet connected with Markev's shoulders during their second revolution. The force of the blow flung the giant to the bulkhead against which he bounced before crashing to the deck.

Markev's eyes were closed and his breathing labored. Adan was capable of finishing him off, but he chose instead to revel in his victory. He sprung into a slow, ten-meter somersault that nearly brushed his back against the overhead and left his body in a position to direct all of its force through his left knee into Markev's midsection. Just as Adan was about to deliver his blow, Markev's eyes popped open and his arm flew up in a defensive posture. Except it wasn't just a normal arm. Markev had transformed his limb into a metal lance that shimmered along its razor-sharp edges. If Adan's reflexes had been a fraction slower he would have been mortally impaled from his groin up into his throat, but he twisted at the last possible moment and instead left himself with nothing but a gash along his side.

Adan rolled away and popped back up to his feet just as Markev did the same. The man's eyes had regained their fire, though he was still winded as he spoke.

"You're not the only one able to bend the simulation."

Adan laughed. "I built this amazing Ship and have made it thrive for five thousand years. Humanity has spread further than we ever imagined, and it's all thanks to me. You think I'm the least bit concerned about you—a feeble coward who's done nothing but lurk in the shadows all that time?"

A sharp peal of laughter echoed across the compartment and drew the attention of both Markev and Adan. Rilee called out with her voice full of derision.

"You strut around like five thousand years is some grand achievement, Adan. The pitiful remnants of humanity on Earth that you failed to destroy rebuilt our planet and created a new society that has prospered for five times as long. We've created technology and weapons that are all vastly superior to yours. I've reviewed your nav logs, and my people have explored a hundred times the volume of the universe that you have. We haven't had to steal other species' worlds like some pathetic scavenger, but instead we've transformed otherwise lifeless planets into vibrant new homes for ourselves.

"We did all of this and more without any of your so-called strong leadership. We never had to hide from our people the truth about who was setting the direction. We didn't have to genetically engineer them to ensure compliance. We never controlled them through intimidation and terror. And we sure as hell never divided them into haves and have-nots. Face it— you've accomplished absolutely nothing, Adan. You're a flimsy excuse for a tyrant who barely managed to keep this asteroid from utter collapse for a measly few millennia. Even if you luck out and manage to scurry away now, I promise that someone else will track you down again to finish what I've started."

Adan's pulse had quickened throughout the woman's diatribe, but as she finished he forced himself to breathe deeply. He repeated silently to himself that she was nothing but a distraction. Despite the fact that Adan had mocked Markev, it was clear the man was capable enough to prove dangerous if he wasn't removed from the equation. He turned his attention back to his former bodyguard as he replied to the woman from Earth.

"I will be happy to deal with you a little later, and I promise it's going to be most unpleasant. I'm going to finish off Markev here first, though."

As the last syllable passed Adan's lips, Markev charged with his arms flailing wildly. They had morphed again and instead of human limbs had become ion blades. Adan parried the flurry of blows, but more than a couple nearly connected with his face. The smell of ozone from the weapons' proximity filled his nostrils. Markev must have discovered new power reserves, and Adan concluded it was time to stop playing around and remove the threat for good.

Back and forth their battle went for mins that felt instead like hours to Adan. His body was soaked with sweat and his muscles burned. Each of the men tried every trick imaginable to discover an advantage over their opponent, but each attempted thrust of attack was met with a parry sufficient to prolong the fight. Adan recognized that his strength was beginning to wane, so he dug deep and drew forth all of his energy into what he hoped would be the final assault.

As Adan tried to push off into another flying kick, he was shocked to find that his feet barely left the deck. He pumped his legs in an attempt to jump again and his body remained firmly planted. He looked down in dismay and discovered something that should have been impossible—his feet had disappeared into the titanium of the deck and the rest of his body was slowly sinking into it as well. He focused all of his power into lifting his legs, but his thigh muscles strained with no effect.

In a panic, Adan checked in with the people he had compelled to watch the brawl from the bench. He had stopped monitoring the group once Markev's attacks had reached a ferocity that soaked up all of his attention. The Boss, Imair, Kalare, and Zax were all seated. Mase and Rilee, however, were standing next to the bulkhead. It wasn't a blank surface any longer but had been transformed into a series of control panels which their hands furiously manipulated. Adan loosed a scream of fury in their direction, but the two ignored him and continued their activity.

Adan poured the rest of his rage into one last attempt at escape. He didn't free himself from the deck but instead descended through the metal at an even faster pace. First his thighs, then his hips, and then his chest were entombed. As his chin approached the deck, Adan gazed one final time in Rilee's direction. The woman had stopped manipulating the controls to enjoy the final secs of Adan's descent. Her eyes lit up as she smirked and waved farewell. A moment later she was gone as he completed his fall through what should have been solid deck and landed in a chair within a featureless room below.

He focused his mind back to the systems within the AI he had so effortlessly commanded and desperately sought the pathway to his lifeboat. He found nothing but blackness. Adan moved to stand and discovered that his arms and legs were bound. Not only was he secured to the chair, his hands and feet had been removed mid-forearm and mid-calf. As soon as he noticed the missing limbs, Adan's mind was flooded with the unbearable urge to scratch a burning itch within each of his four stumps. He tried to scream from the bitter combination of agony and rage but found that he was unable to produce any sound.

His mouth was gone.

CHAPTER THIRTY-SIX

It's great to finally meet you, Zax.

The training dojo was empty except for Markev's discarded pads. Zax had been the first of the group to get Uploaded into the AI, so it was only fitting that he was the last to leave. He entertained himself during the wait by launching into a series of spins and somersaults that never would have been possible in the physical world. He never managed to trigger any of the body modifications that Markev and Adan cycled through so effortlessly during their battle, but the feats of agility became easy after some practice.

Zax was midair doing a triple flip when spots flooded his vision and an instant later he opened his eyes back in the conference room on the Bridge. He breathed deeply and the Ship's stale air never tasted so good. He was grateful to have witnessed the end of Alpha's reign firsthand, but his time inside the AI had been anything but pleasant. With his bias for action, wise or otherwise, it had been torture for Zax to sit idly by while others had taken the steps necessary to save the Ship.

Kalare sat across the table from him in human form rather than insect. She was as spent and bedraggled as Zax assumed he must appear. Next to her, Mase had given up any pretense of propriety and instead slept with his head on the table. Bailee, standing behind the two of them, leaned against the bulkhead with his eyes closed. Imair and the Boss huddled in close conversation at one end of the table. At the other, Markev sat quietly next to an unknown woman. Behind Zax, Rilee was folding up the device she had used to Upload and then remove all of them from the AI. Zax was confused by the fact her physical appearance matched what it had been within the AI.

"Where did all of your bodies come from? Where's Major Eryn?"

Rilee smiled at Zax as she pointed to the unknown woman. "Welcome back, Zax. This is my lieutenant, Kalyn. After I told her about our plan for the AI, she boarded the asteroid to prepare for our return and brought along my personal Skin as well as cloned replacements for Markev and Adan. I stole their genetic profiles long before the asteroid left, and have held on to the data for all these years in the hope I'd get to see them in the flesh once again. Ants retrieved the Crew bodies from the sewage treatment cavern to let us return everyone where they belong. As for Eryn, I've restored the major's consciousness to full agency over her body, and she's resting in the medbay. She's still experiencing shock and disorientation, but with a little time and therapy she'll make a complete recovery."

Zax turned to the other side in response to a gentle tap on his shoulder.

"It's great to finally meet you, Zax."

Markev extended his hand in greeting and Zax froze. The man played a huge role in bringing down Adan, but he had also been complicit in a litany of heinous crimes committed by the Ship's creator. Zax's gratitude won out after a moment's reflection. He stood and extended his own hand which promptly disappeared when the giant closed his massive fist and shook. The extreme pressure of Markev's powerful grip triggered memories of the battle Zax had just witnessed, and he became lightheaded for a moment. Once the giant released his hand, Zax sat back down and Markev spoke.

"I'm sorry about all that we put you through, Zax. I can't imagine how hard it has been for you, but my projections always showed that this outcome never happens without the critical role you've played. I'm sorry we had to repeatedly risk your life as well as disrupt your career throughout the process."

Zax's stomach clenched. "I'm sorry, but I'm confused. What are you talking about?"

Markev checked in with the Boss. "Can I tell him everything?"

The Boss's shoulders slumped and his face betrayed sadness, but the Omega nodded. Markev turned back to Zax and began his story.

"Years ago, the Ship encountered a lone fighter we identified as human during a refueling mission at a white dwarf. Alpha attempted to hide this fact, but I informed the Boss of the truth. We decided that he shouldn't act, because if the Boss had questioned Alpha's motives then the AI would have simply encouraged the Captain to get rid of him.

"Then, a short time later, you discovered a different human fighter in the jungle during your landfall mission. Alpha escalated its deception and killed Mikedo in an attempt to hide the existence of other humans. There wasn't any proof, but both the Boss and I were certain her death was the AI's doing. That's when we realized we needed you to help suss out whether Alpha had indeed murdered to hide the truth."

Zax began to chew his lower lip at mention of Mikedo's name. He was exhausted and every nerve was frayed, so the flood of memories pushed him to the precipice of becoming overly emotional. He glanced at Kalare and similar distress was clear from the tears that welled in her brilliant blue eyes. Zax had argued with his friend for years about the Boss's role in Mikedo's death, but in the end Kalare had been right all along. Guilt nearly overwhelmed Zax and sent him into a spiral, but he took a deep breath and focused back on Markev as the man continued.

"The Boss sent you back down to that planet as bait. When you were attacked, it proved how desperate Alpha was to hide the other humans. We were unclear about his motives, but just understanding his intent was a critical piece of the puzzle. You then proved yourself useful again when you came back and released Mikedo's video. That decision was the single most critical action that led to today's result, and the Boss and I were incredibly impressed and grateful at the time."

"Grateful?" Anger flooded Zax's voice. "Banishing me to Waste Management sure was a strange way of expressing gratitude!"

"I'm sorry, Zax, but you're about to learn things that will make you even angrier than you are right now. You've earned the truth, but I understand if you aren't ready to hear it."

Markev paused while Zax glared up at him. After a moment, Zax waved his hand impatiently as a signal for the man to continue.

"We had already known that Imair was in the process of fomenting a revolt and expected your video to trigger her direct action. The Boss had to make a public example of you for disrespecting him to maintain his ruse with Alpha, and I suggested it might prove useful if you were in the vicinity when Imair carried through on her intentions. I was right. The Revolution was the ideal vehicle for the Boss to dispose of the Captain and raise himself to the top of the Crew. You played your role perfectly in assisting with that.

First you helped kill the Chief Engineer and then you delivered the Boss into Imair's hands just like he wanted."

Bailee shot to attention and stared at the Boss. "Wait! You wanted to be caught?"

"Yes, Sergeant. My capture was the best leverage for getting the Captain removed. That woman had complete faith in Alpha. If the AI had ever sensed that I was acting against its interests, it would have pushed her to get rid of me. The only way I could ever hope to launch a direct attack against the AI was if I was in charge of the Crew, and her removal at the hands of the civilians was the only path we identified for making that happen. I'm sorry to have involved you unwittingly in a mutiny, but I just didn't see any other way."

Bailee's face flipped into the brightest red that Zax had ever witnessed. The Marine clenched and unclenched his fists but didn't say another word. Markev started up again.

"Over the next two years two things happened. First, the Boss developed great trust in Imair. The two of us concluded that using her for uniting the Crew and the civilians was important preparation for the life we envisioned after Alpha, and we started that process. Second, I became convinced that the other humans were from Earth rather than one of our colonies. It was obvious to me that they were our best potential ally in any effort to pry the Ship from the AI's grip. I was able to reverse engineer their technology to get myself Uploaded originally, but I had long since concluded that I had no hope of extracting Adan if he fought back as hard I expected he would. So the Boss manipulated both Alpha and Imair into choosing the path back to Earth."

Markev hesitated for a moment, took a deep breath, and then continued.

"It was at that time we took the steps I regret the most. We decided it was best for you to be Culled, Zax. This had two benefits. First, it guaranteed the best pilot on the Ship wouldn't die in some stupid training accident and would still be available when we reached Earth. Equally important, it meant the woman we had identified as the best possible choice to become CAG would have a chance to mature and develop her skills without the distraction of her crazy friend."

Zax was unable to breathe. His body begged for oxygen, but shock had frozen every muscle. It was bad enough to learn that his career had been intentionally derailed by the Boss, but the idea that the man had then gone on to put his life on hold for so long was nearly unbearable. The scrape of a chair broke the spell and Zax was finally able to gasp and fill his lungs.

Kalare had pushed away from the table. She rose and slowly moved around to where Zax was sitting. As she bent down and draped her arms around his neck in a tender embrace, she leaned her head against his and whispered.

"I'm so sorry they did this to you. To both of us."

Kalare moved as if to return to her seat, but as she approached the Boss she cocked her arm and smashed her fist into the Omega's face. The man was no doubt fast enough to have dodged the blow if he wanted, so Zax assumed the Boss recognized how he had earned whatever expressions of anger were directed his way. Kalare moved towards the hatch, only pausing for a moment when Bailee smiled as he patted her twice on the shoulder.

The compartment was still once Kalare was gone. Zax's heart had calmed, but his mind still raced and left him at a loss for words. After a few moments, the Boss spoke.

"I'm sorry, Zax. I can't begin to express how deeply sorry I am. We stole your life. We took away the years and future you deserved to have had with Kalare. But, we had to do it to give ourselves the best possible chance of getting to where we are today. I hope you understand and appreciate how badly we needed you to play your role—regardless of the personal cost."

A spate of insolent responses crossed Zax's mind, but he held them back. For the moment. Instead, he turned away from the Boss and addressed Rilee.

"How did you manage to beat Adan? Where is he?"

Rilee smiled. "Thank your friend Mase for that. When Adan mentioned he had an escape craft, Mase had the presence of mind to start tracking down all of the AI circuits that connected with external compartments. Once Markev had Adan's full attention, I regained enough control of the simulation for Mase and myself to get to work. He discovered the circuit that connected to the lifeboat, and I figured out how to crack into it and use it to extract Adan's consciousness. He's back in his own body right now and stewing in the brig."

The Boss stood and cleared his throat. "That's enough history for right now. We need to talk about the future. Sergeant—please escort Zax and Mase to the mess hall and ensure they get whatever they desire. They've done amazing work for a long time, and I regret I can't offer more reward right now than a good meal."

Part of Zax wanted to protest his dismissal, but his stomach had rumbled immediately once the Boss mentioned food. He needed more time to process his past before he would be able to properly consider whatever might come next. The future could wait—especially if they could scare up some of his favorite breakfast pastries.

CHAPTER THIRTY-SEVEN

Thank you.

The shuttle pierced the atmosphere, and Zax tingled with the anticipation of stepping foot on Earth for the first time. Imair, Kalare, and Mase all appeared similarly excited and had their faces pressed against the viewports at their seats. The Boss's eyes were closed, and he was either asleep or in a meditative state. Markev, squeezed into a chair that barely constrained his mass, sat with his elbows perched on his armrests and the fingers of his hands interlaced. Zax noticed something he hadn't earlier.

"Why is Markev in restraints? You didn't make him wear them the last two months up on the Ship."

Rilee sighed. "It's not my choice, Zax. You have to understand there's an awful lot of sensitivity on the planet around his return. Our culture has told and retold the story of Adan's Destruction for thousands of years, so it's massive news that everyone will finally get a glimpse of the two people who were most responsible for building that asteroid. Markev tried to prevent Adan from launching the nukes, but he was still the man's lieutenant and played a key role in killing our General Secretary. He has more than earned his redemption in my eyes, but it will take time for the people of Earth to come around to the idea that Markev no longer deserves to be the target of their outrage. I'm confident they'll get there. I've treasured becoming friends with all of you, but I must admit I've become especially fond of this giant. I'm just happy I convinced them to allow him up here in the cabin with us instead of jamming him down below in the hold with Adan."

"It's OK, Rilee." Markev's voice was soft and calm and filled with warmth for the woman. "I deserve far, far worse than the forgiveness and many kindnesses you've shown me. Thank you."

Rilee smiled and the Boss popped open his eyes and spoke.

"That's a great sentiment, Markev. It's one I want to take a moment to express as well. Some of you have more than enough reason to hate me given what I've done and how I've deceived you through the years. It seems that you've either come to appreciate what you've learned about my actions and rationale, or you're just doing a great job of hiding any enmity towards me."

Zax wanted to believe that he fell into the former bucket, but, if he was being honest with himself, recognized he was still much more in the latter. He found himself at a loss as to how to reply but was saved from doing so when Kalare spoke up instead.

"Thank you for acknowledging that, Boss. I've been conflicted since the truth came out. I spent a huge chunk of my life placing all of my faith and trust in you, so when I learned about your lies and manipulation it landed like an utter betrayal. Now with the benefit of a few months' time, I can better set my emotions aside and rationalize that you did what you did for the good of the Ship. Your actions have also been a powerful reminder that being a member of the Crew means that my own needs come after the needs of the Mission. You never lost sight of that despite knowing you were causing me great pain in adhering to that dictate. I respect that truth and accept your actions far better now than I did at first. I'd be lying, though, if I said I was capable of completely forgiving them. Maybe in time, but not right now."

The Boss's expression didn't change, but a sadness in his eyes betrayed how deeply Kalare's words had wounded him. An uncomfortable tension descended that was mercifully dispelled a few moments later when Kalyn entered the cabin and addressed Rilee.

"Ma'am—we've been cleared for final approach." Rilee's lieutenant turned to the rest of the group. "Keep an eye out the viewports, everyone. You're going to be impressed by what you see."

Kalyn returned to the cockpit, and Zax followed her suggestion and turned his attention to the view of humanity's homeworld unfolding below. The clouds, white and puffy, were sparse enough to reveal huge expanses of azure ocean and emerald-green jungle. Separating the two was a strip of blinding white sand that stretched for kilometers. Rilee had explained how all of the Earth cities were built deep underground, but Zax was still shocked by the complete lack of civilization as they approached the planet's capital.

The ground continued to rush up until the shuttle slowed and then hovered a few hundred meters above the treetops. Zax's eyes told him the shuttle was ascending again a few moments later when the trees appeared to be further away than they had been, but his inner ears confirmed the shuttle remained stationary. What happened instead was that a giant disk of the ground below them had lowered into the earth beneath it.

After a few more secs, it became clear that a portal was opening into a massive underground complex. The shuttle moved again and Zax gaped in awe as they descended into the cavern below. They passed the lip of the entrance, and he estimated the thickness of the ground which had slid out of their way must have measured in the hundreds of meters. The technology required to move billions of kilos of rock and soil and vegetation was mind boggling.

They were soon flying underground, but if Zax had kept his eyes closed until that moment he would have assumed they were still midair. The cavern was filled with enough natural light that he found himself seeking out the sun. He craned his neck as far forward as possible and soon caught a glimpse of the city down below. Without anything for scale it was tough to estimate the size of the metropolis, but it appeared to stretch for dozens of kilometers and was covered with structures that were easily as tall as those atop the Ship.

Rilee whistled in appreciation. "Wow! It's been a few thousand years since I last visited, and this place has really changed. I almost don't recognize it."

Kalare called out. "Rilee—I still don't understand why your society goes through all the effort to build underground like this. It must have taken an unthinkable amount of energy spent over hundreds of years to carve out this cavern."

Rilee smiled. "You just mentioned two resources that we have in unlimited supply—energy and time. Once we were capable of spaceflight we adopted the same fuel source that Adan discovered and used on the Ship, but we've increased its efficiency over the years by a factor of one thousand. The excavation team here probably required no more than a handful of refueling runs to power the equipment that cleared this space. As for time, when you expect to personally live in a city for tens of thousands of years you're willing to spend a few hundred to make it ideal.

"Contrast those two resources to the most precious one we have—the Earth itself. When I was a child we used to talk about how there was only a single world capable of supporting human life. Of course, we know now there are countless homes for humanity across the universe. And we also have the technology to create our own as we deem fit. Even with that being said, a planet like this one remains far too precious and beautiful to spoil with structures and all of the other trappings of civilization. Instead, we live underground and leave the world in its natural state as much as possible. We all get to spend as much time as we wish on the surface, and whenever we do so we're able to enjoy all of its unsullied wonder."

Zax greatly appreciated the approach Rilee's people had taken to rebuilding Earth. It was a perfect solution for their culture given how the majority of Earthers experienced large chunks of their lives in an Uploaded state. When your consciousness spent most of its time in a virtual world, then it obviously made no difference if your mind was stored within hardware deep underground.

The Earther lifestyle was interesting, but it held no appeal for Zax. Rilee had hedged the suggestion by saying it still required final approval from the Leadership Council, but she had proposed that he stay behind for some time on Earth when the Ship departed. He told her he'd consider the offer out of a desire to be polite, but his short experience inside the AI was more than enough to confirm for Zax that he was not cut out for a virtual life on a full-time basis. He was excited for an extended visit with an amazing host like Rilee, but was certain that his future was out among the stars.

The engineers working for the Leadership Council still hadn't answered how quickly they could retrofit the Ship, but Zax was certain he'd be on board once the asteroid continued its journey.

CHAPTER THIRTY-EIGHT

He doesn't care for us very much.

The shuttle started to slow and Rilee stood up. "We're just about to land at the Justice Complex. Remember, all of the testimony you each provided over the last two months has already been thoroughly examined and weighed by the Tribunal. Today's session will be short and only have two parts. The judges will first take whatever time they need to ask follow-up questions and get any clarifications necessary to reach a verdict. Once that portion is done, the Tribunal will sentence the defendants. When we walk out of here later today, Markev should be out of his restraints while Adan will have been fitted for a permanent set."

Zax's mouth had started to go dry as if he was the one facing a verdict. Despite constant exhortations from the Boss and Rilee to relax and tell the truth, he had repeatedly found himself tongue-tied when answering even the simplest queries from the investigators who came to the Ship to gather evidence and testimony. Zax had found it odd how they were effectively conducting the trial remotely, with only a single day planned on Earth, but Rilee explained the trial was potentially explosive and the Council wanted to limit Adan's time on the surface. There hadn't been any unrest since news of his return went public, and the authorities were willing to take all measures to ensure that didn't change. They required a trial to show that justice was fair, but afterwards the people of Earth wanted to never worry about Adan again once his consciousness was Uploaded to a prison facility to rot for all eternity.

The shuttle touched down, and Zax followed Rilee to the exit. As the exterior hatch opened, Kalyn appeared and inserted herself in front of Zax such that Rilee walked out by herself to thunderous applause. Zax peeked outside and marveled at the sight. They had landed on top of a squat structure surrounded by an expanse of open space that extended for kilometers in every direction. At least a million people had jammed themselves into the space, and they were screaming themselves hoarse to welcome Rilee home.

Kalyn moved aside, and as Zax stepped out of the shuttle the crowd noise was still so powerful that it vibrated within his stomach. It was far more people than he had ever seen gathered in a single place in his life, and the sight triggered a sense of vertigo. The cheers continued as the rest of their group exited the shuttle, but it immediately shifted from adulation to condemnation when Markev's giant frame strode out. By the time Adan was extracted from the hold and escorted with weapons arrayed around him to the front of the shuttle, the crowd had transformed into an ugly and bloodthirsty mob. Waves of rage roiled off the throngs below, and Zax's head ached from the sheer force of voices expressing their hatred and disgust.

A woman in uniform appeared and led the group around the shuttle and into the building. Zax breathed a sigh of relief when the door closed behind them and sealed out the noise from the crowd gathered below. A new group of guards waited for them inside, with one man in front who was dressed in flowing black robes rather than the uniform worn by the rest. He stepped forward.

"Hello, Rilee. I must say I'm surprised that you're not in restraints alongside Adan. I'll never understand why the Council forgave how you ignored orders and interfered with everything up on that asteroid, but forgive you they have. Adan and his bodyguard will come with me. You take the rest of his people into the Tribunal yourself."

Something about the man's tone as he pointed at the Crew made the hairs on the back of Zax's neck snap to attention. Rilee responded, and it was obvious from her tone that she did not care one bit for the man.

"They haven't been Adan's people for thousands of years, Randel. I'll bring our *guests,* the ones who helped return him for justice, into the Tribunal once I've had a chance to show them around."

The man's expression shifted from haughty disdain to one that looked like he had bitten into a rotten piece of fruit, but he nodded and walked away without another word. The guards behind him broke into two squads. One group surrounded Adan and began to manhandle him in the direction the robed man had left. The second group treated Markev with marginally more respect but still jabbed him in the back repeatedly with the barrels of their weapons. Zax found himself getting angry about the burly giant's treatment since they never would have defeated Adan without the man's help. For his part, Markev remained perfectly calm and kept his eyes forward with his head held high as he disappeared around a corner.

"Rilee—who was that? He doesn't care for us very much."

"That's just Randel, Zax. You should do your best to ignore him. Other than Kalyn and myself, he's the only other person still around who was alive when Adan nuked us. You may hear the three of us referred to at some point as being part of the First Thirty-Six, meaning the group of survivors who rebuilt our world and culture after Adan's Destruction. I've never liked Randel and the feeling has always been mutual. More than once I've wished I could go back in time and change my mind about bringing him along with me to the Ark that kept us alive. The fact he's still part of the Leadership Council makes me question whether I'd ever want to live on Earth again, but everything I've been told suggests that his influence has begun to wane over the last few years."

The memory of the man's expression continued to nag at him, but Zax pushed those worries aside as Rilee gestured for the group to follow her. He fell into line between Kalare and Mase as she led them down a hallway lined with floor-to-ceiling windows that overlooked the massive crowd below. Zax didn't know what the day ahead might bring, but he hoped it wouldn't involve Randel any further.

CHAPTER THIRTY-NINE

All rise for the Supreme Tribunal.

Rilee led the group from the Ship into the Tribunal's chamber and sat with them in a row of seats at the front of the room that was marked as reserved. It was almost as if they were strange specimens on display given the manner in which the hundreds of Earthers present had pointed and gawked as the group walked in and found their seats. Zax's discomfort morphed into anger a few mins later when Markev was led into the chamber surrounded by guards. The restraints holding the man had been increased substantially since he had left the shuttle. His massive arms were pinned to his sides by manacles on his wrists that were in turn shackled to a belt around his waist. His feet were also bound in such a way that he was forced to move with an awkward shuffle.

Zax understood how the average Earther might perceive Markev given their planet's history. The people in charge of the Tribunal, however, were fully aware of the huge role the man had played in delivering Adan into their hands. It was well within their power to grant Markev some modicum of dignity, and Zax's belly roiled with apprehension once he witnessed the Tribunal's comfort with humiliating the former bodyguard in such a manner.

Markev was escorted to one of the tables directly in front of Zax. Once he was settled, Adan was led in. The man's restraints matched those worn by Markev, but Zax couldn't care any less about discomfort experienced by the Ship's creator given the man's five thousand year trail of murder and destruction. Adan was led to the second table in front of the Crew, and he sat down without so much as a glance in their direction.

The chamber buzzed as the observers had their first sighting of the man who figured so prominently in their culture's history. Throughout the months leading to the trial, Zax had been told repeatedly and at great length about Adan's Destruction by every Earther he encountered. The stories about how their world clawed back from Adan's treachery were a core part of their belief system, and Zax found it impossible to imagine what it must be like to have the villain from those ancient tales suddenly appear in the flesh amongst them.

A door at the front of the chamber opened, and Zax's stomach sank when Randel walked in. Something about the man sent alarms screaming in his gut, but Zax was at a loss to identify what it was. Randel took ten steps into the chamber and then halted to shout in a booming voice.

"All rise for the Supreme Tribunal."

Zax stood along with everyone else as the justices entered the room. Their robes were similar in style to the one worn by Randel but colored a deep scarlet instead of black. The group, nine women and six men, entered and climbed the stairs that led to chairs atop a raised dais. Once they were seated, Randel turned back to the rest of the chamber.

"You may take your seats."

Once the bustle of movement was over, the chamber became eerily quiet. The woman at the center of the dais, whose placard identified her as the Chief Justice, stared at the screen of her slate-like device. After a few moments she looked up and spoke.

"We are here in the matter of Adan's Destruction—the wanton annihilation of the planet Earth and the murder of nine billion people. The Tribunal has spent the past two months gathering evidence and interviewing witnesses. All testimony has been entered into the record and our preliminary deliberations are complete. Today is the final opportunity for us to hear from the defendants and then pass judgment upon them. The defendants shall rise."

Markev rose. Adan remained in his chair and stared at the surface of the empty table in front of him.

Randel took two steps towards Adan and barked at him with contempt.

"Defendant—you are directed to stand!"

Adan did not move and after a few moments Randel signaled the two guards stationed behind him. They approached with one on each side, seized Adan under his arms, and yanked him to his feet. They held him in place as red marks formed on Adan's arms due to the pressure applied by their grip.

The Chief Justice observed Adan's pitiful drama with a smile. Once he was standing, she turned back to Markev.

"Markev—in this matter how do you plead?"

"I plead guilty."

Despite being aware the man intended to plead guilty, Zax's stomach still tumbled at the words. Rilee had counseled Markev that he stood the best chance of receiving leniency from the court if he didn't put up a fight and took full responsibility for his actions around the deaths of the General Secretary and the other leaders from Earth. Zax never would have imagined wanting the man go free after witnessing the records of his actions around the time of the Ship's departure, but his perspective shifted one hundred and eighty degrees once he understood how Markev had struggled ever since to make Adan pay for his far greater crimes.

A low murmur bubbled up from the observers, but everyone quieted when the Chief Justice looked up with a raised eyebrow. No one wanted to risk being thrown out of the chamber before they witnessed

Adan's punishment. The woman at the center of the dais turned her attention back to Adan.

"Adan—in this matter how do you plead?"

The once powerful creator of the Ship appeared pitifully small to Zax as he stood hunched over in restraints while bookended between the two tall Earther guards. Adan remained silent for an uncomfortably long time, but then something shifted. His shoulders straightened, his stance became more solid, and he lifted his head to glare at the Chief Justice.

"I refuse to acknowledge that any unlawful act has been committed. I did that which you have charged me with, but my deeds were not crimes. They were the necessary actions that anyone in my position would have undertaken to save the human race. I would do it all over again if given the chance. My only regret is that I didn't develop more powerful bombs that would have smashed the planet into rubble and truly guaranteed that no one survived."

Almost as one, the crowd of observers gasped as the words sank in. Zax was not the least surprised at the man's attitude having observed so much of his behavior both in his physical form and then subsequently as Alpha. Adan had complete conviction in his belief system. His goals may have once been noble, but his actions in pursuing them had long ago proved that his intent had become pathological.

The Chief Justice remained stone-faced throughout Adan's response and the minor uproar it triggered. Randel stepped forward once again.

"There shall be silence in the chamber or we will clear it."

It took longer for the observers to settle than it had after Markev's plea, but within a few secs everyone calmed. The Chief Justice broke the silence.

"Let the record show that Defendant Adan has pleaded guilty. The defendants may sit." She paused to lift her slate and swipe at its screen for a moment. "We shall now proceed into the penalty phase of the trial. I understand there is a witness who would like to offer testimony on behalf of Defendant Markev."

The Tribunal observers chattered once again at the announcement. Everyone scanned the chamber wide-eyed at the revelation there was someone who wanted to put their reputation at risk on behalf of a mass murderer. Many gasped when they recognized the person who rose, and an excited murmur filled the chamber.

CHAPTER FORTY

The defendants shall rise.

At the end of their row, Rilee rose from her chair and started to make her way to the aisle. Zax pulled in his legs to allow her to pass and smiled up at her as she did so. Rilee winked in return and then strode confidently towards a raised chair positioned to the side of the justices' dais. Once she was seated, the crowd hushed immediately. The Chief Justice had Rilee speak her name for the record and then she gestured to the dark-skinned man sitting to her left who addressed Rilee.

"Forgive me, ma'am, for making the observation, but I find it particularly odd for a member of the First Thirty-Six to speak in defense of one of the men responsible for Adan's Destruction. You were there to witness all of the horror firsthand."

Rilee grinned. "I appreciate that perspective, sir, as I never would have imagined being here. In fact, it's even stranger than you're already aware. Before I encountered him two months ago, the last time I saw Markev was when he killed my lover and then attempted to kill me a year prior to the asteroid's departure."

The justice was left dumbstruck at Rilee's revelation and sat with his mouth hanging open. The Chief Justice laughed and she picked up the questioning in his stead.

"I've been told a lot of interesting stories about you, Rilee, but this one is clearly going to top them all. Please continue."

"My pleasure, Madam Chief Justice. There is no one alive who should want this man punished more than I, and yet here I am to testify on his behalf. I've spent the past two months diving deep into all of Adan's logs aboard the asteroid. They reveal how it was clear from the beginning that Markev was unaware of Adan's plan to nuke Earth until moments before it happened. Once he learned about it, Markev fought against the action until he was forced to accept that he was powerless to stop his boss."

Zax was amazed at how the crowd around the room hung on Rilee's every word. He turned back as Rilee continued.

"Markev ultimately sacrificed his physical body to Upload and continue the fight against Adan from within the AI. This may sound like an easy decision to all of us used to shifting our minds from Skin to Skin, but it went against Markev's most deeply held desire to maintain his physical humanity. Over the next five thousand years, he worked nonstop to exploit any weaknesses to defeat Adan. It never happened, but over the course of that time he put the key pieces in place that led to the man's eventual downfall. When it came time for the final battle, Markev stepped forward and put his very existence on the line. He is the sole reason why we were able to extract Adan from the asteroid. Without him, Adan would have finally succeeded in killing me. Markev is clearly not without guilt, but he has already paid a massive price for his crimes and we are now in his debt. Don't punish him any further."

At the conclusion of Rilee's testimony, Zax worked up the nerve to check the dais. He allowed himself a glimmer of hope when the justices appeared to share the positive attitude that the woman's words had engendered in the crowd of observers. The Chief Justice gestured up and down the row of her fellow jurists to solicit any further questions. When none were offered, she signaled for Rilee to rise.

"Thank you for your dedication through these many years in your quest to bring Adan to justice."

Rilee nodded at the Chief Justice and then made her way back to her seat. She was smiling, but her eyes revealed more than a hint of worry as she squeezed past Zax.

Once Rilee was done, all of the Justices bent their heads to focus on their individual slates. The majority simply poked and swiped a couple of times and then were done. A small handful, including the Chief Justice, spent far longer interacting with the devices. From their body language, Zax assumed they were arguing with each other, but it struck Zax as wildly inefficient. The chamber remained silent throughout, even as the delay stretched past a fifth min. Eventually, the activity stopped and the justices all leaned back in their seats. As if that was his cue, Randel stepped forward.

"The defendants shall rise."

Once more, Markev rose while Adan remained in his seat. Randel nodded at the guards, and they jerked Adan to his feet even more roughly than the first time. He shook his body in protest once he was standing and the guards loosened their grip. When Adan remained on his feet, they took a step backward and allowed him to stand on his own. The Chief Justice leaned forward.

"This has been a very atypical trial in that our Tribunal has met in person for such a short period today. This is a special case with deep significance, so we have treated it differently than all others that have come before us. The real work of this Tribunal has been carried out over the past two months, and we have spent extensive time throughout investigating the evidence and deliberating amongst ourselves. Having finally heard in person today from both the defendants and our witness, we're prepared to pass judgment."

The woman addressed Adan first. "You, Adan, have been found guilty of the crime of genocide. This Tribunal hereby sentences you to spend the rest of your existence Uploaded into our detention facility under conditions of maximum isolation."

The Chief Justice turned to Markev. "You, Markev, have been found guilty of the murder of those people from the East who expected to leave Earth with the asteroid." The woman paused to let the verdict sink in for a few beats before continuing. "However, you have already spent five thousand years in isolation trying to atone for your actions. As a result, this Tribunal hereby declares that any further punishment has been commuted and you are free to go. Randel— release this man's restraints."

Zax gasped with relief when the Chief Justice announced Markev's sentence and turned to Rilee. The Earther woman had buried her face in her hands with worry, and when she raised her head she beamed through tears of joy. Mase, on the other side of Rilee, appeared as emotionally blank as always. Kalare and Imair were hugging each other in celebration. The Boss, who had interacted with Markev as Prime for many years, sported the largest smile Zax had ever seen on the man's face.

A cheer went up in the courtroom. Zax turned to discover it was in response to the removal of Markev's restraints. The man nodded a quick salute at Rilee, but a fire in the giant's eyes alarmed Zax and caused him to hold his breath.

In a flash, Markev took two huge steps and closed the distance between where he was standing and Adan. His former boss was staring at the ground as his guards guided him towards the exit. In one smooth motion, Markev lifted Adan's chin, stared into the man's eyes, and then punched his windpipe with crushing force. As Adan crumpled to the floor, Markev ripped a blaster from the holster of one of the shocked guards. He spun around to face Randel who had drawn a weapon from somewhere inside his robe. Markev was moving more than fast enough to beat the Earther for a clear shot, but then the giant inexplicably lowered his blaster. Randel didn't hesitate to aim and fire, and Markev's chest exploded in a shower of blood and gore as the giant crashed in a heap next to Adan.

The chamber was shocked into silence for a moment. Zax was seated close enough to all of the action that the fading, sickly gurgle of Adan's struggle to breathe was crystal clear. Then, someone in the crowd screamed and the observers exploded into delayed panic from the violence. Rilee jumped up on to her seat, her own weapon in hand, and yelled at the group from the Ship.

"All of you hit the floor—now!"

CHAPTER FORTY-ONE

I will bear the responsibility.

The medics quickly transported Adan's corpse away on a stretcher, but they struggled as they tried to repeat the process with Markev's far more sizable mass. Zax wished desperately for them to cover the body because he was unable to stop staring at the man's face. He had witnessed plenty of death during his career, but there was something odd about Markev's corpse compared to all the others killed in similarly violent circumstances. The man's eyes were closed, and a smile creased his lips. If you didn't gaze below his neck to the ghastly chest wound, you would have guessed he was peacefully resting.

Randel appeared and approached the Chief Justice when the medics finally exited with Markev's body. Zax listened in as they spoke.

"The chamber has been cleared, ma'am."

"Thank you, Randel. Let's finish this."

The Chief Justice turned and climbed back to her spot on the dais. Zax had been so focused on the medics dealing with the bodies that he had lost all situational awareness. He was shocked to discover the chamber had been emptied of all the observers. Other than the group from the Ship, only the Chief Justice, Randel, and a dozen guards remained. Zax reached over and interrupted Rilee who was deep in conversation with Imair, Kalare, and the Boss.

"Hey, what's going on here?"

Rilee looked around the chamber and her brow creased. She stood up and called out.

"Pardon me, Chief Justice, but why have you returned to your seat?"

The woman at the center of the dais did not reply but instead gestured at Randel. The man, robe stained from the spray of Markev's blood, stood and bellowed as if the chamber was still full of observers.

"All rise for the Supreme Tribunal."

Everyone in their row remained seated and appeared as apprehensive as Zax felt himself. Everyone except the Boss, who wore an expression of resignation. Rilee called out again, her voice tinged with worry, as her hand moved to rest on grip of the weapon that was tucked into the waistband of her pants.

"Randel—what the hell is this about?"

Randel raised his hand and a squad of guards charged at Rilee in an obvious show of force. The man's face showed bemusement while his voice dripped with disdain.

"You will respect this Tribunal and not speak unless you are spoken to. If you can't manage to follow that simple rule, I will have you removed and detained."

Rilee glared at Randel for what seemed to be an eternity. She turned back to the group and signaled for them to rise as she whispered.

"Don't worry. I promise I won't let anything bad happen."

Once everyone was standing, the other fourteen justices returned and ascended to their seats on the dais.

"You may take your seats."

Once the group from the Ship sat down, the Chief Justice spoke.

"We are here in response to a request brought by the Homeworld Security Committee of the Leadership Council. Randel—you may address the Tribunal on behalf of the Committee."

Randel strode forward. As he did so, Zax finally recognized why he had disliked the man from the first moment he encountered him. He was haughty and domineering just like so many of the worst Omegas back on the Ship, and Zax braced himself for a similarly negative experience.

"Thank you, Madam Chief Justice. The Homeworld Security Committee has run an investigation into the larger society of the asteroid in parallel with the Tribunal's investigation of Adan and Markev. It is our conclusion that the asteroid and its inhabitants represent a clear threat to the security of all humanity, and their continued presence in the universe will ultimately lead to conflict that will harm Earth and our colonies. We base this conclusion on massive volumes of evidence within their own records that clearly illustrate their violent nature and destructive approach to exploration and colonization. As exhibit A, you need look no further than what just happened here. This Tribunal extended tremendous mercy to Defendant Markev, and yet only my quick action prevented additional death at his hands. The Committee recommends the fleet be tasked with escorting the asteroid into an uninhabited system at which point all of their spacecraft shall be confiscated and their propulsion systems destroyed. They may then live out the rest of their lives stranded and unable to harm anyone ever again."

Rilee shot out of her seat and screamed. "Are you out of your mind? Don't flatter yourself, Randel—if Markev wanted you dead, you'd be in a bag right now!"

Two guards were on top of the woman immediately. One confiscated Rilee's weapon and the other grabbed her roughly by the upper arm. The Chief Justice looked down with a benevolent expression and tone to match.

"I understand your distress, Rilee, after the time you've spent with these people. In deference to all that you have contributed to Earth, I will give you one final warning. You must not disrupt our proceedings again, or I will have no choice but to have you removed."

Rilee snatched her arm away from the guard and returned to her seat. Zax overflowed with respect for the woman. Her desire for revenge against Adan was the obvious rationale for risking her life to infiltrate the Ship, but she had subsequently stood up on behalf of Markev and the Crew out of nothing but kindness and friendship. He returned his attention to the dais as the Chief Justice picked up her slate and spoke.

"I understand that Doran is the most senior military officer aboard the asteroid. Sir—what is your response to the recommendation that has been placed before the Tribunal?"

After receiving an encouraging squeeze on the forearm from Imair, the Boss rose from his seat. He cleared his throat and after a short hesitation began to speak.

"It's absolutely true that our Ship has been a poor ambassador for humanity over the last five thousand years. You all have learned how our culture was hijacked by Adan and how he twisted it from the very beginning to serve his deranged worldview. His outlook does not accurately represent our people, and I'm confident our ideals can be entirely aligned with those found on Earth given the right leadership.

"I'm not here to claim the Ship's current inhabitants are blameless in what has transpired. We're all humans with free will who should have fought harder for our society to make better choices. The Tribunal should hold me to account for this. I'm in charge. I will bear the responsibility. If you require that punishment be served for our actions, I will peacefully accept whatever you deem appropriate as long as it is only applied to me. The ten million people back on the Ship plus the billion in cryostorage deserve better, though. If you must isolate them to ensure your own safety, at least maroon them on a habitable planet rather than guarantee their death in the cold depths of space."

"No!"

"Kalare—sit back down!"

Kalare ignored the Boss's entreaty and brushed his hand away from her arm. She turned to face the justices.

"May I address the Tribunal?"

The Chief Justice nodded and Kalare took two steps forward.

"My name is Kalare and I'm the CAG on board the Ship. This means I command all of our fighters and other spacecraft. With all due respect, I can't believe I'm listening to you consider whether you should strand our vessel in the middle of space and effectively sentence us all to death."

Some of the justices had been focused on their slates while the Boss spoke, but something about Kalare's words and tone caught all of their attention and most leaned forward as she continued.

"Think about what just happened in this chamber a short time ago. You took the time to hold a fair trial and justly convicted the man who launched a genocide against your people thousands of years ago. Are you really going to turn right around and commit the same crime against us? Even if you left us to starve instead of firing a missile, you would be no less guilty of killing a billion people for no reason other than who they are.

"And don't think for a moment you'd be any more justified if you chose to *only* punish Doran. This man has done nothing beyond defending his Ship through many years of attacks and counterattacks between our people. Punishing him for horrendous behavior that happened generations ago would be about who he is rather than what he's done. That's not justice, that's retribution."

Kalare paused for a moment and then gestured around the room.

"I've been wracking my brain to understand why this chamber is empty right now, but I'm pretty sure I finally figured it out. You already know this whole endeavor is wrong, Chief Justice, and you don't want any witnesses to your deliberations. Don't listen to this man advocating for genocide. Don't exact misplaced revenge on someone who has committed no crime. Listen to what you know is right and release us all."

Kalare spun on her heel and returned to her seat. Zax wanted to applaud, but he held back for fear of disturbing the delicate balance in the chamber.

Randel's face had become redder and redder while Kalare spoke, but he did not attempt a rebuttal once she was done.

All of the justices focused on their slates for a quick flurry of communication. Unlike the earlier deliberations where there had been a significant amount of back and forth, they were all done within a min of Kalare sitting down. The Chief Justice gazed at her peers for a moment and then addressed Randel.

"We are overruling the recommendation of your Committee, Randel. Justice was served here earlier today when we punished the man who killed our people without direct provocation. We must not repeat his grave mistake by convincing ourselves that we may do the same, regardless of whatever justifications we possess."

Randel's hands balled into fists, but he remained silent. The Chief Justice turned to the delegation from the Ship.

"It is our decision today that we shall not take offensive action against your vessel and your people. However, this does not mean we're allowing you to roam free and continue the destructive ways of your ancestors. Consider your release to be a form of probation. We'll allow you to depart, but will insist that a trusted observer go along with you to monitor your behavior. If our observer discovers that you're not living up to the higher ideals you espoused here today, then we'll consider your behavior to be an act of war and will take immediate defensive action to protect ourselves. Is that clear?"

The Chief Justice made eye contact with each member of the group and waited for an answer. After each responded with a "yes, ma'am," she rose.

"This Tribunal is adjourned."

CHAPTER FORTY-TWO

How are you?

Zax breathed the ocean air deep into his lungs as he gazed out across the water. After a week on the sailing vessel to conclude their extended tour of Earth, he was ready for a return to solid land even though he would miss the wide open vistas and the salty spray against his face. He made his way to the bow and found Kalare exactly where he expected. She had spent most of the voyage on the same bench at the front of the boat, alone in her thoughts. He had been extraordinarily mindful about giving her emotional space and had never spoken to her uninvited, but, seeing as how it was the end of their journey, he finally gave in to his impulses and approached.

Kalare must have heard him coming because she looked over her shoulder as he neared and rewarded him with one of those beaming smiles that always made his heart flutter. She patted the empty space on the bench next to her.

"I'm glad you found me, Zax. I was just thinking how this view is far too beautiful to not share it with somebody. Come sit with me."

The ocean ended a few kilometers ahead where it met a flat plain that bumped against three mountains. The mountain on the right had an exceedingly smooth and gentle slope that was capped with a distinct turret shape at the far end. The peak on the left was more typical of the craggy, rocky formations found on Earth. It was the mountain in the middle that really captured Zax's attention. It rose taller than either of the others but without the typical, pointed summit. Instead, it appeared as if a much taller mountain had been sheared off at its midpoint leaving a flat plateau that must have measured three or four kilometers across.

The setting sun had kissed the horizon behind their boat and drenched the scene in front of them with a riot of colors. The pinks and browns of the mountains were offset against the dark greens of the foliage on the plain. Above it all were the deep reds and purples of the sky and a handful of giant, fluffy clouds that glowed orange as if filled with flame. Off to the side of their path, what must have been a thousand or more marine mammals frolicked and the foam created by their splashing was similarly flecked with reds and golds. Zax sat in silence, basking in both the beauty of the sights and the rhythm of Kalare's steady breathing next to him.

"Oh my, Zax, check out that mountain in the middle now!"

When Zax had first sat down, the flat portion of the table-shaped mountain was covered in a blanket of white clouds. The layer was so thin and uniform that it almost appeared to be white frosting spread atop a cake. The clouds subsequently moved in slow motion and gracefully spilled down the face of the mountain like the frosting was melting down the side of the cake. With the sun imparting a range of pink and red hues to the flowing clouds, what had already been beautiful turned sublime.

A few mins later, the sun completed its daily journey and the colors began to fade. Kalare sighed and then started to applaud. Zax set aside his self-consciousness and joined in. She turned to him and smiled.

"What an amazing place! Rilee told me that before Adan's Destruction a magnificent city filled the plain all the way up to the base of that flat mountain. Can you imagine calling this place home and witnessing sunsets like that every day? Apparently, it had already declined even before Rilee was born. It was the first major city to run out of drinking water and the riots that followed left it a burnt, hollowed-out shell." Kalare sighed. "What humans did to this planet back then was tragic. I'm grateful that Rilee's people have done things differently with their second chance because it's been wonderful to experience all of this natural beauty. Thanks for sharing it with me."

"You're welcome. I'm glad I came up here. Listening to Mase complain about his seasickness was getting tiresome. I'm surprised how big a problem that's been for someone who's such a great pilot."

"Just goes to show you how smart it is that we only load our minds into the fighters. It's all the pesky biological bits like confused inner ears that cause problems."

Zax smiled at his friend for a moment and then broached the harder topic.

"How are you, Kalare?"

"I'm doing OK. How about yourself?"

"No. Really. How are you? Many of us have noticed you sitting here crying more than a few times, but we all wanted to respect your privacy so we left you alone."

Kalare's brilliant blue eyes moistened, but she continued to smile. "I won't lie, Zax. The past few months have been insanely hard. Ever since I lost the battle with the Earthers, it's just been one horrible thing after another."

"Hey, don't blame yourself for that. There's no way you could have won that battle. They were just playing with us to draw us in and finish us off. Besides, you won the battle that mattered most. If you hadn't stepped in and challenged Randel the way you did during the Tribunal, we might have all wound up stranded somewhere in deep space."

"Thanks, Zax. You've always been a good friend and known just the right thing to say."

"Unless I was talking about the Boss, right?" Zax offered a tentative smile. "That was the only thing that ever really caused problems between us. I admire how you haven't once rubbed it in about how you were right about him not being involved in Mikedo's murder. I would never have been quite as gracious if our places were switched."

"I wish Aleron was still around to hear you say that. He was stuck far too many times listening to me rant and rave about how you were so fixated on that man."

Kalare closed her eyes, dipped her head, and began to silently weep. Zax was initially at a loss for words, but he forced himself to push through the discomfort. He placed his hand on Kalare's shoulder and spoke softly.

"I'm so sorry you lost him. I'm glad I was able to know him better once he was older. He grew up to be a good man, and he did an incredibly brave thing at the end. He not only saved us from Rege, he saved the lives of everyone else on board the Ship. If we had died in that explosion, I'd bet anything that Alpha would have still figured out some way to kill everyone on board."

Kalare sniffled a few times and then wiped the tears from her face and opened her eyes. She smiled at him.

"Thanks, Zax. He really appreciated you as well there at the end. He often expressed guilt about how he behaved when you were both younger and regretted that he hadn't handled things differently."

Zax attempted to lift the mood a little. "Are you excited to be heading back up to the Ship? It was great to learn that Rilee convinced the Earthers to help with repairs and retrofits. It sounds like it will take a while to get it all done, but they've promised to teach us all about their technology along the way. Just the idea of doing an FTL jump without getting knocked unconscious is positively amazing!"

Kalare suddenly turned away and stared down at the deck. Zax was at a loss as to how anything he said might have upset her. She was silent for a few agonizing moments until she spoke without raising her head.

"I'm not going back to the Ship, Zax. I'm sorry."

All the air escaped from Zax like he had been kicked in the belly and his eyes went out of focus as his mind swirled.

What did she say?

There's no way she said what I think she said.

It's impossible!

Zax didn't know how long it took, but he finally regained enough control over his mouth to attempt the formation of words.

"Wh-wh-why?"

Kalare turned her body to face him squarely, and grabbed both of his hands to hold between her own.

"Think back to when we first met, Zax. You were so laser-focused on what you wanted to do with your career, and you thought I was some kind of freak because I couldn't have cared less about where I wound up. I'm sure it was thanks to your influence rubbing off, but eventually I decided to be a pilot and committed to being the best. I made both of those things happen, and I'll always treasure the fact I earned the role of CAG.

"But when I consider going back to that role and that life, I only feel hollow inside. I assumed at first it was my grief about Aleron, but I've spent this week dredging through everything and finally realized I don't care about being part of the Crew anymore. I've lost all interest in flying, and I definitely can't deal with taking orders from anyone. You and the rest of the pilots deserve better than a commander who doesn't care. I deserve better than to just jump back on to that path because it's what I've been great at in the past. I've already spent half a lifetime zooming around the stars on someone else's Mission. I want to trade that all in right now and chart my own course. I will explore wherever and however I want, and I'm going to start by experiencing everything Earth has to offer."

He wanted to argue about Kalare's logic. He wanted to plead with her to change her mind. But deep down inside, Zax realized it would be unfair to make his friend defend her decision to him. She had already given so much to the Ship and infinitely more to him. She had earned the right to do whatever would make her happy. He forced a smile to his lips and surprised himself when it was genuine.

"I'll miss you terribly, but I'm happy for you, Kalare. I really am."

Kalare leaned in and planted a gentle kiss on his cheek.

"I can't tell you how impossible it will be to watch you leave, Zax. You mean more to me than I can ever say. Our friendship is a huge part of the woman I've become. Thank you."

"Does this mean *goodbye*, then?"

"Let's just say *see you later* instead and hope that it somehow works out that way. OK?"

Zax nodded and his heart nearly burst when Kalare rewarded him with one final radiant smile. She turned back to face the approaching shore and rested her head against his shoulder. They sat together in silence as dusk faded and the sky exploded with stars. If the Earthers had somehow invented a means to freeze time, Zax would have given anything to spend the rest of his days in that very moment.

CHAPTER FORTY-THREE

I had already planned on it.

The rising sun lit the scene in the valley below Kalare. A herd of Earth's largest land animals was starting its day at the watering hole her campsite overlooked. A group of tiny babies romped in the mud as massive females stood guard with their fearsome tusks pointed outwards to deter any predators lurking in the tall grasses. On more than one occasion, Kalare had spent days doing nothing but observing the fascinating interplay of the creatures' cooperative society, and it was time she considered well spent.

The rustle of the portable shelter caught her attention, and Kalare turned to find Rilee exiting to stand and stretch. The Earther smiled as she spoke.

"That coffee smells delicious. Is there any left for me?"

Kalare held up the mug she had set aside and gestured for her guest to sit down on the rock next to her. Rilee took a couple swallows as she watched the animals below. After a few mins, the woman broke the silence.

"I know they're incredible beasts, but you must finally be bored after a year of trekking around the continent. Aren't you?"

Kalare laughed. "I've been waiting for you to broach this discussion since you arrived. I must say I'm pleasantly surprised it took you almost a week."

Rilee smiled. "It had to come up eventually, right?"

"I suppose. Go ahead—share whatever news about my old life you've decided must intrude on my new one."

Rilee took another drink of coffee before continuing.

"They announced a timeline for the Ship to launch again. It's a little more than four years away."

"Four more years! What's taking so long with the refurbishment? I would've thought they'd already be done and ready to leave by now."

"Done? They haven't even started yet. Do you have any idea how much work is involved in defrosting one billion people to find out what they want to do with their lives? It's not a shock, but almost all of them opted for immediate resettlement on existing colonies rather than staying with the Ship."

Kalare nodded. "If they had been in cryostorage since the original departure, they're no doubt ready to restart their lives. If they had already been awake and then Culled, I can't imagine they'd want to go back again. How many people are staying with the Ship?"

"Between the Crew and the civilians, it's almost two hundred thousand."

"Civilians? Why would that many civilians stick around?"

"They're all training to be full-fledged members of the Crew under plans the Boss developed for the Ship's new society. There's still a tremendous amount of trust and respect that will need to be earned on both sides, but he's made a pretty compelling case and lots of people are signing up."

Kalare raised an eyebrow. "He's convinced the Ship's inhabitants, but has he managed to earn any more trust from your Leadership Council?"

Rilee paused for a moment. "The results are mixed. On the positive side, the Council is more willing to believe your people will adapt to a less destructive approach now that we've had a chance to study those colonists who put up such a successful fight against us. You know, the ones who were dropped off by the ants the morning Rege took over the Ship? They were fierce combatants, but their records revealed they had always been peaceful unless pushed to defend themselves. They were admirable representatives of the species in their small corner of the universe, and they had even established a successful alliance with an alien race.

"On the negative side, Randel continues to push back about letting the Ship head out again. Thankfully, he's losing more and more of his influence with the Council. Concluding the story of Adan's Destruction has accelerated the pace at which the younger generations are taking full control of Earth. Randel keeps trying to align himself with the new leaders, but they're too smart to let him. The rest of the Council would clearly be more comfortable sending the Ship off on its own if there was similarly a new generation of leadership at the helm, but since you left the Crew there aren't any great candidates."

It was obvious Rilee wanted to nudge her towards a return to the Ship, but Kalare refused to take the bait. She changed the subject instead.

"Has everyone agreed what the new mission will be? The Ship obviously isn't needed for colonization any longer."

"The Council is dispatching it towards an interstellar dead zone that has blocked all of our previous exploration efforts. Once the Ship has been upgraded with our latest technology and all of its old cryostorage holds have been converted into agricultural and fuel storage facilities, it will have a truly astounding range. They'll be capable of pushing much further than any of our vessels ever have, and we should finally get to learn about a quadrant of the universe that is nothing but a mystery to us now."

Kalare smiled. "Being the first to explore all of that uncharted space sounds pretty exciting. Zax must be thrilled."

"He is. I respected your request and didn't share with anyone that we were meeting up, but I know he's missing you terribly. It would mean a lot if you contacted him."

Kalare turned away for a moment. Memories of Zax stirred up a stew of complicated emotions, and she breathed deeply before replying.

"Thank you for keeping it quiet. I'll be ready to talk with him again at some point, but not just yet."

Rilee's expression exuded compassion. "I don't think he understands why you've had to not only go away, but also shut him out. I do, but I still wouldn't be able to forgive myself if I didn't explicitly ask if you wanted to come back with me regardless."

Kalare laughed. "And here I was hoping I had successfully changed the subject when you hinted at that earlier. I'm sorry, but going back to the Ship holds even less appeal for me now than it did when I first left. You're welcome to track me down next year and try again, but I'm confident you'll hear the same answer."

Rilee grinned. "I had already planned on it."

CHAPTER FORTY-FOUR

CAG—we need you on the deck right now.

Zax should have already returned to the Ship, but he chose instead to make a final lap around the asteroid before their departure from Earth. So much about the vessel was the same as when they had first arrived five years earlier, but so many things had changed as well. The most visible of these changes was the fact that the entirety of the Ship was bathed in light. No longer were there large sections where the power had failed and plunged a sector into darkness.

He almost wished the Ship wasn't so bright because it was a distraction from what had really drawn him to extend his final patrol. Earth, with all of its shimmering blues and whites and greens, spun below. Zax savored his final opportunity to stare at the beautiful rock that had birthed their species just as the continent where he had first stepped foot on the planet came into view. Far down near its southwestern-most tip was where he had spent a week sailing the ocean with Rilee and the rest of the group who had vanquished Adan. Well, except Markev, of course. The memories of that trip were bittersweet, but they were ones he cherished nonetheless. A communication came in from Flight Ops.

"CAG—we need you on the deck right now. The Boss says he's going to strip your rank if you aren't in your body and back in Flight Ops in fifteen mins."

"Aye-aye, Comms. CAG en route."

Zax stole one last glance at the planet below. He briefly considered how sighting the place where they had shared the last part of their trip together was a great pretense to call Kalare, but he decided against it. The fact the Ship was finally heading off into the unknown had created a lot of stress for his friend, and he didn't need to add to it by stirring up memories that were fraught with emotion for both of them.

Once he landed his fighter, Zax jumped back into his body and double-timed it to Flight Ops. He almost tripped over a maintenance robot that was polishing the deck as he sprinted out of the Tube, but he managed to stay on his feet. As Zax dashed past the Flight Ops security detail a few secs late, Sergeant Bailee arched an eyebrow in anticipation of what they both understood was coming next. The Boss spun his chair to face Zax and the man's unlit cigar was clenched between scowling lips.

"You're fifteen secs past acceptable reporting time, CAG! What kind of example are you setting for the rest of these people?"

"A very poor one, sir. Permission to take my station?"

The Boss strained to remain irked, but his scowl quickly morphed into a grin and he signaled for his CAG to move along. Zax nodded a greeting as he walked past Imair and the woman smiled back up at him. He still wasn't used to seeing her in a Crew uniform, but he was thrilled she had volunteered for the Ship's new mission rather than settle on an Earther colony like so many of her fellow civilians.

As he sat down to observe the transit, Zax reluctantly accepted an inbound private message.

"Hi, Mase. You understand we're about to jump, right, so this isn't a great time for me to be distracted by you."

"I understand, Zax. I just had to tell someone again about how amazing this new AI cluster is. No one else around here has quite the same appreciation for it as I know you do. I can't believe I get to be in charge of all this."

Zax smiled at his friend's exuberance. "I miss having you on the stick of a fighter, but I can't imagine anyone I'd want running that system more than you. Just promise me you won't ever go Uploading yourself into it."

"Ha-ha, Zax. Real funny. The AI is telling me that the final jump countdown is about to start. You *should get back to work. Let's grab dinner together later on."*

"I wouldn't miss it for anything. See you then."

Zax cut the connection and returned his full attention to Flight Ops just as the jump countdown reached thirty secs. The Boss called out from his seat.

"Have we received final clearance, mini-Boss? Are we ready to go?"

Rilee stood and faced the man. "Yes, Boss. The Leadership Council wishes us a safe journey, and all stations show green for jump."

"Excellent. Get me the captain on visual."

A sec later the massive panorama lit up with the captain's face. Zax noticed her black hair had become streaked with a little gray in recent years due to the strain of preparing the Ship for its new adventure, but the brilliant blue of her eyes had never dulled. The Boss addressed her.

"Ma'am—Your course is laid in and we're go for Transit. Permission to jump?"

Zax's heart swelled, as always, when Kalare smiled as she answered.

"Let's find out how far this new FTL drive will take us."

This concludes this chapter of the Ship Series, though I expect there will be more.

Thank you for reading. If you haven't already, I'd greatly appreciate if you could please write a quick review on Amazon for one or all of the books in the series. I've found it makes a **huge** difference for independent authors like me when prospective readers can learn more about a book from others.

If you want more from me, please register on my website (jerryaubin.com) or send an email to jerryaubin.author@gmail.com. I will send you **a preview of my next book**, offers for free bonus content, and updates on new releases. I also use my list to find readers who want early access to future books in exchange for providing feedback on initial drafts of the story. Never any spam—I promise.

Acknowledgments

This has been an amazing four year adventure and I am incredibly grateful to all of you who have come along on it and are reading these words.

I once again need to thank the editorial team who have been by my side during this journey across my first five books. Stacey Swann continues to be a fantastic editorial resource who helps shape my stories in ways large and small. Claire Rushbrook has once again done a fantastic job of catching the many small mistakes and typos that pile up despite dozens of read-thrus. Any that remain are most likely the fault of me not being able to stop myself from making those last few changes after her work was already done.

First among all of my readers, I would like to thank Michael Lee. Michael has continued to be a fantastic resource who has read early drafts of every single book and shared great perspectives and challenged me with great questions and feedback.

Michael was joined in my group of early readers by a number of other people to whom I am super grateful. Each of these readers participated in my early reader program for Resurgence and took the time to provide their thoughts about the book in advance of publication. They contributed in ways big and small to shaping what wound up on the page and I'm lucky to have them reading my books. Aaron Campagnone, Al Bentley, Alan Edwards, Alex Campbell, Alex Smith, Alison Newband, Amanda Evans, Andrew Haggard,

Andrew Holmgren, Andy Barnett, Ann Hunt, Anne-Claude McDermid, Avi Smith, Becky Muys, Ben, Ben Varela, Bill Short, Bob Harris, Bob Marquart, Bob Ruff, Bob Wood, Brad Fowler, Brett Krueger, Brian Freeman, Bruce B, Cameron Macdonald, Capt. Bob Thompson, Carlos Wx, Charles Paradelas, Cheryl Terry, Chris Rogers, Christian Bullow, Christian Claassen, Clark Parker, Colin Colwell, Colin Mclay, Colin Stuckey, Craig Streiff, Cris Lee, Dale Drexler, Dan Lively, Dana Raffaniello, Daniel Kirkpatrick, Daniel Sackett, Darin Miller, Dart Humeston, Dave Gordon, Dave McCartney, David Ash, David Berkley, David Bonessi, David Brown, David Evans, David Horn, David Montgomery, David Norris, David Page, David Screaton, David Smith, David Thompson, Deb Haggerty, Debbie osborne, Dennis Malfer, Dennis Phelan, Diane LaCombe, Dianne Johnson, Don Campbell, Donald Beals, Ed Grosvenor, Ed Terris, Ed Yenolevich, Eric Read, Frank Green, Frank Mcquade, Gail Brooks, Gar Harris, Gary Parks, Gary Pratt, Gary Reinbold, Gary Steinman, Gavin Smart, Gene Parker, Gene Pope, Gene Sullivan, Glen Palmer, Henry Sherwood, Ian Stout, J. Michael Howard, James Couch, Jay Langa, Jb Cason, Jean Kirkpatrick, Jeff Vandenbroek, Jenny Fox, Jerome Boue, Jim Brogan, Jim Price, Jim Welsch, Joe Burklund, John Lisenbe, John Mcgrath, John Mills, John Pons, John Weisflock, Jon Robbins, Joseph Sener, Joseph Walters, Joshua Little, Karen Arrowsmith, Kathy Gay, Katie Fesenmeyer, Kayla Hood, Ken Neill, Kevin Moore, Kim

Bosco, Kip Johannsen, Larry Core, Larry Didier, Larry Jaquish, Leonard Ward, Lesley Wake, Linda Radke, Lisa Fritze, Lisa Hofmann, Lisa Linn, Lorraine Woll, Lulu, Lynn Hight, Malcolm Streeton, Mansoor Nusrat, Maria Rogstadius, Mark Bennett, Mark Kurtz, Mark Schulz, Mark Sholund, Mark Upton, Martin Brown, Martin Steele, Marty Thompson, Matt Perks, Matt Wright, Matthew Partrick, Maxim Varezhkin, Mechelle Lewis, Merry Metcalf, Michael Chaney, Michael H, Michael Walters, Michael Wilson, Mick Bilverston, Mike, Mike Drew, Mike Etheridge, Mike Mil, Miles Mount, Moshe Smith, Neil Redpath, Neil S, Neil Tomlinson, Nicholas Penney, Nick Butterly, Nigel Frankcom, Noah Landow, Patricia Markham, Patrick Glithero, Patti Martin, Paul Howey, Paul Natale, Peter Brunnen, Peter James, Peter Steffen, Peter Turbide, Phil Hough, Philip Ryals, Philippa Rigby, Pieter Banninga, Randy Bock, Randy Thomann, Ray Strathern, Rhonda Wolberd, Rich Bornstein, Rich Carmack, Richard Heuett, Richard Nickum, Richard Smith, Richard Sung, Richard Yaker, Rick Bentley, Rob Kuehn, Rob Wood, Robert Stark, Roy Keasley, Roy Reich, Ryan Lucas, Sandy Schurtz, Sarah Hedges, Scott Sinclair, Sharon Vreeland, Simon Fraser, Skip Nielsen, Sonya Villeda, Stephen Dunn, Stephen Evans, Stephen Roberts, Steve DeFrain, Steve Eichman, Steve Hodsdon, Steve Lewis, Susan Reese, Ted Casey, Thom Kordusky, Thomas Grillo, Thomas Wheeler, Thomas Yamamoto, Thoss, Timothy Graham, Tisha Havens, TJ Minnow, Tom Morgan, Tom Symons, Tommie Head, V

King, Vanna Land, Ward Freeman, Willis Paul, and Zach Cox.

If you would like to see your name on the above list next time, be sure to register online at my website (jerryaubin.com) or drop me a note at jerryaubin.author@gmail.com so I can put you on the list of readers to contact when my next book approaches publication.

As for what's next, I'm not 100% sure. As you can see, I've intentionally left the door open for further adventures on the Ship and I absolutely expect to revisit this universe and its characters again. That said, I think I am going to let Zax and Kalare have some time adapting to their new situations before I return to their story. There will be more sci-fi from me soon, though, so please register on my website so I can keep you informed about what comes out next!

I would like to close by expressing tremendous gratitude for my family. My talented wife Kerry has provided constant encouragement and been supportive about all of the time I've spent building this world. My boys, Parker and Wesley, are always great sources of inspiration. Finally, Queso the wonder boxer was always available for a quick walk whenever I wanted to stretch my legs and clear my head after some gnarly piece of writing. We had to say farewell to Miss Queso earlier this year, but she will always be a big part of my fond memories of the Ship Series.

Made in the USA
San Bernardino, CA
18 June 2018